THE PERENNIAL BOARDER

THE
PERENNIAL
BOARDER

An Asey Mayo Mystery

PHOEBE ATWOOD TAYLOR

The Countryman Press
Woodstock, Vermont

ISBN-10 0-88150-079-8
ISBN-13 978-0-88150-079-0

Cover design by Honi Werner

This edition published in 2006 by
The Countryman Press
P.O. Box 748, Woodstock, Vermont 05091

Distributed by W. W. Norton & Company, Inc.
500 Fifth Avenue, New York, New York 10110

Printed in the United States of America

10 9 8 7 6 5 4 3 2 1

TO

KATHERINE BARNARD

THE PERENNIAL BOARDER

1

Asey Mayo pretended not to hear her, but neither the distant chugging of the evening freight nor the rattle of hailstones against the truck's throbbing hood nor even his own disinclination to listen could drown out the shrill, persistent stream of orders that issued from his Cousin Jennie.

"Bang it, Asey! Bang it! Take the wrench an' bang it, I tell you! Bang it! We only got fifteen minutes left to get over there! Bang it with the wrench!"

Ignoring her impatient knuckle-rappings on the windshield above his head, Asey continued his slow, gentle adjustment of the rusty nut under his fingers, and the recalcitrant windshield wiper continued to scrape grudgingly over a triangle half the size of an ice-cream cone.

"Wrench, wrench, wrench!" Jennie shrilled. "Bang it with the wrench—oh, come here, Asey!"

With a weary sigh, Asey straightened up and brushed the accumulated hailstones from the shoulders of his best gray suit. Then, glancing at the winding curves of the Tonset road ahead, he climbed back into the truck.

"*See?*" Jennie pointed accusingly at the wiper. "Look

at it! It don't hardly even *waggle* now! All your tinkerin's only makin' it worse! I tell you, you got to take the wrench an' bang at it, like Syl always does. It's quarter to six, Asey, an' we're three miles from Quisset. Bang that wiper an' get along!"

Asey leaned back against the slatted seat and shook his head.

"Jennie, I—"

"It certainly doesn't seem a lot to ask you!" Jennie said hotly. "Just to deliver a few clams on time for your poor Cousin Syl, lyin' home there with his ankle all sprained, worryin' if he's goin' to lose his Inn clam business or not! Six is as late as Mrs. Doane'll wait, an' I had a terrible time persuadin' her to wait at all. Six o'clock, she told me over the phone, or she'll get a new clam man!"

"But Jennie, I—"

"Trouble is," Jennie continued, "you're so busy bein' important these days, bein' a director of Porter Motors an' gettin' your picture taken in Washington with Bill Porter an' all those other engine bigwigs, you don't care a snap for me an' Syl!"

"Now look here," Asey said as she paused for breath. "Ten seconds after Bill Porter left me an' my bag at the door, before my hand touched the knob, you were rushin' me off to deliver Syl's clams. You wouldn't listen to my shiftin' the clams to my roadster an' takin' the main road. You insisted on this truck an' this curvin' short cut. You wouldn't believe my warnin' about the hailstorm Bill an' I drove through!"

"Well, who would?" Jennie retorted. "Who'd expect hail the middle of June? The radio man said drizzle!"

"Whatever he said, hail's what you got," Asey said. "I want to beat this clam dead line, but I don't feel up to pilotin' this vehicle over these curves with two blind crossin's an' three bridges ahead, without seein' more than a half inch of road! An' I cannot make that wiper work!"

"Because you won't *bang* it! You got to *bang* it with the wrench!"

"One tap," Asey said, "just one tap, an' that wiper'll break down entirely. Why, it's so near expirin' right now that a cross word'd finish it forev—"

"Oh, give me the wrench!" Jennie said in exasperation. "I'll show you! Give me the wrench, I say! *I'll* do it!"

"Jennie, if you bust that wiper, we're goin' to stay right here, clams or no clams, till I can see to drive! That wiper can't be banged by any wren—"

"Give me that wrench!"

Asey shrugged.

"Very well," he said. "Here you are. Bang away to your heart's content. An' I'll promise you this. If you can bang that wiper into wipin', I'll get Syl's clams to Quisset by six, even if I have to fly through the hail with 'em gripped in my bare teeth!"

"You remember that!" Jennie said as she clambered out.

Asey winced as she hacked viciously at the wiper, half expecting the windshield itself to shatter under the force of her blows.

Then he opened his eyes wide as the wiper, after a preliminary, palpitating spasm, began flipping evenly back and forth in clean, sweeping strokes.

"*See?*" Panting a little, Jennie plumped herself down beside him again. "Now, you get me an' Syl's clams to the Whale Inn, an' hustle up—no, don't you start any more fussin'! You promised!"

"All I said," Asey told her with a chuckle, "was 'Uncle.' I'll try to get you there on time, but don't expect any Superman miracles from this jalopy. An' hang on tight."

Swaying around some of the curves and skidding around others, the truck rumbled along the shore road toward Quisset with an accompanying clamor out of all proportion to its speed.

Asey heaved a sigh of relief when the rutted short cut ended and he swung the truck back onto a tarred highway.

"Next time we set out on any clam deliverin' expeditions," he told Jennie as he relaxed his grip on the wheel, "let's give ourselves a break an' drive somethin' faster an' more flexible than this truck. A steam roller, say. How much time we got left?"

"It's eight of six," Jennie said. "We can just about make it. I knew we could if you'd only put your mind to it—for mercy's sakes, what're you slowin' down for *now?* If it's that pesky four corners red light, don't waste time stoppin' for it! You sail right through, Asey!"

"I meant to. Only," Asey leaned forward and rubbed the steam from the windshield, "only—here, lean over an' look, Jennie. See those fellers swingin' the red lanterns?"

"What for? What's the matter?"

"Army," Asey said briefly. "They're just startin' to pass."

"One of them columns? One of them long strings of cars an' trucks an' guns?" Jennie's voice rose in a crescendo of dismay.

"Uh-huh. Golly, Jennie, it's the same outfit that Bill an' I spent an hour passin' a week ago today. See, now those fellers with the lanterns are switchin' the control box lights to red all around. I guess they're goin' to hold up everythin' on all sides. There's the bus from Boston pullin' up to our left. I'll get out an' see what our chances are of cuttin' through."

Turning up his coat collar, Asey walked across to the nearest soldier, who was energetically swinging his red lantern at the bus.

A minute later he reported back to Jennie.

"Looks like we got to wait till the bitter end. It's a timed problem, an' the column's runnin' late because of the hail, an' they won't let the bus through even though that wouldn't mean stoppin' the column. Huh! If only I had my roadster, Jennie, I could beat it up the West Tonset road an' circle ahead of 'em, but I couldn't ever make it in this truck of Syl's."

"Did you tell that fellow who you *was?*" Jennie demanded. "Did you tell him your picture was in the paper with the Defense Commission yesterday, an' that you was Cape Cod's detective?"

Asey chuckled. "Nope," he said. "I didn't bring up

the Hayseed Sleuth angle, Jennie. We just got to wait. Everybody's got to wait. It's too bad about the clams, but we'll explain to Mrs. Doane how we got thwarted by the Army. She can't carp at that. The Army takes precedence over anybody's clams. So—Jennie, where you goin'? Jennie, come back here an' sit down! Jennie!"

"You leave go of my arm!"

"Jennie, this hail's changin' to rain—look outside. It's already pourin' pitchforks an' gun shovels, an' the only thing you'll get from goin' out an' fussin' at those fellers with the lanterns is a good drenchin'! Now, sit down an' be patient!"

"After all I been through today, with Syl an' his ankle, an' the doctor takin' so long to come, an' tryin' to get someone to deliver these clams, an' then you an' that wiper, no Army," Jennie said with finality, "is goin' to stop me now, not with the Inn almost in sight! I'm goin' to deliver these clams by six!"

With a stride that reflected her belligerent determination, Jennie marched over to the soldier Asey had talked to.

Asey sighed and turned up his coat collar again as snatches of her shrill protests reached him even over the clatter of the passing column. He had no desire to sally forth into the downpour, but when Jennie began to pump her fist up and down in people's faces someone had to step in and curtail her.

He arrived on the scene just in time to hear the soldier's patient answer to her verbal onslaught.

"Lady, for the purposes of this problem, we're theoretically at war, and you can't pass through this column. This column's at war, see? You got to wait—hey! Hey, you! Lady!"

Frantically swinging his lantern, the soldier alternately yelled and blew his whistle at a small sedan that had crept around the Boston bus and was now slowly edging behind him, in front of Syl's truck.

Under the impetus of the soldier's shouted orders, the sedan was rather reluctantly backed up alongside the bus.

"Women drivers!" the soldier said wearily to Asey. "Women're the worst! Always got something they got to get to. Baby to feed. Cake in the oven. They got to do this, they got to do that! They *got* to get past! My God, I can't seem to make 'em understand they're smack in the middle of a theoretical Blitzkrieg! They—"

"Young man!" The driver of the sedan, a slight woman whose face was barely visible under her large umbrella, had been politely clearing her throat to get the soldier's attention. Now, apparently realizing the futility of throatclearing in competition with so many varieties of engine noises, she reached across Asey and was tugging at the soldier's raincoat. "Young man, I fully understand—can you hear me? I understand the justice of your stopping cross traffic, but considering that I am driving on the same road, and that my passing this intersection will in no way impede the Army's progress, I feel that you might reconsider and allow me to go through."

"Lady, orders is orders."

The woman bit her lip.

"But I simply *must* get on! I've got to! Consider. They," the woman pointed toward the Army, "they are headed toward Boston and are using one side of the road. I am headed for Provincetown and I'm on the other side of the road. I shall drive with great care on the extreme right of the road, my car is not large, and I shall not get in the Army's way! I—"

"Orders, lady." The soldier's patience was wearing very thin.

"Oh, it's no use talkin' with him!" Jennie said. "Red tape, red tape! Minute you run into the Army, you run into silly old red tape! Asey, give me the newspaper out of your pocket to put over my hat, will you? My hat's—"

"Please," the woman held out her umbrella. "Won't you share this? And as for you, young man, you'd best look out for that dog. If he's not caught before he jumps out in front of those trucks, your theoretical problem may have an actual incident!"

Asey and the soldier rushed to grab the playful black-and-white setter pup which, having just discovered the Army, gave no indication of ever wanting to give up its new-found pleasure of bounding at every canvas-covered truck that passed. Three times he allowed his prospective captors to lay their hands on him, and each time, with a joyous yelp, he wriggled his wet body out of their grasp and bounded away after more trucks.

Five minutes later, Asey, breathless and soaked to the skin, placed the dog bodily in the arms of two soldiers and returned to where he had left Jennie by the traffic light.

She and the woman with the umbrella were shaking hands like old friends about to part for many years, and as Asey watched the pair curiously, Jennie turned, calmly removed her hat from her head, and tossed it into the path of the still passing column.

Then, before Asey could stop her, and with a sublime disregard for her own safety, Jennie dove after the hat.

The exact sequence of the ensuing events was something Asey never quite sorted out in his mind. There was a multiple shrieking of brakes, a great deal of whistle blowing and order shouting, and then the third truck back from Jennie's hat suddenly skidded on the glassy asphalt and headed, with a certain drunken dignity, for an adjacent telephone pole.

Although the impact seemed slight enough, the pole broke neatly in two. There was a flash of blue sparks, and at once the street lights and the traffic lights went out, and the gas station and stores and houses on the opposite corner were plunged into inky darkness.

But, over and above the subsequent din, Jennie's voice still managed to ring out shrill and clear.

"Cross over quick, Asey! I'm on the corner! Cross over quick! Hurry! Cross over!"

Asey found himself feeling a little guilty, as he ran for Syl's truck, but he consoled himself with the thought that there were literally no red lights barring his way across the intersection. Those trucks which had passed before Jennie put on her hat-retrieving act had already rumbled out of sight, and the remainder of the column had halted while the soldiers with the red lanterns busied themselves with the ditched truck.

As he struggled with Syl's starter, Asey suddenly realized that the small sedan of Jennie's new-found friend had sneaked past in front of him and was now speeding along the road toward Provincetown.

Asey grinned. She was an opportunist, that woman was, and he hoped that Jennie's spur of the moment act wouldn't get her into any trouble with the Army as she passed the column. Jennie should have known better. Jennie, he told himself as he guided the truck past the blacked-out traffic lights, was going to get a talking-to.

"Here I am!" Jennie jumped on the running board and plopped herself down on the seat beside him with a satisfied sigh. "Now! Up the street an' take the first left turn, an' it's just a little way down from there. Hustle!"

"Jennie," Asey said gravely, "I don't know what's goin' to happen to you, but I think you're liable to court-martial! I saw you. You deliberately threw that hat!"

"An' it wasn't hurt a bit," Jennie said cheerfully. "Didn't even bend the feather. Hurry, Asey! Did she get away?"

"Why bother to hurry now? It's been a lot more than eight minutes since we stopped. Nearer twenty, I'd say."

"Yes, yes, yes, but there's the extra fifteen minutes!"

"The what?" Asey demanded.

"The extra fifteen minutes! You *know* I always keep my watch fifteen minutes fast," Jennie said, "so I don't miss radio programs. I think it pays to keep watches fast. We got three minutes. Did she get away?"

"Your girl friend with the umbrella? Uh-huh. She sneaked across. Jennie, you want to think twice before you do things like that hat-tossin'! It wasn't just dangerous for you—"

"Oh, it wasn't either! I only pretended I was goin' to jump after that hat! An' no one saw me, Asey, an' even if they did, they'd still have an awful hard time provin' it didn't blow off. An' anyway, I knew I was safe with you there. I knew you'd stick up for me if anyone made any fuss. Hurry up!"

"But s'pose someone did see you!" Asey persisted. "I know this business of the Army rushin' around seems like a lot of play actin', but they mean it! S'pose some uppity officer decided to make an example of you. What do you think would've happened?"

"Well," Jennie said complacently, "I s'pose he'd just have to arrest me as a Fifth Column, wouldn't he? Turn here."

Asey mentally decided that his talking-to was not making much progress.

"Now look," he said. "Consider. If some officer—"

"Don't miss the driveway," Jennie interrupted. "It's somewheres ahead on the left, an' if the lights was only on, you could see that cunning little whale-shaped light they got. I wish I'd thought to ask her name, Asey."

"The whale's?"

" 'Course not! The woman's! I liked her. Schoolteacher, I think she was. Had steel-rimmed glasses on, an' she talked kind of precise. I didn't get a real *good* look at her, but her hat was that smooth, expensive kind of felt, even if it was kind of plain an' unbecomin'. Her gloves an' her bag was nice, too, an' that tweed coat couldn't have cost a penny less than fifty dollars unless she got it at a sale. With different glasses an' her hair done sort of up instead of all down at the nape of her neck, she'd look lots smarter. How old did you think she was?"

"Don't you try to get me off the track by talkin' about her!" Asey admonished. "You done a crazy thing, Jennie, an' you know it. An' even if that woman in the sedan didn't have a thing to do with it, they'd have got her in Dutch along with you if they'd picked you up, an' all on account of this fool spur of the minute impulse of yours. Don't you dare ever do anythin' like it again!"

"All right, all right, I won't! But we *did* get across, didn't we? Turn now, Asey. Here. I s'pose," Jennie added, "we ought to go around to the back door, but I don't know just where it is, an' with the rain an' no lights to guide you, maybe you better just stop by that covered part ahead. There!"

Asey obediently drew the truck up beneath a porte-cochere.

"Now what?" he inquired.

"Why, get them clams out, ninny! What did you think?"

"Wa-el," Asey drawled, "considerin' what we been through to get here, it seems to me we ought to blow a trumpet or have a fanfare. Don't you think I should give 'em a blast of Syl's exhaust whistle?"

"Asey, don't you dare toot that awful thing!" Jennie said in a scandalized voice. "You get the clams out an' put 'em on the steps. I'll go inside an' find Mrs. Doane an' tell her we're right on time. Don't it look nice in there, with all the candles?"

It did look nice, Asey thought, as he hauled out the first of eight buckets of clams from the rear of the truck.

After hailstorms and wet dogs and pouring rain, the Whale Inn's glowing candles and chintz-covered chairs and lighted fires that he could see through the wide French doors were all a pleasant and welcome sight.

He had the last bucket lined up on the steps when Jennie bustled out.

"Asey, there isn't anyone in there! Not a soul!"

"Sure there is," Asey said. "Must be. Look around for a bell or somethin'. An' Jennie, I just got an idea. I'm goin' to take you to dinner here. I just remembered I'm starvin' hungry. Bill Porter was in such a hurry to get home, he omitted lunch. I want—"

"Asey, forget your old stomach an' come in here! I tell you, there isn't a soul around, an' no bells! You come see!"

Asey followed her up the steps and through the French doors into the large, comfortable room, and looked around appreciatively.

"Why, I remember this place, Jennie! Used to be Mrs. Mercer's Boardin' House. I used to take the boarders on fishin' trips, years ago. This room had dark-green wallpaper, an' a lot of rush-seated wooden rockers, an' grass mats on the floor. There was a Rogers group in that corner, next to a water cooler, an' a player piano in the alcove yonder. Some difference, with all these hooked rugs, an' antiques, an' bowls of flowers. Might be Bill Porter's livin' room over in—"

"Asey, there must be somebody here! See this work-basket on the table?" Jennie stooped over suddenly and picked up something from the floor. "Why! Oh."

"What's that?"

"I thought 'twas a tomato, but it's only a pincushion fell out of the basket. Asey, where *is* everybody?"

"Wa-el, that must be their official desk." He pointed to a corner where a cupboard had unobtrusively been cut down to form a little cubbyhole. "That shelf's got the register on it, an' a phone. Ain't there a bell? Ought to be one."

"There ain't. I looked."

"I get it," Asey said. "Look, there's wirin' to the door. They got a buzzer there, but with the current off it don't buzz. After someone lighted the candles, they remembered the buzzer wouldn't work, an' now they're scurryin' around findin' a bell. That's the answer, Jennie."

"Huh!" Jennie said. "It's after six, Asey. S'pose she won't believe we got here at six because she didn't hear us come?"

"She will." Asey leaned his head back and opened his mouth wide.

"No! Don't!" Jennie said. "You mustn't let out one of those awful quarter-deck bellows in *here!* It wouldn't be right!"

"Well," Asey said, "what you goin' to do? You goin' to make your presence known, or you goin' to stand here an' worry about it? Make up your mind! Me, I'm soakin' wet an' starvin' hungry, an' I want to get these clams delivered so's I can dry out an' get fed. Which way's the dinin' room, I wonder? Ought to be someone there, or in the kitchen, this time of evenin'!"

"This way, I think."

Jennie started hesitantly for the closed door at her left, and then she paused.

"Asey, I don't know which way it is. *You* go find someone! If you used to know this place, you ought to know where the dinin' room was—"

She broke off as the telephone started to ring.

"This'll unearth someone," Asey said, as the phone continued to ring and ring.

He and Jennie looked expectantly at the four closed doors.

But no one came.

"Well, for mercy's sakes!" Jennie said. "This place is beginnin' to get on my nerves! What'll we do about that phone?"

"Answer it," Asey said.

"You think we ought to?" Jennie asked as he strode across the room.

Asey picked up the receiver.

"Hello," he said briskly. "This is the Whale Inn speakin'. What? What's that?"

Jennie nudged him. "Who is it? What do they want?"

Asey turned to her and held out the receiver.

"Somethin' about a beetle. See if you can make sense of it."

Jennie listened, said what-what-what a number of times, and then passed the receiver back to Asey.

"He's hung up," she said helplessly. "He swore an' hung up. What's a mess beetle, Asey? I thought first he said best needle, but then it sounded more like mess beetle. The man's either got the wrong number or else he's mad as a hatter. Mess beetle! Asey, what we goin' to do? I think this is awful queer! Seems as if there ought to be somebody around here somewheres, in a place supposed to be so tony as this!"

"Wa-el," Asey said, "I'm goin' to dry myself over by the fire, an' when someone does condescend to come, I'm goin' to order us some dinner. I'm not goin' to tackle that road home in Syl's vehicle till I'm sure the Army's out of the way. I wouldn't put it beyond that earnest soldier with the lantern to be there waitin' for you."

"I don't care about that soldier! Asey, now I'm beginnin' to get mad! Don't you think we ought to find someone?"

"I think it's high time someone was findin' us." Asey strolled over to the fire. "Whyn't you try some of these doors an' see where they lead to?"

"An' s'pose," Jennie returned with asperity, "that I land up in somebody's bedroom?"

Asey suggested that she could always knock first.

"I don't remember anythin' about the layout of this floor," he said, "an' I suspect it's been made over considerable, but I don't think there'd be bedrooms here.

Anyways, if I had this deep-seated urge of yours to find folks, I certainly should."

"Well, I'm certainly not goin' to stand here twiddlin' my thumbs any longer!" Jennie said. "When I think of what I went through to get these clams here by six o'clock! Why, we could have waited for two whole armies to pass by that red light!"

Thrusting out her hand, she grasped the door knob nearest her, and then she hesitated.

"You really think it's all right to go lookin' around?"

"Sure," Asey said. "Go on."

Jennie yanked open the door.

"It's just a closet—Asey!" Her scream split his eardrums. "Asey, look!"

Grabbing up the candelabrum from the mantelpiece, Asey held it high and strode over beside her.

The closet, which was about four feet square, clearly served as the Inn's public telephone booth.

And sitting on a little chair, with her head slumped forward against the coin box, was a woman.

Jennie pointed a shaking forefinger at her.

"Asey! It's that woman that was at the red light, the one with the umbrella! She's dead! And look—there's a gun in the corner, next to her glasses!"

2

WITH an exclamation of disbelief, Asey leaned forward and peered at the woman, and then, as the hot candle wax dripped down on his hand from the tilted candelabrum, he held it out toward Jennie.

"Take this an' raise it up, will you, so's I can get in there an' see? Higher! Jennie, this somehow don't hardly seem like it could be possible!"

"There she *is!*" Jennie's voice was shriller and a full octave higher than usual. "There she *is!* An' it's *her!*"

"I s'pose," Asey stared at the stain on the back of the woman's tweed coat, below her left shoulder blade. "I s'pose it's possible she could've cut off the main road an' raced back here before we trundled up in Syl's truck. That's possible. I could've done it myself in my car, easy. An' it looks like that woman. But—Jennie, are you sure she's the same one?"

"Look at that pocketbook with the white stitchin'! Look at them low-heeled shoes! An' that felt hat, an' the tweed coat, an' her gray hair low on her neck! An' them steel-rimmed glasses! You didn't really get a chance to see her face, Asey, what with catchin' that dog. But I did! An' I tell you, this is her! An' I think it's awful!"

"Jennie, hold that candelabra thing high, an' hold it straight, an' don't sob so! This is the strangest business I ever—"

"It's terrible!" Jennie said. "Look, there's a stain on the back of her coat, see it? Somebody shot her, Asey!"

"Uh-huh. I know it. Shot her in the back. An' someone's trod on her glasses. The rim's all bent. But, Jennie, I still—"

"There's a nickel in her right hand!" Jennie interrupted. "She was goin' to phone, an' someone come in here an' killed her. That's why there isn't anybody here! Everyone's run away!"

The furrow between Asey's eyes deepened.

"Jennie, put that candle thing on the table, an' bring the rest of the candles over here. This is just plain strange. Did you see that little sedan outside anywhere when we come? I don't remember it."

"My mind wasn't on cars when we come here," Jennie returned. "My mind was on clams. I wouldn't have noticed a dozen cars. I s'pose hers is parked around toward the back somewheres. It must be."

Asey turned around and stood framed in the closet doorway as Jennie brought over a third candelabrum and set it on the table.

"Know what I think?" he said. "I think this must be that woman's twin. I don't think this is the same woman we seen. I'm almost positive sure it can't be her, Jennie."

"That so?" Jennie said. "Well, you take a look at the initials on that bag. O.E.B. The woman at the red lights had initials on her pocketbook with the white stitchin', an' they was O.E.B., too! I near twisted my neck out of joint tryin' to see what they was without gettin' rained on. I thought of twins right away when I opened that closet door, but when I seen them initials on that bag, I knew it was the same one."

Asey leaned against the door jamb and looked again at the slumped figure in the closet, and tried to conjure up a mental picture of the slight figure under the umbrella. He could remember her voice. It was a little breathless, but low and firm and as determined as Jennie's had been. He remembered what she said to the soldier with the red lantern when she urged him to let her pass the four corners intersection. It was a condensed, logical appeal with no touch of emotionalism like Jennie's frenzied exhortations about the imperative need for delivering her husband's clams.

And Asey could remember the rain pouring off her umbrella in a series of little jetting streams, and her quick impulsive gesture as she extended her umbrella toward Jennie.

Vaguely, he remembered her tweed coat. But other than the fact that she seemed adequately clad, Asey could recall nothing personal about her at all.

But women noticed things, personal things, about other women, and Jennie's power of observing insignificant detail was nothing short of phenomenal. Jennie could tell unerringly what dress a member of the Sewing Circle wore to a meeting the week before Christmas. She could remember, item by item, the menus of dinners she had eaten twenty years ago, just how everything was cooked, and just what the pattern was of the plates they had been served in. She remembered how furniture was placed, and what flowers grew in what spot in people's gardens.

And when she was confronted by a strange woman, Jennie's observational powers reached heights.

In short, Jennie was probably not mistaken.

"Except," Asey said, "there's one thing. Her shoes, Jennie. That's the rub. She's dry! Her shoes an' stockin's an' all!"

"Nylon stockin's," Jennie said promptly. "They dry in two shakes. An' when I said to her that we'd probably both catch our death of cold from wet feet, she said she was lucky enough to have a dry pair of shoes in her car. Said she'd picked 'em up from the cobbler's this afternoon. An' the tweed in her coat's most likely been waterproofed by that process they have. Like Syl's Mackinaw. It never even gets damp. I tell you, Asey, it's her, an' no mistake about it! It's her! I know—"

She broke off suddenly, and when she spoke again Asey could barely hear her husky whisper.

"Asey, you hear that noise?"

"Noise? I hear rain, an' gutters gurglin'," Asey said.

"I don't mean that. I mean outside. Listen. Someone's out there on those front steps! Don't twist around an' look. Just you listen!"

Asey listened.

"I can't hear a thing, Jennie," he said at last. "I think it's just your imagination. An' I'll grant you," he added, "that this's enough to set anyone's imagination leapin' around in circles. I still—"

From the steps outside there came a thud and a rattle, and then smaller rattles, and finally a good-sized bang.

"There *was* someone!" Jennie said. "He's knocked over a bucket of clams!"

Asey raced for the door.

There was no one in sight, but he could hear the sound of footsteps pounding around the side of the Inn.

Disregarding Jennie's plaintive protests that she didn't want to be left alone in that place, Asey promptly set off in pursuit.

He followed the sound of the footsteps as they crunched along the Inn's heavily graveled driveway, and swung off to the right when they did. For a moment the noise of the rain and the wind drowned them out, but then he heard crackling sounds, as if someone had plunged into a pile of branches, so he set off again.

That was just what had happened, he told himself as he ran toward the continued snapping. This fellow had slammed into a brush pile, and now he was foundering his way through.

Asey lengthened his stride, and almost at once fell headlong into a puddle.

Picking himself up, he shook the water off his coat, brushed the mud from his chin, and listened.

From somewhere behind him, a Quisset church bell began to peal out urgently, completely drowning out any other possible sounds.

Asey wiped his face with a muddy handkerchief and waited for the bell to stop. Then he realized that the bell was signaling, four long peals and two short ones. That meant that the Quisset Fire Department, unable to use its regular siren with the electric current off, was utilizing the church bell to call its members and tell them where the blaze was. And, Asey thought, if he knew anything about fire departments, that bell would be rung until every last man jack in the department had phoned in that he was on the way.

With a shrug, Asey turned back toward the Inn. It was pretty much of a wild-goose chase anyway, this was, and he shouldn't have left Jennie there all alone. At least he should have waited long enough to tell her to phone Hanson of the state police and report this business.

The bell finally stopped, as he strode along, and at once he heard footsteps, very near and moving toward him.

Swinging around, Asey dashed for the person, who nimbly ducked and raced away.

And again the church bell started ringing, a carefree, concerted pealing which Asey diagnosed either as Quisset's "All Out" or its "False Alarm" signal. There was no doubt, in any event, but what the fire department meant everyone within a radius of ten miles to know that the situation was under control.

He was glad for Quisset, but under the circumstances he couldn't have followed the sound of a scissors-grinder with a bell.

"Huh!" Asey said aloud, and marched for the Inn.

For his part, he couldn't imagine why anyone should be sneaking around the front door of the Whale Inn, anyway. A person who belonged there would have entered without any preliminary lurking. Conversely, a person who didn't belong there, and had designs on the silver, say, would hardly reconnoiter around the front door. And, finally, anyone involved with the shooting of the woman in the telephone booth would, if he had any sense, stay away from the place.

He was so busy thinking about the Inn, the prowler, and the woman in the telephone booth that it didn't dawn on Asey for some time that, in spite of his being constantly in motion, he didn't appear to be reaching the Inn.

He stopped and looked around him.

There were no lights to be seen, anywhere. No houses, not even a tree, loomed in the rain.

Asey sighed.

It had been many years since he'd been forced to use a compass on Cape Cod, but he had to admit the need of one now. He was lost.

He fished around in his breastpocket for a full minute before he remembered that he wasn't wearing his everyday clothes or carrying his big old-fashioned watch with the compass face.

"Oh, well," Asey murmured wearily, and turned to the right. Quisset was a small village, but it wasn't so small that you could lose touch with it entirely in such a brief tramp.

He walked on, sloshed through a small brook, and then, ahead, he saw someone duck nimbly behind a pine tree.

He was just gathering himself together to lunge forward and grab the man, when the man lunged first and grabbed Asey.

"No chickens tonight, brother!" The man's flashlight found Asey's face. "No more free chickens for you out of *my* coop—say, you, what's your name?"

"Mayo," Asey said. "I'll admit to trespassin', mister, but I ain't after your chickens. I'm just tryin' to find my way—"

"I knew who you was! Asey Mayo! Knew you in a minute! Say, you don't remember me, do you?"

"Considerin'," Asey said, "that I can't see your face, no."

The man obligingly swung the flashlight so that it illuminated his long, narrow, clean-shaven face and his shining bald head, on the side of which a blue knitted cap perched cockily.

"There!" the man said. "I guess you remember me now, all right! Well, well, Asey! I always meant to get over to see you since I settled here, but I don't get much of a chance to get away very often." He paused. "I guess you know my wife."

"No, 'fraid I don't." Asey gently eased himself from the man's grasp.

"If you did, you'd understand—say, come along to my shed. That's where I spend my spare time when I'm not workin' my fingers to the bone. You know, I always thought someday you'd turn up like this."

Asey chuckled.

"I don't think," he said, "I ever turned up like this before anywheres, least of all in Quisset. Except for drivin' up the main street, I don't ever see much of the town. Say, where's the Whale Inn?"

"Down the line." The man pointed with his flashlight. "This is all my land here. I'm doing pretty well, Asey. Own place, own garden, own chickens—say, I thought you were the feller that's been swipin' 'em. What do you know about that? The shed's this way. Come over an' dry out an' let's have a chat about old times. Certainly can't beat the old days!"

Taking Asey's arm, he propelled him toward the shed, happily repeating his conviction that nothing was like the old days.

"I'd like nothin' better than to chat with you," Asey said, "some time. But—"

"What's the matter with right now?"

"Wa-el," Asey said, "right now I got some pressin' business I got to get along to. So—"

"No time like the present!" the man said. "After not seeing me for thirty years, you certainly got a few minutes to talk over old times with me, or you're not the man I take you for! Come on!"

Asey had a sudden inspiration.

"Listen!" he said. "Hear that? I think I *do* hear someone after your chickens! You go that way an' I'll go this way an' head him off!"

"Take my flash." The man pressed it into Asey's hand. "I got a little twenty-two here, and if you'll locate him, I'll scare him off for good with a pot shot!"

"Give me time, now!" Asey said.

He waited until the man had hurried away, and then he proceeded in the direction of the Inn.

This was no time, Asey reflected as he strode through a series of puddles, to renew old friendships, even if he had the faintest idea who the man might be. Never, to the best of his knowledge, had he ever seen this hearty, bald person before in his life.

Before he reached the Inn, the electric current returned to Quisset. The street lights came on, the church spire on the main street revealed itself in a glow of floodlights, and somewhere a thwarted clock chimed twenty-two before someone mercifully put a stop to it.

The rain even began to let up as he turned into the Inn's driveway, past the little whale-shaped light Jennie had mentioned. Not that the rain's stopping would make any difference now to his thoroughly saturated, best gray suit, Asey thought, as he passed Syl's truck and briskly mounted the steps.

He was prepared and ready for one of Jennie's more vehement onslaughts, for a torrent of slightly querulous questions as to where he had been anyway, and what he'd been doing, and why on earth he'd dared to leave her alone so long in that place.

But Jennie wasn't in the living room.

Softly shaded electric lamps were burning, the candles and candelabra were back in their proper places, the telephone closet door was closed.

But there was no sign of Jennie.

In two strides Asey crossed the room and yanked open the door of the phone closet.

He breathed a sigh of relief as he closed the door.

The body was still there, anyway!

"May I help you?"

Asey pivoted around so quickly that he nearly lost his balance.

Over in the far corner of the room, her head and shoulders just visible behind the cupboard shelf where the Inn telephone and register reposed, was a pleasant-looking, dark-haired girl.

"May I help you?" the girl repeated, and stood up.

Her rose-colored linen dress was crisp, the girl herself was completely poised and unruffled. She neither looked nor sounded as if she had any inkling of the presence of that slumped-over figure in the telephone closet across the room.

The girl cleared her throat and spoke a little louder.

"May I help you? May I direct you anywhere?"

The inflection of her voice suggested that directing Asey to two other places would be the only possible help she could offer him.

Asey removed from his head the soaked, shapeless thing which had, until recently, been his best gray hat.

"Perhaps," he said, "you could direct me to my Cousin Jennie."

"Does she live in Quisset?" the girl said. "If she does, and you'll tell me her full name, I'd be glad to look her up in the telephone book for you."

Asey half-leaned and half-sat on a corner of the center table and looked curiously at the girl.

The best actress in the world, if she had seen or come in contact with Jennie Mayo, couldn't pretend otherwise. Jennie wasn't a person you passed over lightly. And the best actress in the world, if she knew of that body in the closet, couldn't pretend otherwise. That body was something else you didn't pass over lightly.

"Now, I sort of wonder," Asey said aloud, "how this all transpires. D'you mind tellin' me who you are, an' how long you been here?"

"My name is Doane," the girl said. "My mother, Mrs. Doane, manages this Inn. It's the Whale Inn, by the way, and I rather think it's not the place you're hunting for. You want the Commercial House, don't you? That's over on the main street by the bus station. I'd be glad to phone them, if you wish, and ask if your cousin is there. Or," she added pointedly, "I'll send one of the boys over with you."

Asey chuckled. "I must," he said, "look pretty much of a tramp."

The girl didn't deny it.

"But," Asey continued, "my appearance is deceivin'. I've done some trampin' this evenin', only I ain't one. Miss Doane, how long have you been in this room?"

"Since three this afternoon," the girl said tranquilly. "And now, I'm sure you're in a hurry to get to the Commercial—"

"You mean," Asey said, "you been in this room since three this afternoon? All the time?"

"Yes," the girl said firmly.

Asey's eyes narrowed.

"And if you'll be good enough to come to the door," the girl continued, "I'll point out the direction of the Commercial House."

Asey leaned back his head and opened his mouth wide.

"Jennie! Ahoy, Jen-nie!"

The girl jumped as his quarter-deck bellow roared out.

"Jennie!" Asey took another breath. "Jen-nie!"

"Look here," the girl said sharply, "you've got to stop that din! I can assure you that there is no one named Jennie here!"

"Asey! A-sey!"

"Who's that?" the girl demanded.

"That," Asey said, "is Jennie. Ahoy, Jennie, where are you?"

"Upstairs! Come up here, Asey! I got her, right here!"

The girl ducked down, opened the low-swinging cupboard doors, squeezed herself through them, and ran over to the staircase in front of Asey.

"Absolutely, you can't go up—"

"Aside, youngster," Asey said, and took the stairs three at a time.

He found Jennie on her knees with her eyes focused on the keyhole of a room down the corridor to his right.

"What's goin' on, Jennie? What're you glued to that keyhole for? Who's in there?"

Jennie put her finger to her lips.

"Sshh!" she said. "She's in this bedroom! Right in here! Sshh!"

"What's the use of shushin'?" Asey wanted to know. "Between your yells an' mine, I guess somebody knows we're in this general vicinity! Jennie, who's in there? What you been doin'?"

"Look!" Jennie got to her feet and held out something she'd picked up from the floor beside her. "Look!"

Asey took the white-stitched leather pocketbook from her and glanced at the initials.

"O.E.B. This's the one from the phone booth?"

"Listen," Miss Doane had been desperately trying to get a word in edgeways. "Listen, will the two of you simply *stop* this and—"

"Oh," Asey said. "I forgot you. Go downstairs, will you, an' phone Hanson of the state police, an' Doc Cummings, the medical examiner, over in Wellfleet. Tell 'em Asey Mayo wants 'em at the Whale Inn right away. Hurry, will you? Now, Jennie, what'd you take this from the phone booth for?"

"I never did, Asey! I took it from *her!*" she pointed toward the door at whose keyhole she had been watching.

Miss Doane broke in before Asey had a chance to speak.

"You don't look like Asey Mayo!" she said. "I've seen innumerable pictures of him. He wears a yachting cap, and a duck coat with lots of little pockets, and he carries a gun. And, besides, he's in Washington right this minute! I saw a picture of him in the paper this morning, shaking hands with people who make engines or something!"

"I'm back," Asey informed her, "an' these are my city clothes. Now, hustle with those calls, will you?"

"Well, all right." But she still looked skeptical as she turned and walked back along the hall to the stairs.

"Now, Jennie," Asey went on, "let me get *this* straightened out. What's the story on this pocketbook, anyway?"

"I tell you, I took it from the woman that's in the bedroom in there! I didn't take it from the phone booth woman!"

Asey sighed.

"Let's start at the beginnin'," he said patiently. "Somebody knocks over a bucket of clams, an' I rush out into the rain. What did you do then?"

"The minute you left," Jennie said, "I somehow begun to feel awful scared an' trembly. All alone there with those candles flickerin', an' her in that booth! Why, for a minute or two, I just shook! An' then I shut the closet door, an' then I begun to feel a little better. An' then—in she come!"

"Who?" Asey demanded. "This Doane girl that was just here?"

"No, no, no! The woman at the red lights! The one with the umbrella! The one—"

"Look, Jennie," Asey said soothingly, "I don't blame you for bein' confused. I tell you what I'll do. I'll phone Sam over at the garage an' have him drive my roadster here an' take you home. You need to lie down. You had a hard day even before you got to this place, an' what's happened since hasn't made it any easier. I'm not a bit surprised you seen a ghost! Come on downstairs, an' I'll call Sam."

It was not until he took hold of Jennie's arm that Asey realized his error. The sudden gleam in Jennie's eyes was not gratitude for his consideration, but sheer, unadulterated anger.

"You think I'm a fool, Asey Mayo? You think I don't know what I seen? You think I don't know what I'm talkin' about? I tell you, it was that woman, an' it wasn't no ghost!"

"You mean, she recognized you, an' spoke to you?" Asey asked.

Jennie shook her head.

"She walked straight past me, Asey! Never said a word. I don't think she knew I was there! Straight past me, an' across that livin' room, an' up the stairs!"

"What did you do?" Asey demanded. "Did you speak to her, or put out your hand an' touch her? What did you say?"

"I was so flabbergasted," Jennie said, "I didn't do a thing but gape, an' I think my eyes nearly popped out of my head, Asey. They ain't felt right since. Why, there one minute I'd closed the door of that booth, an' the next minute there she was, comin' in the front door an' walkin' past me! *I* thought it was a ghost, first. But that woman was just as real as could be."

"Honest, Jennie, d'you—"

"I kept thinkin' of things to say," Jennie went on. "Only they all stuck in my throat. She was halfway up the stairs before I could unloosen my tongue an' find my voice. Then I let out a scream. A good loud scream. It even scared me! Scared her, too. She went up the rest of the stairs like a streak of greased lightning. Then I come to an' rushed up the stairs after her. An' right on the stairs was this pocketbook here. I guess that proves she was real, don't it? Ghosts don't carry pocketbooks!"

Asey restrained himself from remarking that ghosts had been known to carry far stranger objects than ladies' handbags.

"Huh," he said. "Then you didn't actually take this bag from her, did you, Jennie? You just found it on the stairs."

"Same thing!" Jennie retorted. "She dropped it when I let out that scream! Don't you look so doubtful, Asey. She had on that felt hat an' that tweed coat. I tell you, it was *her*."

Asey frowned, and played with the clasp on the pocketbook.

"An' you saw her go into this room?" he asked, as he casually opened the pocketbook and peered inside. "Where is she now?"

"Oh, I didn't *see* her go in, because she reached the top of the stairs before I even got started," Jennie said. "But I know she's in this room. This is the way she ran. An' I been in every room on this floor that's unlocked, an' I listened outside every room that's locked, an' this is where she is. I heard a rustlin' sound. Twice."

"There's nothin' in this pocketbook," Asey said. "It's empty. Tell me, just where did you find it?"

"On the curve of the stairs, to one side, just where she dropped it when I yelled," Jennie told him. "An' I wish you'd stop askin' a lot of fool questions an' either tell her to come out, or break that door in. I knocked an' banged, but she didn't pay a speck of attention!"

Asey reached out and rapped his knuckles against the door.

"A self-respectin' flea," Jennie said with scorn, "wouldn't hear *that* knockin'. An' if it did, it wouldn't pay any attention to it! Tell her to come out here!"

"Will the occupant of Room Five," Asey said, "be good enough to open the door?"

Nothing happened.

Asey repeated his request, and then he drew a long breath.

"Honest, Jennie, don't you think that maybe perhaps it was just possibly an imaginary woman, sort of a picture in your mind?"

"I do not! She dropped that pocketbook!"

"Maybe. But someone might've been goin' out in a hurry, an' shifted things from one pocketbook to another—I've known you to do that, Jennie—an' left the empty bag on the stairs."

"I tell you, she dropped it! An' she dripped!"

"She what?"

"She dripped rain. She was wet."

"Let me tell you what I think," Asey said, "an' don't interrupt me till I get through. I think it was perfectly natural, after your closin' the door of that phone closet, to look up an' think you seen that woman's image. Most likely you did. Remember those cardboard things kids used to spin, just triangles an' circles, an' after you spun 'em, you looked away an' seen a face? Well, this woman you thought you seen was an image like that. An' with all that rain pourin' down, I don't doubt your image dripped some. Everythin' else was drippin'. So let's call this little episode over with, an' go back downstairs. I got a number of things to look into."

Jennie's lips pursed themselves into a thin, stubborn line.

"I'm goin' to stay here till I see who comes out of this room. An' if it ain't that woman that was at the red lights, I'm goin' to eat my—my—"

Asey never knew what Jennie intended to devour, for her sentence petered out in mid-air as bedsprings suddenly creaked inside Room Five.

Then someone moved.

Jennie smiled triumphantly.

The door key was turned, the door knob was twisted, and then the door itself was flung open.

A tall, pale, black-haired woman, dressed in a wide-skirted housecoat of crimson-and-white striped satin, stood and surveyed Asey and Jennie with an expression of one who had been tried beyond human endurance.

Jennie's eyes bulged, and Asey bit his lip to keep from smiling. This woman didn't even bear a passing resemblance to the slight woman under the umbrella at the red lights.

"What you two are doing here," the woman said icily, "and why you have chosen this hallway to imitate a pair of screaming panthers in a cage, I cannot imagine. Move out of my way, please. I shall see what Mrs. Doane has to say about this!"

Jennie gulped audibly as the woman sailed past her and disappeared, with a great swishing of her billowing skirt, around a corner of the hall.

"Well, did you ever! Well, for goodness' sakes, what do you know about that! Asey, what you suppose happened to the woman I seen? Run after her quick an' ask her where that woman went to!"

"I think," Asey took her arm, "that we'd better get

out of here before she comes sailin' back with Mrs. Doane. From the look on her face, I think we'll be lucky if she don't come sailin' back with a fire ax. Come on downstairs, Jennie!"

He steered her toward the landing.

"But Asey! I—"

"No buts," Asey said. "What you seen is technically known as a mirage, an' what you been doin' is harassin' an innocent bystander. That's that. Now, get along!"

Before they reached the foot of the stairs, snatches of a heated conversation taking place outside on the front steps floated up to them through the open front door.

Jennie nudged Asey as she caught sight of a broad-shouldered figure in a raincoat.

"That's Mrs. Doane, Asey! Syl says she's the bossiest woman he ever met. Listen. That girl's catchin' it good an' plenty."

The girl, Asey thought as he walked quietly across the living room, certainly was.

Mrs. Doane, with a sweeping, peremptory gesture that included Syl's truck, the buckets of clams, and the clams strewn over the steps, wished to know exactly what her daughter was thinking about to permit such an evil-smelling scene.

The trouble with her daughter Freddy, Mrs. Doane announced, was not that she lacked brains. Freddy merely refused to use them. The result was a lackadaisical incompetence which sometimes terrified Mrs. Doane. Sometimes, Mrs. Doane said, she waked in the middle of the night shivering to think what would happen to the Whale Inn and its clientele, which she had so carefully built up throughout the years, if she herself were called away just for a single day. At once, Mrs. Doane was certain, the Whale Inn's old and valued clientele would depart forever. They would be gone with the wind. The hard, constant work of twenty long years would in the space of a few brief hours be irrevocably and forever blotted out. It would all have been for nothing.

Outtalking her daughter's attempts to protest, Mrs. Doane went on to add, sadly, that whoever said that ingratitude was sharper than serpents' teeth was entirely right. Freddy had been given every advantage. Freddy had been sent to one of the best schools. Through college. And had Freddy ever shown the slightest indication of gratitude? Had she, even with all her contacts, ever managed to bring the Whale Inn one single guest? Freddy, Mrs. Doane said, had not. What did Freddy want to do? Sometimes Mrs. Doane thought that Freddy's sole purpose in life was to bite the hand that fed her and bring about the complete destruction of the Whale Inn.

If that was not so, Mrs. Doane wound up, then why had Freddy allowed the clam man to park his hideous, smelly fish truck out in front of the Whale Inn, not to mention all those smelly clams littering the place?

"Dear me, Mother," Freddy said, "you're in rare form! That was practically like launching the curse of Rome. Was it a flat tire? I wondered what was keeping you."

Mrs. Doane said that owing to the incompetence of an ungrateful daughter, who utterly refused to pay any attention to detail, she had run out of gasoline and been forced to walk miles through a downpour whose like she had never seen, in order to remedy the situation.

"And with the current off, they couldn't draw any gasoline from the pump. I simply had to sit there and wait. Freddy, why did you ever allow Mayo to park there? *Why?* What would people think if they saw that thing out there?"

"I didn't have a thing to do with it, Mother. I didn't even know it was there till you showed me. I hadn't looked out. But cheer up, I'll drive the truck around back and sweep up the clams, and no one will ever guess how untidy we've been, dear."

"But didn't you hear it come? What have you been doing?"

"Trying to get the old Delco system working," Freddy said. "The current was off here, too, and when I phoned and asked about it, they said it would be three or four hours before it came back. So Dad and I went to work on the Delco. We thought you'd be so pleased that we thought of it. I didn't hear the truck. But I did wonder what those two came in."

"What two?"

"Well," Freddy said hesitantly, "I was trying to tell you about them when you went off on a tangent about serpents' teeth. Come inside, Mother, and I'll—"

Mrs. Doane stopped short on the threshold and stared at Asey and Jennie.

Apparently the sight of them did nothing to improve Mrs. Doane's state of mind.

"Who are these people?" she snapped the question at Freddy.

"They're the two, Mother. The woman was upstairs. I don't know what she was doing there, or when she went up. She must have slipped in while I was out trying to get the Delco going. Then he came in. He says he's—"

"Mrs. Doane!"

The woman in the crimson-and-white house coat spoke from the stairs.

At the sound of her voice, Mrs. Doane's expression changed from that of the presiding officer at a court-martial to one of friendly and kindly benevolence. It was so swift and complete a change that Asey found himself looking at Mrs. Doane with new interest.

"Oh, Mrs. Hingham!" Mrs. Doane walked quickly over to the foot of the stairs. "Is your headache better? Should you like more coffee?"

"I shall have to ask you," Mrs. Hingham said frigidly, "to call a doctor. What with this pair screeching up and down the hallway, my migraine is worse. I do think your local friends—they *are* local people, aren't they? I do think you should request them to be more considerate of your guests."

"Freddy," Mrs. Doane said, "help Mrs. Hingham up to her room, and get her some fresh hot-water bottles. I'll be right up with some coffee as soon as I've called the doctor."

She waited until Freddy and Mrs. Hingham disappeared from sight, and then she turned and faced Asey and Jennie.

"Mrs. Doane," Asey said before she could open her mouth, "I should've made myself known to you before now, but I wanted to find out if you was as much in the dark about things as your daughter seemed to be. I'm Syl Mayo's cousin. This is his wife. We came here at six with Syl's clams—"

"Whatever your connections may be with that irresponsible clam man," Mrs. Doane said brusquely, "I do not wish to know about them. You may take your clams, all of them, including those you threw over the steps, and leave. I don't wish to hear any of your explanations."

"I'm afraid," Asey said, "that you're the one that's goin' to make the explanations, an' I can tell you I wish to hear 'em, Mrs. Doane. No, just you wait, please, until you see what I have to show you."

Walking over to the telephone closet, he swung open the door and turned to Mrs. Doane.

"If you'll come over here an' look, Mrs. Doane," he said, "you'll find out why I—well, for the love of Pete!"

He looked blankly at Jennie, and she looked blankly back at him.

The telephone closet was empty.

The body was gone!

3

Now, take your clams and your truck and get out!"
Mrs. Doane said. "I don't know and I don't care
what startling things you expected to bring to
light in my telephone booth! Certainly there's no body
there!"

"No what?" Asey inquired.

There was a purring note in his voice which made
Jennie prick up her ears. She knew that purr as an
indication that Asey was getting down to brass tacks.

"Nobody!" Mrs. Doane said. "Now, get along, the
two of you, and take your clams with you!"

"Mo-ther!" Freddy Doane called from the stairs.
"Mo-ther! Mrs. Hingham's having hysterics or something—will you come quick?"

"Right away." Mrs. Doane reached out and slammed
the phone closet door shut, and then, marching over to
the front door, she swung it open wide and stood there,
tapping her foot. "Come along, you two!"

Asey hooked his arm through Jennie's.

"Come on, Cousin," he said. "Lady wants us to leave.
Let's."

He expected that Jennie would register an immediate protest against a retreat, but Jennie waited until they were on the top step and the door had been slammed to behind them by Mrs. Doane before she let out a loud sniff of indignation.

"Asey, you goin' to stand for this?"

"Nope," Asey said. "Climb into the truck while I pack up our clams. I just wanted to see how anxious she was to get us out of the way."

"What you goin' to do? You don't intend to leave, not knowin' what become of that woman in the phone booth!"

"Wa-el," Asey said, "to make Mrs. Doane feel good, we'll leave temporarily. Right now, I think it's best that she thinks she's won. Later—"

"Later what?" Jennie asked, after Asey had returned the clams to the truck and got in himself. "Asey, what happened to that body? That woman's body was in that phone booth when you an' I come, an' it was there when I closed that door!"

"Uh-huh." Asey's foot bore down on the starter. "An' it was there when I come back from rushin' around outside. Let's see. I was gone fifteen minutes or so. Huh. I probably come back around six-twenty-five, I'd say. It was only six-forty when we left the livin' room just now, an' we'd been downstairs listenin' to Mrs. Doane talkin' to her daughter for four or five minutes. I think, Jennie, this kind of resolves itself into what you might call a time problem."

"I don't see how it's any time problem," Jennie said as Asey backed the truck out of the Inn driveway.

"Seems to me as if it was more of a body problem. Asey, where did that body *go?*"

Asey chuckled.

"It didn't go. It got moved, Jennie."

"Where? Ain't you goin' to try an' *find* it? Where are you goin', anyways?"

"I'm goin' to turn this corner," Asey said, "an' park the truck. Then you're goin' to the nearest store, an' phone Hanson up at the barracks. I got a suspicion that girl Freddy didn't phone him. You find out. If Hanson's there, tell him where the truck is, an' then go back an' wait for him. When he comes, tell him what's happened. If they say at the barracks that he's on his way, you try an' hail him when he goes past. By rights, he ought to go past here."

"An' just where are you goin'?"

"Back to the Inn," Asey said, "to sort of meander around. I got a hunch. You know, Jennie, no matter how you look at it, someone only had at the most about eight or nine minutes to move that body in. That'd be from the time after I looked in there, before I bellowed for you, till the time we come downstairs after rousin' that Mrs.—what was her name?"

"Hingham. An' you know what? I think I know who she is," Jennie said. "I heard 'em talkin' about her at the Sewin' Circle. She's the one that's been divorced so many times an' has all that money an'—"

"I'm goin' to park right here," Asey said, "an' I only hope Syl's lights last. They're the feeblest lights I ever seen on a four-wheeled vehicle. The point about all this body-movin', Jennie, is that people didn't have much time."

"Who moved it? An' why didn't someone see 'em?" Jennie demanded. "Why, after you come upstairs, that girl went right down again, didn't she? She was there!"

"We took it for granted that she was," Asey said, "but I don't know."

"You think she moved it?"

Asey smiled. "You ever move a body, Jennie?"

"I should hope not!"

"Wa-el," Asey said, "it ain't one of the easiest things in this world to do. Not for one person. Unless you was a city fireman, say, or an ambulance worker, or had some kind of special trainin' in luggin' people by yourself, I should think it would take a good eight or nine minutes for you to figure out where to start hoistin'. That phone booth would add a kind of confinin' angle, too. Somehow, Jennie, I don't think that body's gone so far that with a little meanderin' I can't locate it. You get started, now, an' call Hanson."

"I don't suppose," Jennie said tentatively, "it could have been her I seen."

"You still think you seen someone walk through that room?"

"I still *know* I did!"

"Don't try to tell Hanson about it," Asey said. "There's no use confusin' him at the start. Oh—before you go. You better call Sam at the garage home an' have him drive my roadster over. He can hang around till Hanson's come, an' then drive you back in the truck, or he can drive you back in the roadster. Figure it out between you, but get my car here."

Jennie protested vigorously at his suggestion that she go home in any sort of vehicle at all.

"Why, the idea of my leavin' now!" she said. "I want to know what happens! I don't want to go kitin' home now!"

"What about your poor husband an' his sprained ankle?" Asey inquired.

Jennie uttered a little cry of remorse.

"I forgot all about him! An' the poor man ain't had a speck of supper! Oh, my goodness! I guess Sam had better drive me right home in your roadster—but, Asey, you'll phone me when you find out what become of that poor woman, won't you?"

Asey promised that he would. "Hustle along an' call Hanson, now," he added.

Jennie took a step or two along the sidewalk path, and then she stopped.

"Seems too bad, don't it, Asey, that she thought up that plan? If she'd just been content to wait right there an' been late for her date, maybe she wouldn't ever have been killed at all. I s'pose it goes to show you that you shouldn't ever try to plan ways to change the course of things."

"Hey, wait!" Asey said. "Jennie, you mean that she thought up that hat-tossin', an' not you?"

Jennie was surprised at his amazement, and she said so.

"Why, I thought you knew she thought it up! It was her idea, but I said I'd better do it instead of her, an' then if there was any fuss, why it would come out all right for me because you was there. I told you all that, Asey!"

"Uh-huh, only you didn't bother to add that it was her original idea. What was this date she was so all-fired anxious to get to? Did she tell you?"

Jennie shook her head.

"No, she just said she didn't want to be late, an' it was very important that she was on time, an' if only she could manage to get across that intersection, she knew she could get there on time. 'Course, I thought she meant that once she was across, she could rip an' tear along to Provincetown, but I guess what she really meant was that once she got past the soldiers with the lanterns, she hoped she could cut across that Army string at the next turn. Asey, I think it's awful strange about those clams!"

"What's the matter with them?"

"Why, Syl's delivered clams for I don't know how many years, an' the worst thing ever happened to him was gettin' bit by the Carleys' police dog. You just deliver clams once, an' look what you run into! I don't see how it happened! There she was alive at the four corners, an' there she was shot dead at the Inn, an' then she walked past me, big as life, an' now—well, heaven only knows where the poor woman is now! Why, I can't believe what I seen with my own two eyes! I can't make head nor tail out of it!"

"Don't try," Asey advised, and turned back toward the Inn.

Jennie's plaintive reactions, he thought as he walked rapidly along, were certainly justified. He felt thwarted himself.

But after you thought things out, they weren't nearly as confusing as they appeared. Not, to be sure, that they made sense. But they at least made more sense than they had at first.

It hadn't seemed possible to him at first that the woman at the four corners could get back to the Inn before he and Jennie reached there in the truck. She had given the definite impression of wanting to go in an entirely different direction. She actually had started out in that direction. But it was easy to see how, on being held up by the Army, she might have said she wanted to go straight ahead even though her goal actually was the Inn. She had wit enough to know that her chance of being permitted to go straight ahead was greater than her chance of being allowed to cut across the column. Once past the intersection, she had probably taken the first left turn, cutting past the stalled Army, stepped on the gas, and been back inside the Whale Inn before he himself had finished picking up Jennie from the opposite corner.

That the woman could have been shot in the phone booth of the Inn's living room without someone having discovered her or having heard the shot also seemed incredible at first. But that situation was clearing up. Mrs. Doane had been out on the road somewhere, waiting to get gasoline for her car. The Doane girl had been outside somewhere, trying to fix up the Delco system. Neither of them had mentioned or summoned any other servants or staff, so it seemed reasonable to assume that none were around. Probably, so early in the season, the Inn wasn't overburdened with guests and the staff was correspondingly small.

So, the woman from the four corners had come into the empty, candle-lit living room, gone to the phone booth, and been shot.

Asey dismissed Jennie's vision of her walking across the living room, and attacked the problem of who could have moved that body in so short a time.

There was the person he had chased, the person who had knocked over the bucket of clams. He might have been waiting around outside just for the opportunity of removing that woman from the phone booth. It was a perfectly good possibility.

"But I wonder," Asey murmured aloud, "if someone hangin' around to steal a body away would be idiot enough to *let* himself trip over a bucket of clams!"

He shook his head and mentally checked off the clam-tripper. The hearty bald man who was trying to snare his chicken thief was too far away.

That left the Doanes, mother and daughter, and Mrs. Hingham, whom Asey at once eliminated. If a little noise in a hallway increased Mrs. Hingham's headache to a point where she felt she had to summon a doctor, the mere sight of a body would probably have knocked her out completely. Besides, she hadn't even gone downstairs.

Asey considered the Doanes.

The girl, he decided, was out. She wasn't the sort of girl who could whisk a body away one minute and gently poke fun at her mother's harangue the next minute.

But Mrs. Doane was an individual you could let yourself brood about. She was a large, powerful woman, and nearly as tall as Asey himself. If anyone around the Inn possessed the physique to move bodies, Mrs. Doane did. And she was the only person who'd made even the faintest slip of the tongue. "No body," under the circumstances, was a lot different from "nobody." That slip, coupled with her eagerness to get rid of Jennie and himself, didn't look so good.

Most important of all, she could switch her mood like a chameleon changed color. She could in an instant change the look on her face and the tone of her voice. To Asey, that ability was more significant than her powerful shoulders.

Of course, there was always the possibility that he was doing Mrs. Doane a great wrong. Perhaps she hadn't moved the body herself. But Asey couldn't help feeling that she knew something about it.

About a hundred feet from the Inn's graveled driveway, he slipped through the tall privet hedge and stood for a moment in its shadow while he surveyed the place.

As Mrs. Mercer's Boarding House, it had been a good-sized colonial house, he remembered. Rather boxlike, bare looking, and girdled about with an open piazza that gave the impression of being one huge rocking chair. But, with the passage of years, Asey guessed that the Inn's total area had been at least doubled. So many additions and corrections had taken place that it was difficult to tell where one ell began and another ell left off.

Now that the rain had stopped and the lights come on and he really had an opportunity to view the Whale Inn, Asey decided that the place could be summed up very briefly.

It bulged.

From where he stood he could see no less than three upper-story sun decks and two captain's catwalks, and as he started to circle around the building Asey began to feel that the amazing part of this business was perhaps not so much that a body had been lost as that a body had ever been found in the first place.

Perhaps, Asey thought, it had been a mistake on his part to assume that the body must necessarily have been removed by one of the people he had come in contact with. Those ells alone were capable of concealing a regiment.

As he neared one of them toward the rear of the building, lights flashed on, and Asey sidled over to the window of what turned out to be the Inn's modern and well-appointed kitchen.

He suppressed an exclamation as the person who had snapped on the lights swung around and revealed himself as the hearty bald man who had been hunting the chicken thief with such vigor.

With the air of one who belonged there and intended to stay, the bald man removed his coat, pulled off a bright-green sweater, unlaced a pair of wading boots and exchanged them for a pair of slippers he picked up from under one of the stoves.

"Huh!" Asey murmured under his breath. "Now who in blazes are you?"

He was considerably more curious when the man, after hanging up his wet overcoat, casually withdrew from its pockets a small pistol, a short, ugly-looking knife, and a blackjack.

Asey whistled softly to himself. Perhaps his abrupt departure from this walking arsenal of a man had been a wiser and a safer action than he ever could have guessed at the time.

Having stowed away his murderous collection in his hip pockets, the bald man put on a chef's white apron and set a chef's white cap on his head. Then he stood for several minutes in front of a mirror, adjusting the cap until he finally achieved that same cocky angle at which he had worn his little blue knitted cap.

When he at last turned around, Asey nearly let out a whoop.

Now he recognized the man.

Now, with that outfit on, he remembered who the bald man was. He was Washy Doane, the cook of his uncle's old five-masted schooner *R. R. Mayo*. Biffer Doane he had been called, owing to his violent tendency to biff over the head with the first object at hand anyone and everyone who disagreed with him. Sometimes, in fact, Washy didn't even bother to wait for any disagreement to take place. Sometimes Washy just biffed.

It wasn't a habit that endeared Washy to his employers, and Asey's uncle Custer Mayo had been about the only person in those far-off days who was willing to sign Washy on. Custer, a fat, philosophic man devoted to what he called his victuals, felt that Washy's cooking was worth a few cracked skulls, and he steadfastly refused to believe or even listen to anyone who pointed out to him that, on numerous occasions, Washy's victims never entirely recovered. Custer said firmly that he wouldn't allow his cook to be libeled.

And here was Washy Doane, Biffer Doane, the central figure of dock brawls from Portland to Sitka, his pockets stuffed with lethal weapons, amiably peeling himself a banana in the spotless, stainless steel kitchen of the Whale Inn!

Asey leaned back against the ell, and shook his head.

He was getting old, he told himself, old and slow. If only he had paid more attention to his Cousin Syl's discourses on the subject of his clam and fish customers, he would have known about Washy Doane. If he had only used his head, he would have caught on to the situation out there in the woods in all that downpour. He should have realized that Washy was talking about the Inn when he mentioned his land, his business, his chickens, and all the rest. If only he had thought twice, he would have guessed that Washy was the girl's father, the "Dad" she referred to as helping her to fix the Delco system when the lights went out. He certainly ought to have realized, after listening to Mrs. Doane, what Washy meant when he mentioned his wife in that tone of voice.

Asey grinned.

No one at sea had ever been able to tame Washy

Doane, but the Biffer had obviously met his match in the strapping Mrs. Doane!

His grin faded as Asey reflected on what complications the presence of Washy Doane might add to an already complicated situation. Innocent as he might appear, sitting there in the kitchen and munching at his banana, Washy was not a person you could pass over lightly.

If it hadn't been for that collection of pocket weapons, Asey wouldn't have considered it quite fair to judge the man on the basis of his past performances. But, with a gun, a knife, and a blackjack tucked away on his person, Asey could only come to the conclusion that Washy was unchanged.

On the other hand, Asey had never heard any gossip of Washy's giving vent to his violent tendencies by engaging in any skull-cracking around Quisset. Probably, with Mrs. Doane at his elbow, Washy hadn't been given much opportunity to let himself go.

No matter how you looked at it, Asey thought, bodies and sudden death were nothing new to Washy Doane. And while it was a little bizarre to think of Washy shooting a gray-haired woman to death in a telephone booth, Asey felt sure that Washy Doane would never balk at the task of moving the body.

He peeked in at the window again.

Washy was sitting at the center table with a small slate in front of him and two cookbooks by his elbow, apparently busily absorbed in the task of menu making. Twice, while Asey watched, Washy got up and checked items in the vast corner refrigerator. During one of his checking trips he poured himself out a tumbler of milk, and when a gray-and-white cat jumped up on the table, Washy obligingly poured some of his milk out on the table top for her to lap.

It certainly was a peaceful scene, Asey thought. It was so very peaceful, and Washy was so very innocent, and everything was so very tranquil and homey that it began to be just a little sinister.

Asey ducked back from the window as the head of Mrs. Doane appeared in the doorway behind Washy. She looked thoughtfully at her husband's back, and then disappeared from sight. She was tiptoeing, Asey concluded, because Washy gave no indication of having heard her.

"Huh!" Asey murmured. "Pussyfootin', are you?"

It might be just as well to find out what for, he figured, and promptly started around the ell.

He circled past an incinerator, a bulkhead, and a couple of woodsheds, hurried by a stretch of what seemed to be some of the original boarding-house piazza, and found himself once more at the front of the house.

A large black sedan was just drawing up to a stop by the front door, and Asey paused by a clump of lilac bushes while a large woman, of the type scornfully referred to by Jennie as overstuffed, was assisted out by an equally overstuffed chauffeur.

"Good night, Alfred," the woman said.

"Good night, ma'am."

The woman walked hesitantly up two steps, and then she turned around.

"Alfred, did you take my blue Bergdorf to the cleaner's?"

"Yes, Mrs. Clutterfield."

The woman still hesitated.

"And it will be quite all right about the pay raise, Alfred. I'm afraid I spoke rather hastily about it yesterday. Of course, times *are* hard, you know, Alfred. You can't be *sure* about things any more. Mr. Fredley at the bank said taxes were going to be simply *ter*rible—"

Asey's fingers drummed impatiently against his sides as Mrs. Clutterfield went into detail on the tax situation as foreseen by Mr. Fredley at the bank.

"But I will manage somehow," Mrs. Clutterfield said. "Er—Alfred, you won't *tell*, will you?"

Asey raised his eyebrows.

"No, Mrs. Clutterfield. You may depend on me."

"It will be our little secret, Alfred. Just a little secret between you and me," Mrs. Clutterfield said coyly.

"Yes, ma'am."

"I suppose you really can manage quite nicely by yourself, Alfred?"

Alfred nodded and assured Mrs. Clutterfield that he could manage all right, only it might take quite a long time.

Although it sounded to Asey like a thoroughly convincing assurance, it didn't appear to dispel the doubts in Mrs. Clutterfield's mind. Instead of proceeding up the steps and into the Inn and out of his way, as Asey fervently wished she would, Mrs. Clutterfield continued to teeter on the second step.

Her next contribution to the conversation was so unexpected that it hit Asey with the effect of a right to the jaw.

"I suppose," she said anxiously, "that body wouldn't really *keep* over night in the trunk, Alfred?"

"Well," Alfred said judicially, "it would, ma'am, but for the sake of the trunk, I think I'd better get a spade and a shovel and bury it like we planned, tonight. After all, Mrs. Clutterfield, we don't want anyone to find that body in our trunk. Remember that old lady in Bar Harbor, and the trouble we had there. Cost us quite a tidy sum in bribes before we was through, that time, and all because we didn't bury the body proper."

Asey pulled himself together and took a step forward, and then he paused as the front door of the Inn opened and Mrs. Doane emerged to inquire from the top step if Mrs. Clutterfield was all right.

"Quite, thank you," Mrs. Clutterfield told her with icy politeness.

"The clams came, after all," Mrs. Doane said brightly. "You should have stayed here for dinner. I *told* you I thought they'd come."

"Really?" Mrs. Clutterfield said. "I had an excellent meal at the Country Club, thank you. Very *good* clams, and *no* waiting."

She turned suddenly and walked down the steps and got back into the car.

"Aren't you coming in?" Mrs. Doane sounded faintly worried.

"I have changed my mind," Mrs. Clutterfield announced. "I am going to accompany Alfred on an errand. I may be quite late."

Asey didn't jump for the car at once. His plan was to saunter up about the time that Alfred was bundling Mrs. Clutterfield up with the lap robe, and request some explanations before either of them could recover their poise.

But his plan didn't even begin to work out. It never had a chance.

With a speed that Asey never expected from a man of Alfred's wide girth, Alfred adjusted the lap robe, got in front, started the car, and had it rolling around the driveway turntable and out of the Inn grounds almost before Mrs. Doane had the front door shut, and seconds before Asey thought of moving.

"Flat foot!" Asey muttered in disgust. "Ole flat foot, that's what you are!"

There was no excuse for him. But at least, he thought as he crossed from the clump of lilacs to an arbor on the other side of the drive, at least Mrs. Clutterfield's license-plate numbers were engraved for all time on his mind, and there still might be time, when Hanson came, to look into this fantastic business of Mrs. Clutterfield and her man Friday.

From where he stood he could see Mrs. Doane talking to Freddy in the living room, and Asey found himself wondering just what would happen if he were to barge in and demand to be shown the body at once. With almost any other woman, and in almost any other house, his bluff would probably work. But at the thought of the combination of Mrs. Doane and all that maze of ells, Asey shook his head. He had nothing to back up his bluff, and they could deny everything till the cows came home. It would be better to wait for Hanson and see what effect his brass buttons and official manner might produce.

Asey leaned against the arbor. To him, the time element was still the most puzzling thing about the removal of that woman's body. If the girl Freddy actually had gone directly downstairs and phoned Hanson when he told her to, and if she had stayed there in the living room until her mother returned, that margin of eight or nine minutes would be sharply reduced to only two or three. The thing, Asey thought, smacked of Thurston and Mulholland and Houdini. A woman was in a a box. You saw her in a box. Then, presto! The box was empty and the woman gone.

"Mayo," he said suddenly aloud, "you're a fool! That's what happened here!"

He could see now, as he looked across at the Inn, that the ell in which the telephone booth was located, at the left of the living room, was far wider than the mere width of the booth. It was certainly three times the width of the booth.

Asey grinned with pleasure as he strode across the driveway. The side of the telephone closet opposite the door opened, and he ought to have known as much, even in candlelight and with a body against it. He had a closet at home in Wellfleet, under his front stairs, that could be entered from the hall on one side and from his sitting room on the other. Neither any latch nor hinges had been visible here at the Inn, but another door was the answer. Asey felt sure it had to be.

He went close to the single little window in the ell

and was reaching up to unhook the screen when the lights conveniently flashed on inside.

Before he ducked down, Asey saw all that he needed to convince him that, for the first time this evening, he had managed to hit the nail on the head.

The telephone booth backed onto a narrow hall, and on the opposite side of that hall was a series of doors, apparently leading into closets, which Asey found himself yearning to explore.

He looked up cautiously to find Mrs. Doane in the hall, removing a dustpan and brush from one of the closets. Then she turned her head and listened to some sound in the house, hurriedly returned the dustpan and brush to their place, and slipped away, leaving the lights on.

A few seconds later, rather to Asey's amazement, Mrs. Hingham slipped into the hall, walked along to the rear door of the phone booth, flipped a latch, and went inside.

Even from the brief glimpse he had of her face, Mrs. Hingham didn't look to Asey like a woman suffering intensely from migraine. She looked to him rather like a woman suffering from intense bad temper.

She looked even angrier when she came out of the phone booth.

Asey looked after her thoughtfully as she flounced up the narrow hall.

He had eliminated Mrs. Hingham from his mental list of people who might have removed the body from the phone booth, but now that he turned the matter over in his mind, it occurred to him that Mrs. Hingham, after sailing out of her room past Jennie and himself, had not appeared again until the conclusion of Mrs. Doane's lecture to her daughter. It would have been no terrific task for Mrs. Hingham, during that interval, to come down some back flight of stairs, as she obviously must have come right now, to have moved that body, then returned upstairs to reappear on the main staircase loudly demanding a doctor. There was no better way to divert suspicion from yourself, Asey thought, than to put yourself on record as being ill enough to require a doctor.

Mrs. Doane was tiptoeing back into the hallway now, and a look of irritation crossed her face as a car horn sounded in the driveway. Asey could see how hard she gritted her teeth as she again departed.

He turned and looked expectantly at the headlights of the arriving car. It ought to be Hanson, but it would be all right with him if it turned out to be the overstuffed Mrs. Clutterfield and her nimble-footed yes man. That pair, Asey frankly admitted to himself, were preying on his mind more than Mrs. Hingham, Mrs. Doane, and Washy the Biffer all put together.

But the car which drew up to the front door was a custom-built Porter which he recognized as belonging to Quisset's leading citizen, Judge Houghton, a frequent visitor at the Porter house. His passenger, a tall, bearded man, jumped out after a brief conversation, ran up the steps and into the Inn. At least, Asey thought as the Judge's car swung around the turntable, the

Whale Inn possessed one guest who seemed to be normal, without headaches or without a body that required burial.

He felt less sure of that conclusion a moment later when the bearded man came out, walked down the steps, and looked cautiously to the left and right as if he expected something ferocious lurking in the bushes to leap out and jump at him.

Then, staring down at the gravel, the man walked slowly along the driveway.

"Lost somethin'?" Asey inquired as the man passed by him.

With a start, the man looked up, located Asey, and smiled.

"Yes, a cigarette lighter," he said. "Last time I lost it, a heavy rain turned it up—I say, I know you! Mayo. Asey Mayo, isn't it? I thought so. I called on you once a couple of summers ago. Remember?"

"I was tryin' to place your beard." Asey made his way around a flower bed and walked over to the man. "First I thought you was Bill Porter's explorer friend. But you're the genealogist, ain't you?"

"That's right. Rankin is the name. Jonathan Rankin." He shook hands with Asey. "I'm pleased you remember me. I remember our chat about the Mayo family, and also your excellent cousin—Jennie, wasn't it? She fed us hot sugar gingerbread and told me more about the Mayos in an hour than I'd learned in six months. What in the world are you doing here, Mayo?"

"Wa-el," Asey drawled a little, "it's sort of an involved story, Mr. Rankin. It's my impression that there's been a murder here, but—"

"What!"

"Uh-huh. But right now," Asey went on dryly, "if you was to ask me for proof, I'd look awful silly."

"What do you mean, man?"

Asey smiled. "I mean we had a body in a phone booth, an' now it ain't."

"You mean it's *gone?*" Rankin demanded. "Where?"

"It might not seem that way to you," Asey said, "but that's what I'm tryin' to find out right this minute. I don't mind tellin' you that I never put in a more startlin' half hour than this last one I spent around here peerin' into windows. I don't think I'd find many odder folks or odder things if I peered through the windows of the state hospital for the insane. Look, you're stayin' here, ain't you? Then," he added as Rankin nodded, "will you, for Pete's sakes, tell me somethin' about this setup?"

"The Inn? Oh, it's rather a decent place. I've put up here off and on for five or six years. Tell me, who's been killed?"

"If you asked my Cousin Jennie," Asey said, "she'd tell you it was a woman she seen first alive, an' then dead, an' then walkin' past her. But don't let's go into that right now. Tell me about this place."

"Well," Rankin said, "Mrs. Doane is a bit of a tartar, but the place is well run. Very well run for a tiny town like this. I've been doing a lot of work on some Massachusetts families, and whenever I have to look up records in this part of the world I make it a point to stay here. The food's excellent. Of course, the place really isn't open and running yet. They usually have a lot of college kids for waitresses and all, and they won't be here for another week. There's just a handful of guests, old reliables like myself, and a few others. Mrs. Doane is rather particular about her guests. There's a legend that she checks up on your rear molar fillings before she'll give you a reservation, and you really have to stay here eight or ten years before she stops viewing you with suspicion and gives you one of the better rooms. I'd still be under a cloud if she hadn't known most of my aunts and uncles for several decades. Who was killed?"

"I don't know," Asey said with perfect truth. "What about Washy?"

"Washy?" Rankin sounded bewildered.

"Mr. Doane."

"Oh." Rankin laughed. "He's an odd duck."

"Did he ever biff you," Asey inquired, "with a rollin' pin?"

"No, the worst time I have with him is to get him to stop telling me yarns about his years at sea," Rankin said. "To hear him talk, you'd think he was a combination of Leif Ericson, Captain Kidd, and Count von Luckner. He spins the most bloodthirsty yarns you ever heard."

"Ever noticed any bloodthirsty tendencies?" Asey said.

"I've noticed that he seems to enjoy killing chickens," Rankin said, "but you could hardly term that homicidal.

The daughter's a nice child. She's having a thwarted love affair at the moment which is inclined to make her slightly distrait, but ordinarily she's very pleasant, and probably the only person who isn't terrified of Mrs. D's tongue. Now look, Mayo, *who* has been killed, Elissa Hingham?"

"What makes you think she might've been?" Asey countered with another question.

"You've heard of people who were born to be killed, haven't you?" Rankin said. "Well, Elissa is one of those. She's been asking to be killed all her life, and I shouldn't be at all surprised to find her lifeless body crumpled in a little heap somewhere, under the present circumstances. Was it Elissa?"

"What do you mean by the present circumstances?" Asey wanted to know.

Rankin took a few steps down the driveway.

"Right around here is where I lost that lighter," he said. "I had my raincoat slung over my shoulder, and it popped out of the pocket—aha! I thought I'd find it!"

He bent over and picked something up from the side of the driveway.

"What about the present circumstances?" Asey persisted.

"See?" Rankin displayed a small chromium pocket lighter. "I mean her husband, Mayo. And if you don't know about him, then I don't think it was Elissa after all. And if there's really been trouble here, I'm not going to prejudice you against her by bandying her private life about. If she hasn't been killed, her domestic problems don't matter. I wish you'd tell me—I say, it wasn't Lady Boop, was it?"

"Who?"

Rankin laughed.

"That's my own private name for Mrs. Clutterfield. Violet Clutterfield. You know her, don't you? You don't? Really? Mayo, I'm beginning to think that you don't get around much in Quisset's upper crust!"

"I don't," Asey told him. "For the last six months, I've been so busy trailin' Bill Porter around that I haven't even been on the Cape at all very much. I know some folks here, of course, but Quisset's never been a town I seem to get to, somehow, an' if I do, I just pass through it without noticin' if it's got an upper crust or a meringue. Tell me about Lady Boop—an' look, let's stroll down the drive a bit so's we ain't quite so visible from the Inn."

"About the only place you're visible from now," Rankin said, "is my bathroom window. Why don't you want to be seen?"

"I'm tryin' out the enough-rope theory," Asey said. "It bein' about all I can do till Lieutenant Hanson of the state cops shows up. What about Lady Boop?"

Rankin smoothed his neat Vandyke and looked at Asey reflectively.

"D'you think it's entirely fair," he asked, "to pump me this way, without telling me who's been killed? I can only give you my opinions, which are largely biased, and might not coincide at all with someone else's opinions. For all I know, I may be either maligning the dead or slipping a noose around someone's throat!

You're out of sight here, by the way, but you can still get a pretty good view of the place, if that's what you're after."

"It is." Asey paused by a clump of pines and looked back at the Inn. "I'm also after a kind of panoramic view of the people here. I want to get 'em sorted out in my mind. An' like I told you, I don't even know who the body is that we haven't got. But I'm considerably interested in Lady Boop."

"Well, she's a large, plushy lady," Rankin said, "whose husband died ten years ago and left her a fortune, and since then her mother and two sisters have all died and left her their fortunes. Also a grandmother and a great-aunt. And last month, I believe it was another great-aunt who contributed. As Freddy Doane quipped, everyone who goes to their reward seems to kick back a good share to Lady Boop."

"Rich as that, is she?"

"She pays more taxes annually," Rankin said with a trace of bitterness, "than you and I will ever earn in all our lives. I can easily picture her dying of apoplexy, but I suppose people with all that money are a constant invitation and challenge to murderers. *Was* it Lady Boop? Because if it wasn't, by the process of elimination, that leaves only Horace and—"

"Hey!" Asey said suddenly.

"What's the matter?"

Asey drew Rankin back into the shadow of the pines and pointed up toward the roof of the Inn.

"Look up there. D'you see somebody on the catwalk by the small chimney?"

Rankin put on a pair of glasses.

"Yes! Yes, I do! It's a woman! For God's sakes, it's Elissa! What's *she* up to?"

"Not so loud!" Asey cautioned.

"She's crazy! She can't get down from there! What's she doing?"

"Shush!" Asey said. "She'll hear!"

"She's *dragging* something—Mayo," Rankin said in horror, "it's a *body!*"

4

C AN'T be!" Asey seemed to be trying to convince himself rather than Rankin. "Can't be!"

"It certainly *is* a body!" Rankin insisted.

Asey peered up at the roof. When the wind blew them just the right way, the leaves of the maple trees in front of the Inn swayed and let the street light shine on the figure on the catwalk. It was Mrs. Hingham, all right, although she'd changed her billowing, satin house coat for something more practical. A trench coat or a polo coat, it looked like. And she certainly was dragging something.

But it couldn't be a body, Asey told himself. At least, it couldn't be the body he and Jennie had seen. That had been downstairs, and its removal up a flight of stairs was a physical feat beyond the ability of Mrs. Hingham. It couldn't be the body, and yet Asey couldn't imagine what Mrs. Hingham was alternately tugging and dragging at if it wasn't a body.

"Rankin," he said suddenly, "would there be an elevator in the Inn?"

"Two of 'em. Let's—"

"Two?" Asey asked in surprise. One was unusual enough in a Cape Inn.

"One to the dining room, and one in the alcove off the living room. For the aged and gouty. They're more what you'd call lifts than elevators. Mayo, let's go and look into this!"

Asey took his arm and pulled him back.

"Wait."

"For the love of God, what for?"

"If we surprise her now," Asey said, "I have a horrid feelin' that by the time we get to the Inn we'll find Mrs. Hingham back in her bed, sufferin' terrible with migraine."

"So she's been pulling her migraine act again, has she?" Rankin demanded. "Hm! But we can see her! She can't deny being there when the two of us saw her there!"

"Maybe she can't," Asey said, "but I bet you she will. Wait, Mr. Rankin. Wait an' see what she's aimin' to do. After all this to-do, I want to see what her underlyin' plan was."

Rankin said in exasperated tones that he didn't see that waiting and watching and generally prolonging the agony would get Asey or anybody else anywhere at all.

"Get her," he added, "get the body, and get to the root of the thing!"

"I'll admit it's sort of the first impulse you get," Asey said. "But consider. If she finds a body in her room, say, an' she thinks it's the best thing to put the body elsewhere, she'll probably drag it along to that adjoinin' sun deck an' leave it there. Could happen, you know. But, on the other hand, if it's a body she's responsible for, as you might say, she's probably got some idea of removin' it to as far distant a place as she can manage. The more effort she makes to take it away, an' the farther she takes it, the redder her hands are, an' the harder it's goin' to be for her to deny anythin'. Then you really got her."

"I think that's nonsense," Rankin said flatly.

"Maybe so, but you," Asey said, "ain't seen what I seen tonight in the line of bodies bein' one place one minute an' elsewhere the next, an' nobody seemin'ly knowin' anythin' about it, or bein' involved with it. Now that I got someone with a body, I want to run 'em to the ground with it. I think—what in time!"

"She's running back to that eave door!" Rankin said. "Something's frightened her!"

Asey pointed to the man marching down the middle of the driveway.

"It's Hanson! Golly, he would turn up now!" he said. "If he goes bargin' into the Inn, he'll spoil everything. An' if Mrs. Hingham spots us rushin' up an' hailin' him, that won't work out, neither—hey, gimme your little lighter, quick, will you?"

Rankin looked puzzled, but he dropped the lighter in Asey's outstretched hand, and Asey promptly raised his arm and pitched the lighter straight at Hanson.

It hit him on the shoulder, and Hanson stopped and looked around him curiously. But he didn't seem particularly startled.

Asey sighed. He should have known that nothing smaller than a barn door would have had any effect on the fellow.

He remembered suddenly that he had in his coat pocket the flashlight Washy had pressed into his hand during the chicken-thief episode.

"That's the thing!" Rankin said as he drew it out. "Flash it at him!"

"Not with Mrs. Hingham up there to see!" Asey said, and raised his arm again.

The flashlight sailed through the air and landed at Hanson's feet. This time he seemed to begin to get the idea. Picking up the flashlight, he walked on down the driveway toward the pines where Rankin and Asey stood.

"Keep on walkin', Hanson," Asey said as he neared them. "Don't stop. Keep walkin' about six feet more, an' then turn around an' march out the way you come. Go down the road as far as that locust grove, then circle around back here to us so's you won't be seen from the Inn. We'll wait here. I'll explain later."

Hanson obeyed without question, a phenomenon as rare in him as it would have been in Jennie.

"D'you mind my saying," Rankin sounded amused, "that this seems really rather involved?"

"Nope," Asey told him, "I don't mind a speck. It is involved. But I hope it's goin' to have a simple endin', which you wouldn't get if you barged inside the Inn right now an' started slattin' around, yellin' for explanations. Think of all the Doanes an' Mrs. Hingham, all denyin' an' affirmin' an' talkin' at once, an' you can see where it'd take you half the night to get any place. Hey —I think she's comin' back! Uh-huh, she is! She fell for it. She's decided Hanson was just some poor sap that turned into the wrong driveway!"

"She's back," Rankin said, "but she isn't *doing* anything! What's she waiting for? Why doesn't she get along with it?"

"Give her time."

"*I* don't think she's going to do anything more," Rankin said impatiently. "Look, Mayo, I think she's stuck. Her car's in the garage. There." Rankin pointed to a building beyond the turntable. "She's got to get that body down from the sun deck, get herself down, get her car, get the body into it—"

His patience was practically exhausted by the time Hanson reached them via his circuitous route.

"Hi," Asey said. "Where's your car?"

"Parked down the road a bit. Jennie seemed to think that was what I ought to do. Asey, Jennie told me all about this, but I don't understand it! And whenever I asked her to explain anything, I couldn't understand it as well as I hadn't before! *What's* happened here?"

"We're endeavorin'," Asey said, "to find out. Hanson, peek up on the roof—no, this way. By the sun deck. See the lady?"

"What's *she* doing?"

"Lady has a body," Asey said. "She's now in the process of broodin'—hey, come back here! Hold on, Hanson. We ain't rushin' in on her. We're goin' to let her brood an' see what she does with it. You go get your car an' ease it up across from the drive, an' be ready to follow her in case she gets to the point of drivin' off. We're goin' to wait here an' watch for developments, an' if they don't develop pretty soon, we'll join up in a bit of confrontin'."

"But, Asey," Hanson began, "I—"

"Pop along an' get the car."

"But look here," Hanson said plaintively, "I only want to know one thing, Asey! Is all that stuff Jennie told me *true?*"

"Most probably," Asey said. "Maybe she's done a little embellishin', but she must've stuck pretty close to facts. If she'd started wonderin', you wouldn't be here now. Say, where's *that* car goin'?"

"What car?" Hanson returned. "I don't hear any car."

"See them headlights, over yonder?"

Asey pointed to the left beyond the kitchen ell.

"Service drive," Rankin said. "It swings along over there."

"How'n time did I miss that?" Asey asked, and at once answered his own question. "That rain the first time, I guess, an' I cut in the other side of it the next time. I was so busy computin' the area of them ells, I suppose it's no wonder I missed a driveway."

"Well, I didn't," Hanson said. "It was full of puddles up to my knees—"

He broke off as Asey grabbed his arm.

"Hey! We got to beat it on the double-quick! Hustle up!"

"What for? She hasn't left that roof, has she? I can see her."

"But she just waved! Now she's goin' down! Hustle, Hanson! Get goin'! Whoever come in that car is goin' to help her! She waved, I tell you! Come on!"

"Can I come too?" Rankin demanded.

"Hustle!"

With Asey leading, the three of them cut back through the woods, circled wide around the Inn, and reached Hanson's police car a split second after a sedan cut out of the service drive.

"I'll drive," Asey said, and started off with part of Hanson and most of Jonathan Rankin clinging perilously to the running board.

Hanson took it as a matter of course. He had driven with Asey too many times before in Asey's own low-slung Porter roadster and when Asey was really in a hurry to be perturbed about a slight catapulting.

But Rankin was frankly shaken by the experience, and he said so, as soon as he regained sufficient breath.

"Do you," he inquired acidly, "always start off like that?"

"Only," Asey told him, "when the car I'm chasin' has the choice of two main roads an' fifty million little ones—that's funny, Hanson. They're goin' down the Cape. They're takin' the Pochet turn."

"How do you know? I can't even see the car!" Rankin complained. "And what made you guess that Elissa might be having help?"

"Wa-el," Asey said, "like you pointed out, she *was* kind of stuck. An' she seemed to be waitin'. An' I seen her make a kind of surreptitious phone call, usin' the back door of that livin' room phone booth, so I put two an' two together an' wondered if she wasn't just possibly waitin' for some help from the person she called. Hanson, this is fishy."

Hanson and Rankin both instantly demanded to know why.

"Because," Asey said, "they're goin' too blessed fast. We're a lap behind 'em, an' look at our speedometer needle."

"I'm trying not to," Rankin said. "And what's so fishy, as you term it, about their haste? After all, they have a body to dispose of, and they want to dispose of it with all possible speed and celerity, don't they?"

"If you had a body to dispose of, an' if you possessed just a quarter of a teaspoonful of common sense, would you drive like a fool an' lay yourself open to accidents, an' village cops' speed traps, not to mention the fellows Hanson plants around these roads just to haul in speeders?" Asey returned. "I'm sure I wouldn't. I'd drive thirty-five miles an hour on the right-hand side of the road, blow my horn pretty at all intersections, an' try to seem like somebody on their way home from Prayer Meetin'. This gets fishier an' fishier, Hanson. They've taken the turn into Pochet village."

Rankin took off his shell-rimmed glasses, wiped them as well as he could in his cramped position next the door, put the glasses back on, and shook his head.

"I'm still damned if *I* can see any car at all!" he said.

"Why, it's right *there!*" Hanson said. "Right on—

let's see. That'd be the Old Mill road, wouldn't it, Asey?"

"Well, yes," Asey said. "Only kind of a little mite more to the left, on the cut-through that runs past the ball park."

"A little mite more to the left, indeed!" Rankin said sarcastically. "You mean a good half mile to the left! Hanson, *you* can't see that car any more than I can, and you know it! And if you really know, Mayo, and if you really are following it, why don't you catch up with it and grab them for speeding, and put an end to this—er—well, I suppose you *could* call it just a ride, but it seems like such an awfully scant and inadequate little word! If this is merely a ride, then I've been traveling on gocarts all these years!"

Asey chuckled.

"Bear up," he said. "I'm goin' to see this thing through to the bitter end. Maybe you better hold on tight, Mr. Rankin. I'm goin' to creep up on 'em a mite. I want to know what they're up to in the village."

"Creep!" Rankin said. "Creep! I'm the one who's creeping! I'm a creeping piece of goose flesh! That speedometer needle won't *go* any farther!"

When it did, Rankin took off his glasses, folded them, and tucked them away in the pocket of his brown tweed coat.

"Hey, I can see the car now! Look!" Hanson pointed.

"My eyes," Rankin told him, "are closed. Tell me when we've landed."

Hanson laughed.

"I wonder what he'd have said, Asey," he suggested, "if he'd been with us that night last December when we were chasing that Portygee in the blizzard, and you got tired of hanging behind the snow plow? We were in Asey's roadster, see, and the top was down because it wasn't snowing when we started, and when we tried to get it up, we couldn't because a brace had jammed. And the snow got so deep on the floor of the car, we had to keep stopping and scooping it out!"

"To me," Rankin said, "it sounds perilously like Baron Munchausen. With just a faint trace of Dick Tracy."

"It was a Dick Tracy finish, all right!" Hanson said. "You'd ought to have seen that finish, Mr.—say, I don't know your name!"

"Meet Mr. Rankin," Asey said. "Mr. Rankin's a genealogist, Hanson."

"Oh," Hanson said, and added, after a pause, "Do things with rocks, huh?"

"No, I do things with families," Rankin said with a trace of laughter in his voice. "People with nothing better to do pay me to track down their family trees. And if I come to a violent end on this little ride, as I fully expect to, there are at least three fat dowagers and two brash Middle Westerners who'll cry themselves to sleep because I never finished their ancestral charts—look, we must be there, aren't we?"

"Uh-huh. You can open your eyes now," Asey said, "I'm parkin'."

Rankin looked around Pochet's main street.

"Where's Elissa?"

"Parked by the station. I drove past 'em. Kind of gay here tonight, ain't it?"

"Gay? It's almost abandoned! What's the reason for all this reckless illumination?" Rankin indicated the brightly lighted stores in front of them. "Stores open, crowds milling around—what's the event? Is there a carnival in town, or is it bank night?"

"Tomorrow's a half holiday in these parts," Asey told him. "Seventeenth of June. May even be a bonfire later, if the boys get ambitious, an' things ain't too wet to burn. They—"

"See here," Rankin interrupted, "now that you've caught up with them, aren't you going to see what they're doing?"

"I'm watchin' right now." Asey indicated the rearview mirror. "Mrs. Hingham's just gone into Fishback's Hardware Store."

"Hardware?" Rankin sounded incredulous. *"Hardware?* Mayo, you've made a mistake, that's all. You picked up some other car and followed that! Elissa Hingham's been a number of places, but she never entered a hardware store in all her life! If you asked me to name three places Elissa would never go, I should unhesitatingly say three hardware stores! What in the name of all that's holy would Elissa be doing in a hardware store?"

"Time will tell," Asey said. "Fishback's is where she went."

Rankin said that he didn't believe it, and that Elissa Hingham didn't know what hardware was.

"Wa-el," Asey said, "she's findin' out fast. She seems to have been purchasin' a pickax. See her?"

Rankin craned his neck. "No."

"Look into the mirror." Hanson obligingly moved over toward Asey.

Rankin wriggled himself around until he finally caught a glimpse of Mrs. Hingham with her newly purchased pickax.

Then, after straightening out his collar and tie and pulling his coat back in place, he shook his head and announced that it was all beyond him.

"All I can say is that the sight of Elissa Hingham bearing a pickax startles me a lot more than the sight of her dead body ever would! Mayo, now that she's got her pickax, what d'you expect she intends to do with it?"

"Wa-el," Asey said, "most usually when people buy pickaxes they plan to dig. But you can't ever tell. Maybe Mrs. Hingham's aimin' to join the W.P.A."

Rankin sighed.

"Mayo, do you always take this sort of thing so lightly? Here you are trailing a body, and you jape! Here's Elissa removing a body, and you don't seem to care a whit!"

"I care deeply," Asey said. "Hold on some more, Mr. Rankin, we're startin' up again, just's soon's they get by."

He and Hanson bumped their heads trying to get a clear view of the car as it went past.

"What did that guy driving have on?" Hanson

asked curiously. "He seemed to have something funny around his neck. Was it a scarf, Asey?"

"Couldn't see."

Asey swung the police car out of its parking space and started after the sedan.

"I got a pretty good look at him," Hanson said. "I think I've seen that guy somewhere before. Did he look like someone you knew, Asey? Did he look familiar?"

"Didn't notice."

His crisp, abrupt answers, in such contrast to his easy, joking manner of a minute before, appeared to trouble Rankin. He looked questioningly at Hanson, who merely shrugged.

"What's wrong?" Rankin formed the words with his lips.

When the car swerved around a corner, Hanson took the occasion to whisper in Rankin's ear as he lurched against him.

"Asey's like that some times."

Asey, keeping just in sight the taillights of the sedan containing Mrs. Hingham and her friend, paid no attention to either of his passengers.

This whole thing was getting fishier by the minute, he thought. Again the driver of the sedan was hurtling along at a terrific speed, cutting corners, slamming past side roads. And he wasn't heading for any remote beach or secluded woods. He was heading into South Pochet village, which was well lighted and well populated, and in general no place to dispose of a body.

That had certainly looked like a body up there on the roof, Asey thought. It had every appearance of a body. Mrs. Hingham had certainly purchased a pickax, which certainly would come in very handy for burying a body.

But gravediggers would hardly set out in costume. And under Mrs. Hingham's trench coat she was wearing something that looked like an evening dress to Asey. And the man driving that car had what seemed to be a ruff around his neck, and his coat looked more like a satin waist.

Those costumes, and that crazy driving! Asey shook his head.

If it should turn out that this excursion was a wild-goose chase, as he now strongly suspected, he was going to look like considerable of a fool. But that wouldn't matter. What would matter was that in racing off from the Inn, he might well have presented to someone, on a silver platter, the opportunity of making away with the body in comparative peace and safety.

And there was always that fantastic possibility rearing its ugly head that Mrs. Clutterfield and her man Friday might have had the body all the time anyway!

The car ahead cut off on a side road, and a little smile began to play around Asey's mouth. He thought he was beginning to understand this.

"Hey, Asey, where's this road go to?" Hanson wanted to know. "Isn't this the way to that dairy farm?"

"It was."

He drew the police car up by the barn just as Mrs. Hingham alighted from the sedan.

"Ah!" Hanson said with relish. "They're going to drag it out. Come on!"

He and Rankin leapt from the car, but Asey stayed behind the wheel.

He was chewing on his pipe stem when they returned a few minutes later.

"Asey," Hanson said breathlessly, "you know what? You know what that was? You know what we been following all this time?"

"Rug, huh?" Asey said.

"How'd *you* know?" Rankin demanded.

"I guessed. What was that bandy-legged fellow in tights supposed to be? No wonder he stayed in the car where nobody could see him!"

"He," Rankin said, "was a page. I asked him from what, and he said, just a page. Mayo, did you *know* this was the South Pochet Barn Theater?"

"It come to me after we hit the side road," Asey said. "I drove Betsey Porter to their formal openin' last summer. Why'd Mrs. Hingham choose such a roundabout way to remove a rug? Was it Mrs. Doane's rug?"

"No, her own," Rankin said. "She bought it last week in Hyannis, and Bram Reid, the director, saw it and wanted it for the set of their first play here. She refused to let him have it, but tonight she decided she was—I quote—a selfish pig, and he could have the rug. Her migraine at once left her, so she phoned for someone to come and help her get the rug."

"Somehow," Asey said, "that don't all follow."

"That's Elissa's story. After troubling Mrs. D. so much with her migraine, she didn't want to trouble Mrs. D. any more. So she hit on the roof route. Maybe that sounds illogical to you, Mayo?"

"It ain't the most sterlin' logic I ever heard," Asey admitted.

"Let me assure you it's characteristic. The pickax, I might add, is a prop."

"Just what kind of a play," Asey started the car, "needs a page boy with a ruff, an' a pickax, an' a Persian rug?"

"Elissa said it was a dear little fantasy," Rankin told him, "and I see no reason to doubt her. Er—now you know a little more about Elissa, don't you, Mayo?"

"She certainly seems like a creature of impulse," Asey said. "What is she, an actress?"

Rankin said that depended entirely on one's point of view.

"Personally, I'd sum her up as a thwarted prima donna. Now what?"

"What I'd like," Hanson said, "is some food. I been up at Camp Edwards all day teaching the traffic squad, and I rushed down here without dinner when Jennie called. We got time enough to get some food, haven't we, Asey?"

"What we got to do," Asey said, "is get straight back to the Inn an' comb the place from attic to cellar an' give Mrs. Doane and everybody else a little re-fined third degreein'. An' if you want to kick me for gettin' sidetracked on this crazy chase, go on. I deserve it."

"Did *you* have dinner?" Hanson inquired coldly.

"Nope."

"Well, then!" Hanson said. "Let's stop anyway at the corner diner and get some sandwiches. It wasn't a crazy chase, Asey, and if it'd taken a little longer, why we'd been longer, wouldn't we? So we certainly got ten minutes to get some sandwiches. Get 'em and eat 'em in the car, huh?"

"Somethin' within me says we shouldn't stop, an' somethin' else says we will." Asey drew up at the corner diner. "Get me anything that's ready, an' some coffee in one of those paper things."

Hanson urged him to come in.

"Nope. If I do," Asey said, "we'll just find ourselves sittin' down gorgin' ourselves on Artie's prize fifty-cent dinner. Bring it out, an' hurry up!"

"Well, all right," Hanson said reluctantly.

It was plain that the idea of gorging himself on one of Artie's regular dinners appealed to Hanson a lot more than the thought of a few ready-made sandwiches to be gulped down en route.

"Rankin," Asey said, "would you step in there after him an' stand at his elbow in a menacin' fashion an' keep him from succumbin' to anythin' that requires time? He knows I'm hungry myself, an' he'll tease me into a full meal if I go in."

Rankin laughed. "After that drive, I should think you'd need a real meal to restore you, anyway! Sure, I'll restrain him for you."

Asey leaned his elbows on the wheel. He needed more than a meal to snap him into this business, he thought. He needed a night's sleep. The last two days had been nothing but a constant rush by plane with Bill Porter from one factory to another, and the trip back to the Cape had been both hectic and tiring.

He sat up with a jerk as a car drove past the diner.

Lurched was maybe a better word than drove, he thought. It had lurched so close to Artie's neon sign that the fender almost scraped the post.

Then Asey noticed the license-plate numbers.

Massachusetts 68807.

It was Mrs. Clutterfield's car!

Asey's hand went to the switch key. He started the car, and then, when the big sedan had lurched on down the road a way, he unostentatiously slid the police car out of Artie's driveway after it.

Something was certainly the matter with Mrs. Clutterfield's chauffeur. Something was basically and radically wrong.

The sedan wandered from one side of the road to the other, but mostly it preferred the left side, to the infinite annoyance of the several drivers who practically had to force their cars up trees in order to escape emminent collision.

Recognizing the police car, one of the drivers howled angrily at Asey to pull that damn drunk off the road before she hurt somebody.

Asey waved reassuringly, and continued on.

The silk shade in the sedan's rear window was drawn, thus blocking his view, but he had suspected, even before the driver howled, that the car was not being piloted by Alfred. The drunkest chauffeur in the world couldn't steer that way! It must be Mrs. Clutterfield herself.

And for the safety of the general public, Asey decided, it would be best to pull her off the road entirely.

He blew the horn urgently and started alongside.

At once, Mrs. Clutterfield steered sharply to the left.

Asey braked, muttered things under his breath, and started to cut past her on the right.

Mrs. Clutterfield steered sharply to the right.

Asey tried again to pass on the left, with very nearly disastrous results.

"By golly," Asey said, "I'll *force* you over!"

He abandoned that plan when it became apparent that the only person who was going to suffer was himself. Hanson's light car couldn't stand up against that heavy, long, wheel-based thing.

As far as nifty blocking was concerned, he thought, Mrs. Clutterfield might have spent three years in Stanford's backfield!

"Okay," Asey said with resignation. "Okay, Sister Jane. I'll follow you!"

He did, cautiously, and with growing admiration for her hairbreadth escapes.

Her turn off the main road reminded Asey of an old-fashioned movie comedy when the cross-eyed comedian's car would swing up a crowded avenue, weaving in and out of a conglomeration of streetcars, fire engines, trucks, baby carriages, and pedestrians.

Her final jackknife swerve between two trucks was something he himself would never, in his wildest moment, have attempted.

He followed her up a rutted lane. Sometimes the sedan's two front wheels canted over the ruts to the right, sometimes they canted to the left. In general, Mrs. Clutterfield's progress resembled that of a mortally sick earthworm.

Finally, at an angle which completely blocked his way, the sedan came to rest with its front wheels sloping gently toward a ditch. Something about it reminded Asey irresistibly of a dog playing dead.

He swung open the car door and got out, and was halfway to the sedan when the fat figure of Alfred appeared from the bushes to his left.

"Inspector!" Alfred said breathlessly. "Inspector! Hey, Inspector!"

Asey turned around.

"Inspector," Alfred went on, "let me explain all this to you, Inspector! Here."

Asey stared down at the heap of bills, clearly visible in the glow of the headlights, in Alfred's outstretched hand.

"I knew your lights," Alfred said. "I know the fog lights on your cars. Here, Inspector. You take this and let me explain. I was afraid this'd happen. I tried to stop her, but she got away from me. Let me explain, Inspector, will you?"

"Go on," Asey said.

"The trouble is," Alfred lowered his voice confidentially, "the madam can't drive, see? She can't get a license. She's been turned down for a license about ten thousand times, see? But she's crazy to drive. Can't keep her hands off a wheel, see? And just now when my back was turned, off she went, see?"

"You mean, you'd left her alone in the car? What did you get out for?" Asey demanded.

Alfred said in hurt tones that he'd just stepped out of the car for a moment, that was all, and when he came back, the car was steaming up the lane.

"The madam's all right, you understand, Inspector!" he added. "There's nothing the matter with her only she just can't drive, and she's crazy to—uh—what'd she hit?"

"Plenty," Asey said gravely. "Plenty."

Alfred's hand dug into his pocket.

"Listen, Inspector, let's you and me settle this, huh, shall we? My name's Moriarty, by the way. Most likely you know my brother, Captain Moriarty, Station Forty, up in Boston? Anyway you know my brother in the registry. Everybody knows Pat. Say, maybe we can settle everything, huh?"

"Meanin'," Asey said, "that if we can't settle it now, it'll get settled anyways?"

"Oh, I wouldn't say *that!*" Alfred said hurriedly. "You got me all wrong, Inspector! Only there's more than one of your boys around here that's maybe going to get into trouble if we do. There's more than one of your boys wearing hundred-dollar suits of clothes because of the madam's little weakness. Yes, sir!"

"So?" Asey, who knew intimately most of Hanson's troopers in the vicinity, was pretty sure that Alfred was lying.

"And if you don't mind my saying so," Alfred observed, "you could do with a hundred-dollar suit yourself, Inspector. Maybe a couple of 'em, huh?"

"Alfred!" Mrs. Clutterfield called out plaintively. "Alfred! Alfred! Where are you, Alfred! I can't work the door!"

"Oh, God, she's stuck again!" Alfred scurried off.

Asey watched while Alfred jiggled the sedan's door handle and extricated Mrs. Clutterfield from the front seat. Gripping her firmly by the elbow, he put her in the back seat, said something to her, and pointedly closed the door.

He was mopping his forehead when he returned to where Asey stood.

"Now, Inspector," he said, "let's us—"

"Just what," Asey interrupted sternly, "was you buryin', somethin' she run over?"

Alfred's eyes almost popped out of his head, and he wet his lips nervously.

"Cat?" Asey said. "Dog?"

"Goat." Alfred seemed suddenly deflated. "Say, how'd you know I buried anything?"

"I know a lot," Asey said darkly. "Where is it?"

Alfred produced a flashlight and led the way to a little mound near the side of the road.

"Here it is. Look, Inspector, here's the trouble, see? If we go tell people what we run over, they take one look at my uniform, see, and the car, and her diamonds, and why then a cat costs its weight in gold, see? And it isn't like we didn't make it up. We do. Next day we go to the place, see, and we buy an antique."

"What?"

"Yes, that's the way the madam figured it out. Next day we stop at the house and ask if they got any antiques, and then we buy something—any old thing, see? And pay a crazy price for it. We're going to this place where the goat was tomorrow, see, and buy a well sweep."

"Alfred," Asey said, "you're makin' this up as you go along!"

"It's God's truth, Inspector! God's truth, so help me! She has dinner at the club, see? And on the way home—well, maybe she had a cocktail with her dinner, I don't know. Anyway, nothing'll do but she's got to drive, see? Well, it's a long straight stretch there, see, and I thought if I let her drive along it, then she'll shut up and give me some peace for a day or two, maybe. I thought it'd be safe enough there. It's a wide road, and only one house the whole length of it. So I give in and let her take the wheel. And bang! She gets the goat. Look, I'll show you."

He uncovered sufficient evidence to convince Asey.

"There." Alfred smoothed over the loose earth and then shouldered the shovel that had been lying on the ground. "Now I've given you the whole story, I'll get back and see to her."

He fumbled in his pocket.

"What's that?" Asey inquired, pointing to the small bottle Alfred had brought forth.

"Smelling salts. She'll be all to pieces by now. Let me tell you, Inspector," Alfred said in a burst of confidence, "I drove for the best people twenty years, but I never knew what it was to work for a living till I worked for the madam!"

"Tough, huh?"

"Tough! Say, I'm telling you she watches the mileage like a hawk to see I don't waste a drop of gas, but if I was to give you five hundred bucks to keep quiet about the goat and her driving around without a license, she wouldn't never bat an eyelash! Why, she wouldn't give ten cents to a blind beggar froze solid in a snowdrift for a cup of coffee to thaw him out," Alfred said bitterly. "But you know how much cash she gives me to keep in my pants pocket to ease her out of the trouble she gets into with her driving? A grand! And ninety-five per cent of the time there isn't a guy humane enough to cut me in on as much as a sawbuck! And me with a wife and four kids! Honest to God, Inspector, tough ain't the word. If I can't settle you, bang! I'm out on my ear."

"A grand, huh?" Asey said with sudden inspiration. "Alfred, I'll settle."

Alfred beamed, put down the shovel, and proceeded to count out bills.

"There," he said. "A grand."

Asey presented Alfred with a hundred, folded the remainder and tucked it into his wallet. Betsey Porter's ambulance fund, he thought, might just as well profit by this dead goat, and it was better for Mrs. Clutterfield's money to be in circulation than stagnating in Alfred's pants pocket.

"Inspector," Alfred said, "you're a white man. Yes, sir, you're a white man! It's a pleasure to do business with you."

"Thanks," Asey said dryly. "Now, wait a sec before you revive Lady Boop. Let me get somethin' straight. You an' she was at the club for dinner this evenin', wasn't you? Say, around six."

"She was," Alfred said. "I wasn't. Think she'd waste money buying me a meal at the club? Not much she wouldn't. I ate at the boarding house I live at, off the main street over in Quisset."

"You don't live at the Whale Inn, huh?"

"No. At this lousy boarding house—say, how'd *you* know she lived at the Inn?"

"I'm part Yogi," Asey said. "Then neither of you two was anywhere near the Whale Inn around six or so this evenin'?"

"Well, *I* was there—oh, I don't know just what time it was," Alfred said. "The madam had this dress to go to the cleaner's, see? The blue dress she calls her Bergdorf. I forgot it, so after I left her at the club I went back to the Inn and got it—come to think of it, I guess it was around six. The lights went off about then, and I was there when they went out."

"Alfred," Asey said, "sit down on that nice rock yonder an' tell me things. Who'd you see at the Inn? What was goin' on there?"

"Nothing," Alfred said promptly. "Nobody was there at all."

"Come on an' think! Must have been somebody," Asey said. "Freddy Doane, Mr. Doane, someone!"

"Well, I guess Freddy was in the living room. She usually is about that time. I don't know. I didn't see her. I went in the back way. I saw her father," Alfred added with a touch of indignation creeping into his voice. "He damn near killed me. You guys ought to take that gun away from him, Inspector! It ain't safe, the way he shoots around!"

"What do you mean?" Asey demanded.

"Why, he's got this target in the woods, see? And when his wife ain't there, he shoots. And some day he's going to kill somebody. He shot right past me this evening when I got out of the car."

"Was you anywheres near the target?"

"No! The target's in the woods!" Alfred said. "But sometimes he just shoots past people. He thinks it's funny. *I* don't. I think he ought to be stopped. You ought to stop him before somebody gets hurt!"

"I don't know," Asey said, "but what maybe perhaps I won't. Huh. Thanks, Alfred, for tellin' me about that. Now, you went upstairs an' got the dress. That right?"

Alfred nodded.

"And before I got downstairs, the lights went off. I—"

He hesitated.

"You what?" Asey asked.

"I guess Mrs. Doane was there," Alfred said. "I was

trying to think. Yes, I guess it was her I seen at the back door. But there wasn't nobody else there in the whole place, I don't think."

"Alfred," Asey said, "you been a great help an' comfort to me. It's been a real pleasure to do business with you, Alfred. If I didn't think that ambulances was worthier, I might even make you a bigger donation. Get along to Lady Boop, feller. She's most likely swooned with worry by now. An' don't ever let her get hold of a wheel again as long as you live!"

"Say!" Alfred said as Asey turned away. "Say, Inspector, what's your name?"

Asey got into the police car, started it, and grinned as Alfred repeated his question.

"The name," he said, "is Mayo. An' I'm 'fraid it'll most likely break your heart, Alfred, but I ain't an inspector, you know. I ain't even a cop. So long, Alfred. See you again."

Six minutes later he parked Hanson's car beyond the Whale Inn's porte-cochere, and walked over toward the front steps.

He was going to gather the Doane family together and have a little talk with them and get to the root of things. If Washy made a habit of potshotting around recklessly at people—

"Pssst!"

Asey turned around.

"Pssst! Here!"

Someone was beckoning to him from the little strip of open porch he had noticed earlier when he made his circuit of the Inn.

"Pssst! Asey!"

"Jennie!" Asey said in bewilderment and hurried over to her. "Jennie, I thought you'd gone home! What you doin' here?"

"*I* found her," Jennie said with quiet pride. "I found the body!"

5

"WHAT!" Asey stared at her in disbelief.

"I tell you, I *found* the body! I *found* her! Land's sakes, you *deaf?*" Jennie demanded with some asperity. "You want me to *scream* it at you?"

"Havin' got to a point where I sort of don't believe my own eyes," Asey said, "I should hate to think I don't believe my own ears, too. How'd you find it? Where is it?"

"Here," Jennie said. "Right here on this porch. See that Boston rocker?"

"Where?" Asey looked around the porch without seeing anything even remotely resembling a rocker, Boston or otherwise.

"For mercy's sakes, come here!" Jennie said. "Now, watch!"

Lifting a tarpaulin off something Asey had thought was a small table, Jennie revealed an overturned Boston rocker resting on its arms.

Under it was a body.

It was *the* body, too. Asey knew it even before he leaned over and struck a match.

"How in the name of common sense did you find out about this?" he demanded. "*How?*"

"You don't sound a bit pleased," Jennie said.

"I probably never was more pleased an' delighted over anythin' in all my life," Asey assured her, "an' it'll probably please an' delight you to know I just spent considerable time an' effort trackin' down two bodies. One turned out to be a Persian rug, an' the other was a dead goat. So you're way ahead of me. Only, Jennie, I thought you was headed home to feed your husband an' soak his foot."

"I meant to." Jennie appeared unmoved by the insinuation that she was neglecting her husband. "Only then I got to thinkin', Asey. It just seemed too bad to leave here with all this excitement goin' on. After all, I can always get Syl's dinner any time. So I phoned Cousin Hat an' asked her if she'd run over an' feed Syl an' look after him. Hat loves to run over an' look after sick folks. She makes such *good* calves foot jelly, you know, she loves to show it off to folks. It don't seem she's ever so happy as when she can feed someone calves foot jelly. 'Course, Hat—"

"I know Hat," Asey interrupted, "an' I got no doubt but what she's feedin' Syl calves foot jelly this minute, whether he wants it or not. What I want to know, Jennie, is how in time you landed on this body!"

"Well," Jennie took a long breath, "I phoned Hanson, an' I phoned Sam—he took the truck back home an' left your roadster on the corner where the truck was. Then I phoned Hat—my, my, I guess I better talk lower. Well, then I had a couple of sandwiches in the drugstore. I brought some back for you, Asey, an' I must say, I don't know what they slice ham with at that store. Must use a razor. That ham ain't any thicker than a piece of newspaper, an' I don't know but what newspaper'd have as much taste. I made the boy put on a lot of mustard, so anyway there'll be a taste of *somethin'* to it. Asey, what do you think she'll do?"

"Who?" Asey felt confused.

"Mrs. Doane."

"What do you mean, what'll she do?"

"Why, d'you suppose she's goin' to come back an' take this body away, or is she just plannin' to leave it here?"

"What!"

"I think she's comin' back, myself," Jennie said.

"Jennie, what are you talkin' about!"

"Mrs. Doane! She's how I found out about the body! You see, after I did all that phonin', an' waited for Hanson, an' waited for Sam to bring your car over an' all, then I walked over here to the Inn. Didn't seem to be anythin' happenin' inside, an' I couldn't hear any excitement or see you anywheres, so I guessed you'd gone off, an' so I come out back here to wait for you. An'—I was sittin' right over there by the lilacs, on that wooden bench." Jennie pointed to it. "An' out come Mrs. Doane to this porch with a dustpan, an' shook it out. Awful funny time to be dustin', *I* thought."

"Now I wonder if she was," Asey said. "I wonder

if maybe she hadn't been brushin' out that telephone booth!"

"How in the world did you guess that? The daughter come out an' asked what was she doin', an' that's just what Mrs. Doane said. Said she'd been brushin' out the phone booth an' tidyin' it up. She went back inside then, but a little later she sneaked out an' lifted up this tarpaulin, an' looked. When she went in, I come over an' looked, too. An' I can tell you, I don't know how I had the courage not to let out a good scream. You suppose Mrs. Doane lugged the body here? She looks strong enough to lug an ox, goodness knows. You think she did?" Jennie promptly answered her own question. "I do. Because I've been here nearly an hour, an' nobody else's come snoopin' around. She seems to be the only one that knows about it."

"Did she come back?"

"Twice," Jennie said. "She was so quiet the first time I didn't hear her. I don't know how she missed seein' me. But somebody called her, an' she popped back indoors, quick. Little later, she popped out again an' then in again. Just like a jack-in-the-box. What do you think she's goin' to do?"

"Wa-el," Asey considered, "in one way, I don't like to suggest we wait an' see. Seems to me most all I been doin' tonight is waitin' an' seein', an' not gettin' much of anywheres in the process. Huh. Did you say you had some food for me?"

"Right here in my pocketbook."

"Then," Asey said, "suppose we make our way around to that shed, Jennie. I'll eat my sandwiches, an' we'll wait that long, anyway. If she should come out, we got her. If she don't come out, we'll go inside an' see how much of a state we can work her into with some plain an' fancy trippin' up. Come this way, an' don't trip over the wire of that flower bed."

Jennie sighed as she opened her pocketbook a few minutes later in the shadow of the shed.

"I wish there was somethin' we could *set* things on. But I s'pose I can hold things for you."

"What you got?" Asey inquired.

Jennie told him apologetically that it wasn't much.

"Here's a little paper container thing of beef cube soup. It's cold, but you drink it anyways. It's good for you. Here's the sandwiches. All four of 'em," Jennie said with scorn, "wouldn't make a good-sized mouthful for a fly. An' here's a couple of tarts—nasty things with that store raspberry jam all over 'em. Goodness, it's dripped off all over my bag! Here. Here, Asey. I got a container of coffee in my coat pocket. It's that stuff you make with powder, but it's better than nothin'. An' in the other pocket I got a few candy bars an' some potato chips."

"No finger bowls?" Asey inquired quizzically.

"I got paper napkins in my bag," Jennie returned. "Oh, an' there's pickles. Pickles, pickles, where'd I put those pickles? That's too bad. I must have left 'em there on the counter. Asey, tell me what you found out an' what you been doin'."

Between mouthfuls and swallows, Asey told her, and when he concluded his story Jennie shook her head.

"Well, I never! Why, *I've* heard Custer Mayo talk about Washy Doane, an' it does seem as if Syl ought to of known him! But Syl never barely mentioned him. Only person he ever speaks of here is Mrs. Doane. Asey, you know what seems queerest of all to me?"

Asey chuckled. "Sure. The woman who walked past you. Your ghost."

"Still don't believe me, do you?" Jennie retorted. "Well, just you wait! Sooner or later, I'm goin' to prove to you I seen someone. If I don't ever do anythin' else in my life, I'm goin' to get *that* settled up! But what I think is the queerest is Mrs. Doane herself, Asey. She makes a lot of money out of this Inn. She's worked hard to build this place up from a common boardin' house to what it is now, a nice inn with nice guests an' a fine reputation. It's taken her years an' years—why, this woman who's been shot, she's been comin' here more than twenty years, Asey!"

Asey choked on his raspberry tart.

"Jennie, you mean to say you know who she is?" he demanded.

"Why, of course, don't you? Land's sakes, Asey, ain't you even found out who she is yet?" Jennie sounded slightly shocked.

Asey pointed out that having practically only just discovered the body he had hardly had the time to accomplish much in the way of identification.

"You knew what she looked like, didn't you?"

Jennie said. "Why, I met Angie Harris up in the drug-store, an' she knew the woman in a minute when I described her. I said, 'Angie,' I said, 'tell me who's a schoolteachery lookin' woman about fifty-odd wears steel-rimmed glasses an' a tweed coat—' an' before I could say I thought she stayed at the Inn, or anything else about her, Angie spoke right up an' said I must mean Miss Olive. Angie knew right off who I meant. Even the counter boy, he knew her."

"Who is she?"

"Why, she's a schoolteacher lives here at the Inn!" Jennie said. "Everybody knows her. Angie said there wasn't probably anyone in Quisset that didn't know Miss Olive. Miss Olive Beadle, that's who she is."

"Mess beetle!" Asey said. "Mess beetle. Well, well!"

Jennie wanted to know if he felt all right.

"I'm improvin' rapidly," Asey told her, "thanks to you. Remember that phone call we didn't understand, Jennie? Somebody was phonin' her, don't you see? They was askin' for her, only we didn't get it. Huh! Go on, Jennie, tell me more."

"Well, she's been comin' here," Jennie said, "it's either twenty-four or twenty-six years. Angie said it was either the year the ole ice house burned down or the year the livery stable burned down, an' she couldn't remember just which. Anyway, she started comin' here when the Inn was Mrs. Mercer's Boarding House. She's a quiet little body, Angie says, goes to church every Sunday, an' to all the suppers an' fairs, an' to the movies most every night. She pays more attention to the town an' the townfolks than the rest of 'em at the Inn. Angie says the others are awful high-hat. She says one of 'em, a big fat woman that drives around in a big car with a chauffeur, she wouldn't even give a measly little dollar to the ambulance fund drive."

"You'll be glad to know," Asey said, "that the fat lady has made a thumpin' good contribution tonight, though she don't know about it. So Angie thinks this Miss Beadle's all right, huh?"

"Angie likes her. Says she's helped the Women's Club, an' made fancy work for their sales, an' she'd helped some of the town boys through college. She didn't give 'em money—I s'pose she couldn't afford anything like that—but she introduced 'em to people in Boston who got 'em started. She has a little car she drives around a lot, an'—"

"I wonder, where is that car now?" Asey interrupted. "I ain't noticed it anywheres around here."

"Goodness, why worry about her *car!* 'Course, Angie said she was a woman kind of set in her ways. She used to have a special rocker she liked when it was Mrs. Mercer's Boarding House, an' she's made Mrs. Doane keep it on the porch for her even now. I s'pose," Jennie added, "that's the very rocker she's under now. Makes your flesh creep, don't it? Anyway, Angie says you could set a clock by her. She goes to the mail at the same time every day, an' she gets her paper the same time, an' she comes the same day every year, June tenth, an' she goes the same day every fall, September tenth. Quisset people call her the perennial boarder. You payin' any attention to me?"

"Uh-huh. I'm just thinkin'," Asey said, "an' watchin' that porch. A light went on just now in the room beyond."

"That don't mean anything," Jennie said. "It's been on an' off a dozen times. Now, of course, I didn't tell Angie anythin' about what'd happened here tonight, but from what I found out it seemed to me you might say this Miss Olive Beadle was a kind of a star boarder, too. That's what I meant, Asey, when I said I thought it was queerest about Mrs. Doane. If she kills anyone, she just is killin' her business too, isn't she? An' somehow, you wouldn't hardly expect that anyone would kill off their star boarder, would you?"

Asey shook his head.

"No," he said, "you wouldn't."

"I got the idea from Angie," Jennie said, "that this Miss Olive, as Angie called her, she'd sort of stuck to Mrs. Doane through thick an' thin. The place half burned down one year, but Miss Olive, she come just the same on June tenth an' lived in the room she always has, even though half of it was just boarded up an' covered with tar paper. An' one time there was a lot of talk that the water at the Inn was bad. Seems somebody come down with typhoid. Everybody packed up an' left but Miss Olive. She stayed right on. An' when some of them that'd left found she was stayin', why they come back. Angie said Miss Olive an' Mrs. Doane, they got along fine, an' more'n once, Miss Olive's smoothed people over when Mrs. Doane had riled 'em. I tell you, I do think it'd be awful queer for Mrs. Doane to be killing Miss Olive now, Asey! But if she didn't, then why—"

"Hold it," Asey said softly.

"Is she comin' out again? Is—"

"Shush."

Mrs. Doane slipped out the door on to the little porch and softly closed the door behind her.

Removing the tarpaulin that covered the rocker, she bent over and looked down.

Asey moved from the shed to the porch so quietly that she wasn't aware of his presence until he cleared his throat and spoke to her.

"What you doin', Mrs. Doane?"

He startled her so that she jumped, and for a moment Asey thought she was going to rush back into the house.

But her voice, when she answered him, was even and composed.

"What are you doing here?"

"Confrontin'," Asey told her.

"What?"

"Wa-el," Asey said, "call it confrontin' an' confoundin', if you prefer it that way."

"What are you talking about?"

"That's the way they always put it in the newspapers," Asey said. "You don't ever just happen on someone you find who's apparently committed a crime. You confront 'em in the act. You don't ask for explanations when you confront. You confound 'em with the evidence. Like, 'Mrs. Doane, proprietress of Quisset's well-known and highly thought of Whale Inn, was confronted while bending over the body of her star perennial boarder, Miss Olive Beadle, and confounded—'"

"Who are you?" Mrs. Doane demanded.

"Asey Mayo, Syl Mayo's cousin. I told you who I was."

Mrs. Doane stood very still.

"You just said you was his cousin," Jennie, who had just skirted the flower bed, informed Asey. "You didn't say you was Asey. Huh. I guess you confounded her, all right. She kind of looks like she was wiltin'. She looks like—"

Asey motioned for her to be still.

"What you goin' to do, Mrs. Doane?" he inquired. "Goin' to tell me the truth about all this, or do you want to do things the hard way? It's up to you."

In another ten seconds, Asey thought, Mrs. Doane was going to bite clear through her underlip.

"In your place, Mrs. Doane," he went on, "before I made a decision one way or another, I think I'd be inclined to consider one pretty important angle. I think I'd consider just what publicity of this sort would do to my Inn."

"What do you think," Mrs. Doane's voice was vibrant with feeling, "that I am considering? What do you think that I have been considering? Why do you think I moved this body out of the telephone booth in the first place?"

"So it was you who moved it!" Jennie said. "Well, all I've got to say is, I should think you'd ought to be ashamed of yourself!"

"I'm not!" Mrs. Doane said defiantly. "I'm not! I'd do it again! And if you want to know, if you two hadn't come, I should have put her body in the car later, and I should have driven it just as far away from the Inn as I could!"

Jennie was genuinely shocked.

"I think that's awful! You mean, you'd pick up the body of a woman that's been your best boarder, an' stuck by you all these years through thick an' thin, an' you'd go movin' her body like—well, like she was some ole tramp?"

Mrs. Doane burst suddenly and violently into a flood of tears.

Between the intensity of her sobs and the unexpectedness of her breakdown, Asey felt strangely helpless.

But Jennie, after watching Mrs. Doane for several minutes, made a decision and took the situation in hand.

"You got a handkerchief, Asey? Now, Mrs. Doane, here's a handkerchief. You'll feel a lot better if you'll blow your nose an' wipe your eyes. You know perfectly well you wasn't goin' to move poor Miss Olive's body to some ole ditch! You couldn't have gone through with it, could you, really?"

"I didn't want to!" Mrs. Doane said brokenly. "Oh, I didn't want to! I didn't want to move it out here!

I felt awful! But what could I do? I couldn't have left it in there!"

"When'd you find it?" Asey asked quickly. "When'd you move it?"

Punctuated by sobs, the story seemed longer than it actually was, in spite of Asey's promptings.

"I see," he said at last. "Boiled down, you seen Syl's truck out front when you come home, so you went in the back way, intendin' to give blue blazes to whoever brought Syl's clams over for leavin' that truck where it was. An' when you didn't find anybody out back in the kitchen, you begun to wonder if maybe Syl's substitute had had the nerve to sneak into the front part of the Inn. Right? So that was why you went up the little narrow hall an' slid open the back door of the phone booth so cautiouslike. You was goin' to listen, an' then pop out an' confront whoever it was that brought the clams. Only, instead, you found yourself confronted with Miss Olive's body. An' right away, you knelt down, slung the body over your shoulder, an' lugged it out here to the porch. That's the story, ain't it?"

Mrs. Doane nodded.

"I had to move it, don't you see? I couldn't let it stay there! I couldn't leave it there! I couldn't let it be!"

Jennie wanted to know why not.

"Why not?" Mrs. Doane laughed bitterly. "Why not? You stop and think! If something like this happened in the city, it would be in the paper, yes. But would the hotel ever be mentioned by name? No! They'd call it a downtown hotel, or a small hotel near Smith Street, or an old-established hotel. It would never be mentioned by name. Never! But d'you think for a minute that would hold true here? D'you think the papers would just be content to call this a small Cape Cod inn? Never! It will be named. Murder at the Whale Inn. The Whale Inn killing. The Whale Inn shooting. The Whale Inn mystery. There'll be pictures of it in the rotogravure. The radio'll name it fifty times a day. You know that just as well as I do. The reputation I've built up over all these years, the clientele I've built up, everything," she made a help-less little gesture, "that's the end of it, over night. That's why I moved the body, don't you see?"

"I don't know's I ever thought of it," Jennie said slowly, "but they don't ever name city hotels, do they? When people jump out of city hotel windows, they just say it's a Back Bay hotel, or somethin' like that. Huh. I should think you could fix that part of it, Asey."

Mrs. Doane, who had been wiping at her eyes, straightened up suddenly.

"Twenty-six years ago, my sister Mary Mercer died, and left me this place. Mrs. Mercer's Boarding House. Ten dollars a week top, and no plumbing. I saw what it could be, and I set to work. I've seen this place through fires and storms and blizzards and hur-ricanes. I've scrubbed its floors and papered its walls and washed its windows, yes, and I've even got up on the roof and helped shingle that. I've kept scandal from it. I've stood up to whispering campaigns. Three times I've pawned everything I owned to keep the mortgage from being foreclosed, and now the place is mine, free and clear. It isn't much when you compare it to the Waldorf-Astoria, but I've spent twenty-six years making it what it is. That's why I moved her body. *I* didn't kill Miss Olive! I don't know who did. I can't guess who might have. I can't imagine why anyone should. But I moved her body. And I wonder," Mrs. Doane was looking earnestly at Jennie, but Asey knew she was talking straight at him, "I wonder if you wouldn't perhaps have done the very same thing, if you'd been me?"

Jennie thought for a moment, and her answer was exactly what Asey expected.

"I don't know," she said hesitantly, "but what maybe I might have wanted to. When you work awful hard on a thing, you hate to see it smashed into smithereens. But, on the other hand, I don't think I'd have been able to bring myself to move her. Not someone I knew an' liked, who was a friend."

Mrs. Doane's manner underwent another sudden change. There was the same slight touch of the martyr about her that Asey had noticed when she was talking to her daughter Freddy.

"Of course," she said to Jennie, "you've never run an inn, have you? You've never had to run a business! You're not a business woman. Let me assure you that women in business can't always afford the luxury of indulging their feelings! The business must come first!"

"I s'pose," Jennie said, "that's so. That reminds me. Here. This is for you."

Fishing around inside her capacious pocketbook, she finally drew out a folded paper and presented it to Mrs. Doane.

"What's this?" Mrs. Doane demanded in some bewilderment.

"Syl's clam bill," Jennie told her, "an' if you hadn't spoke about business, I'd have forgot all about it. Shows you the kind of a business woman I am, I guess —what you chucklin' about, Asey?"

"I just coughed, that's all," Asey said. "Kind of a tickle in my throat. Mrs. Doane, there's a little somethin' I'd like to ask you about, if you don't mind, an' then I—"

"Before you get started off on some other track," Jennie interrupted, "you *can* see to it they call it just a Cape Cod inn, can't you? You can make Hanson see to that—an' Asey, where *is* Hanson, anyway?"

"Golly!" Asey said. "I forgot all about him an' Rankin! I never give 'em another thought after I drove away from Artie's diner! I just left 'em there!"

"That's what it sounded like when you told me what you'd been doin'," Jennie said, "but I thought I'd heard wrong. What you goin' to do about 'em?"

"Nothin'," Asey said. "I guess they can manage to get themselves back here. Jennie, pop inside an' phone Doc Cummings an' ask him to hustle over here, will you? I didn't want to drag him out till we had somethin' concrete for him to look into. Cummings," he turned to Mrs. Doane, "is medical examiner for this district, you know."

"I didn't know that, but I know him," Mrs. Doane said. "I'll go right in and call him."

"Jennie can go," Asey said. "There's somethin' I want to ask you about, if you don't mind, Mrs. Doane."

"Of course!" But she continued to stand blocking the doorway so that Jennie couldn't get past. "I'll be glad to tell you anything I can, only I think my daughter Freddy probably can tell you more. I wasn't here at the Inn this evening, you know. I'll send her out to you and call the doctor. Two birds," she added rather brightly, "with one stone."

"Just a sec," Asey said, "before you start your stone-throwin'. If you're bound an' determined that you're goin' inside an' call the doc, I suppose you can. Only first, hand over that gun, will you?"

"Gun? What gun?" Mrs. Doane demanded. "Did you say gun?"

"Uh-huh. The one you took out of the pocket of Miss Olive's tweed coat. I don't know how it got there. It was on the floor of the phone booth when I seen it first, but I s'pose you put it in the pocket when you brought her out here. Give it to me, please."

"I'm afraid," Mrs. Doane said, "that you're sadly mistaken! I didn't see any gun!"

"Maybe you didn't get a good look at it in the dark out here," Asey returned, "but it's that thing you drew out of her coat pocket an' put into your sweater pocket just before I spoke to you an' asked what you was doin'. It's a small, hard, metal thing. Just you fumble around in your sweater pocket, an' I think you'll manage to locate it without a lot of trouble."

Mrs. Doane started to protest, and then apparently thought better of it. Without another word, she gave Asey the gun.

"Thanks. Now, you really want the name of your inn kept out of the papers?" Asey inquired.

"You know I do!"

"Then let me give you a few words of good advice," Asey said. "Instead of tryin' to ball things up any more'n you already have, try an' co-operate for a change. I haven't got enough official power so's ir-ritatin' me will make much difference, but don't go irritatin' Lieutenant Hanson when he gets back. Don't try to fool him. Don't lie to him. Don't try to cover anybody up. Tell him the truth. And let him search the whole place, and question everybody. You'll come out a lot better. If you co-operate with Hanson, I think you'll find him willin' to protect you from sight-seers an' thrill-seekers an' candid-camera fans an' such like pests. If you're halfway decent to him, he'll proba-bly try to give you a break about the Inn's name. In short, nobody's goin' to make things hard if you don't. You take anything else?"

"No!"

"Except what?"

Mrs. Doane hesitated.

"Well, there were her glasses," she said. "They were broken on the phone booth floor. I swept the glass up into a dustpan and threw the pieces out here in the bushes. The frames I put in the fireplace and covered with wood ashes."

"Anythin' more?"

"No!"

"What gas station did you wait at for the current to come back so's you could get gas for your car?" Asey asked.

"What's that got to do with—"

"The name of the gas station, please," Asey said.

"Joe's."

"Okay. Now you can go phone the doc. An' I'd like your daughter to step out here."

Jennie sighed as the door closed behind Mrs. Doane.

"Isn't she a changeable one, Asey? There I was, feelin' so sorry for her after she told about the Inn an' how hard she worked for it all these years! Didn't she make it sound hard?"

Asey agreed dryly that it did sort of sound like twenty-six years before the mast.

"An' wasn't you feelin' sorry for her, too?" Jennie asked. "Why, I was almost forgivin' her in my mind for movin' that body—an' then to think she stole that gun! Asey, what do you make of her?"

"Wa-el," Asey said, "I s'pose if you've spent twenty-six years tryin' to please boarders an' guests, an' toadyin' to 'em, you most likely get into the habit of sayin' what you think someone would like to hear, whether you believe it or not. Havin' made this place her lifework, as you might say, I s'pose it's a lot more important to her than anythin' else is, includin' any feelin's she might have had about her star boarder bein' killed."

"But why would she have stolen that gun? If she was intendin' to move the body somewheres else later, like she claimed, then why'd she sneak that gun into her pocket just now?"

Asey shook his head.

"This model she was tryin' to walk off with," he said, "is a twenty-two, Jennie. It's a Colt. It's what they call a Sports Model Woodsman, an' it's the gun that was on the floor when we first found her in the phone booth. To judge from that wound, I'd say, off-hand, that this Miss Olive was shot with a twenty-two, an' it seems's if this ought to be the one someone used."

"Well, for land's sakes, ain't it?"

"Wa-el," Asey said, "the gun I seen Washy stick into his hip pocket might be the twin of this one, Jennie. I know for sure that's a twenty-two, because when I run into him out in the woods, he spoke about takin' a pot shot at a chicken thief with his little twenty-two. An' Mrs. Clutterfield's chauffeur said that Washy'd been target shootin' around reckless this evenin'. Maybe Mrs. Doane thought this gun was her husband's. I don't know. What the average woman thinks about guns is somethin' I never been able to understand much. They don't seem to realize that guns ain't like cups an' saucers, somethin' you can shift around an' nobody be the wiser. No matter how much you try to shift guns around, the truth comes out in the wash, anyway."

"What you mean?"

"As soon as Doc Cummings gets here an' gets his part over with, we'll put Hanson's experts to work on the gun situation," Asey said. "If there was a dozen twenty-twos lyin' loose around this inn, they could tell you in no time just which one of 'em the bullet was fired from that killed her."

"I see," Jennie said dubiously. "I see. Only, if the gun that shot her wasn't there, if Mrs. Doane took it away, they wouldn't know then, would they?"

"That," Asey said, "is hittin' the nail plumb on the head. But at least, Hanson's boys could tell you that she wasn't killed by any of the guns that actually was kickin' around loose. On the other hand, if—"

"Now don't go mixin' me up!" Jennie said. "I know there's this gun, an' Washy's gun, an' they're both alike, an' Mrs. Doane was tryin' to steal this one, an' this one's the one that most likely killed Miss Olive, an' that's confusin' enough without your iffin' around, an' on-the-other-handin'! What's keepin' that daughter, I wonder? You suppose Mrs. Doane's primin' her, maybe?"

Asey shrugged.

"Seems to me," Jennie went on, "she'd ought to have been around. Seems to me someone must have been around this place this evenin'! Miss Olive was at the four corners a little before six. 'Bout ten of six or so. She was here, dead, when we come at six. I do keep thinkin' someone ought to have been here, Asey. What about dinner? Wasn't anybody goin' to eat dinner here?"

"Apparently not, near as I can make out," Asey

said. "From what I gathered up here an' there, Mrs. Clutterfield got sore because there might not be clams —Mrs. Doane had doubts about you gettin' 'em here, I guess—an' so she flounced off to the club. Rankin come back with Judge Houghton, so I gather he had dinner with him. I s'pose with her migraine, Mrs. Hingham wasn't goin' to dine. But Washy was here, shootin' his little twenty-two. An' Mrs. Clutterfield's chauffeur come back for her dress. An' this girl Freddy told me she was there in the livin' room all the time from three o'clock on, but I'm inclined to think she meant she was there all the time except when she was somewheres else. Jennie, want to help me out?"

" 'Course, if I can."

"While I'm busy with the doc, an' Hanson, an' odds an' ends, will you linger around Washy an' Mrs. Doane? Particularly her. Notice anythin' they keep you from seein', or lookin' at. An' bear in mind that Mrs. Doane's used to soft-soapin' an' salvin' an' manipulatin' folks. Act like—well, act like Cousin Hat. Like somebody never stirs out of her own kitchen. Act just as little like a business woman as she thinks you are."

"That won't be hard," Jennie said. "Land's sakes, I *am* in my kitchen most of the time, and goodness knows, I don't know a thing about business! All I know about business is what Father told me about more than three per cent interest wasn't never safe, 'less it was a good, sound, first mortgage, an' think for two weeks before you sell land, an' things like that."

"Uh-huh," Asey said. "Well, don't tell Mrs. Doane

any of them maxims, or what you got for the wood lot when you finally sold it. Or about your dickerin's with that antique dealer you fleeced into buyin' them walnut chairs!"

"Why, Asey!" Jennie said indignantly. "*I* never fleeced him! He somehow just got the impression they was—well, sort of—"

"Uh-huh. Sort of heirlooms. I know. Well, just you hide them portions of your past from Mrs. Doane, Jennie. Don't be too dumb, but don't be terrible bright, either. An' for the love of Pete, don't dicker with her!"

Jennie looked at him curiously for a moment.

"You're lots more suspicious about her than you was, Asey. I can tell by the sound of your voice. You are, ain't you?"

"Wa-el," Asey said, "in a sort of way, yes. You remember when we was waitin' for the Army column at the four corners? When you barged out to talk to the soldier with the lantern, I sat there in the truck an' watched that big sign on the opposite corner. It was one of those neon jiggers that flashes red an' then white, an' then sort of dances, an' makes a figure."

"What of it?"

"That," Asey said, "was Joe's gas station."

Jennie gave a little squeal.

"It was? Why—yes, I remember, now! The 'J' blinked all the time. Why, Asey, if she was waitin' there! Why—she might have seen Miss Olive! Maybe she hailed her! Maybe, after Miss Olive drove across, after the trucks jammed up, maybe Miss Olive picked her up an' brought her here! Why, Asey, it sort of takes my breath away!"

"It does sort of open up new vistas, don't it?" Asey agreed. "Well, you pop inside, Jennie, an' chase that girl out here, an' start in with your eye-peelin'."

"Huh!" Jennie said. "I'll eye-peel, all right! Why, *think* of that!"

The door had scarcely closed behind her when Asey heard the scrunch of gravel as a car rolled up the driveway.

Stepping off the porch, Asey looked around the side of the ell.

It was Hanson and Rankin, getting out of a large, red, grocery supply truck, which backfired several times, then lurched around the turntable and drove away.

Asey whistled to them, and chuckled as he saw them look at each other meaningly before they strolled over to him.

"Mr. Mayo, I presume?" Rankin inquired. "Er— remember us?"

"I'm sorry," Asey said. "I had to see a fat lady about a dead goat—Hanson, Jennie found the body. Come take a look."

Rankin nearly fell off the porch when Hanson's flashlight illuminated the face of the woman under the Boston rocker.

"It's Miss Olive!" he cried. "I thought of everyone else at the Inn, but I never even considered Miss Olive! Mayo, this is ghastly!"

"Who is she?" Hanson demanded.

"She's a schoolteacher." Rankin still sounded dazed. "Miss Olive. Miss Olive Beadle. She comes from somewhere around Boston. One of the Newtons, I think. She stays here at the Inn every summer. Has for years. They call her the perennial boarder. Everybody in town knows Miss Olive. She's an institution here at the Inn."

"You never said a word about her when I asked you who was staying at the Inn!" Hanson said.

"I never thought of her! It's just as I told Mayo, just now! I never thought of her in connection with anything like this! Elissa, or her husband, or Lady Boop—yes! I could understand that! Particularly Elissa! But Miss Olive—why, I just can't believe this! What happened? Was she killed out here?"

"She was shot in the phone booth, in the livin' room," Asey said. "She was there when Jennie an' I first seen her."

"The phone booth?" Rankin sat down heavily on the step. "My God! I saw her go in there!"

"When?" Asey asked.

"I came down the stairs with her! She said she had to phone, and asked me if I had two nickels for a dime, and I did, and I gave 'em to her, and she went into the phone booth! My God!"

"What time was this?" Asey asked again.

"This afternoon—oh, half past four or quarter past four, some time around there. Freddy would know. Freddy was there at the desk in the living room. I gave her the nickels and went on uptown—that was when she was killed, wasn't it, Mayo?"

"I don't think so," Asey said. "Jennie an' I both saw her at the four corners this evenin'. She was killed in the phone booth around six, I'd say. Then Mrs. Doane found the body an' moved it here."

"Mrs. Doane?" Rankin said. "Mrs. D? *She* moved her? Is that how you lost the body? Mrs. *Doane* moved her? My God, I don't understand any of this! What did she move it for? You mean, she really found the body, and she *moved* it?"

Asey's summary of the proceedings to date and the part that Mrs. Doane played was a marvel of brevity and conciseness.

"Say, I don't like this!" Hanson said when he finished. "This don't look so hot to me! You say that chauffeur said he saw Mrs. Doane here when he came to get Mrs. Blutterfield's dress—"

"Clutterfield," Asey said.

"Well, whoever she is. And Mrs. Doane says she was at Joe's gas station—why, there's no reason why this Miss Olive might not have picked her up, right there! I bet you we'll find out the two of 'em had a quarrel, or a fight, or something! That's what I bet!"

"I bet you don't!" Rankin said. "I never knew Miss Olive to fight with anyone. And she's a particularly good friend of Mrs. D. They always got along beautifully together. In fact, I don't think I ever knew anyone to get along any better with Mrs. D."

Hanson shrugged.

"Well, if she was killed in the phone booth around six, let's round up all the people who were around then, Asey, and get to work. Ought to have been plenty of people around about that time."

"Uh-huh," Asey said. "Seems like there ought, don't it? But when Jennie an' I come, we couldn't round up a single, solitary soul."

"You just didn't try," Hanson said. "Of course there was someone around!"

"The Doane girl an' her father were tryin' to work the auxiliary light system," Asey said. "The place was empty, except for this Mrs. Hingham, an' it took a whale of a lot of effort on Jennie's an' my part to drag her to the door of her room half an hour later. She was sick with migraine. An'—"

"I thought you understood, Mayo," Rankin interrupted, "that Elissa's migraine was a fake. I must warn you that Elissa has migraine as a matter of course. Maybe I should say as a matter of excuse. When she doesn't want to do something, or when she's thwarted, she has migraine. Probably she was mad with her husband. They've been quarrelling more than usual lately, Freddy told me today."

"Well, if Mrs. Hingham was here, that gives us something to start with," Hanson said. "She'd ought to know something about this Miss Olive, and what went on."

Rankin smiled.

"If Elissa knows more than her name, or ever troubled to say more than 'Good morning' to Miss Olive, I'll be very much surprised," he said.

"They don't get along, huh?" Hanson asked quickly.

"My dear man," Rankin answered, "it's got nothing to do with their getting along with each other. They simply don't know each other. They moved in different spheres, that's all. As far as their interests and lives and friends and activities are concerned, they live in two different worlds!"

To Asey, who had seen both women, Rankin's statement seemed reasonable enough, but Hanson shook his head.

"Seems queer that two women living in the same place wouldn't have anything to do with each other! Mrs. Hingham must have heard a shot, anyway! Was she the only one here, Asey?"

"Except for the Doane girl and her father," Asey said. "Mrs. Doane says she was at the gas station—you might check up on that, an' if she was around all the time the lights was out."

"I'll tell one of the boys to drop around there when I call back to the barracks," Hanson said. "Asey, I can't excuse Mrs. Doane's moving this body because she was afraid her Inn business'd be ruined if its name got into the papers mixed up with a killing. Why, there was a murder at an inn in Pochet a couple of years ago, and offhand, I can't remember the name of the place. I don't believe anyone remembers it. I can't—"

"I think I hear Cummings's car," Asey said. "Wait —I'll go see."

When he reached the porte-cochere, the short, stocky figure of Dr. Cummings was already bustling up the front steps.

"Hi, Doc," Asey said. "Come around this way."

"Hello," Cummings said. "Why does it always happen like this, I wonder? You go away, and life is peaceful and restful and relaxed, and then you come back, and it hails, and there's murder. Dropped some weight rushing around with Bill, haven't you? Asey, what's the matter with your Cousin Jennie? She said Olive Beadle had been shot!"

"She has," Asey told him.

"Then there must be two Olive Beadles," Cummings said with finality. "The one I know is a schoolteacher. Been here for years. They call her the perennial boarder. She's due in my office tomorrow afternoon for her annual shot of poison-ivy vaccine. Wears steel-rimmed glasses. You don't mean *her*. You can't mean her. What's this Olive Beadle of yours look like?"

"It's the same one," Asey assured him. "She's around back here, under a Boston rocker on the porch. She's been shot in the back."

"Now I know you're wrong!" Cummings said. "I tell you, I know Miss Olive, Asey, and she's not the sort to get murdered. No one would shoot *her*. Not in the *back*, anyway! I think somebody's slipped up on your identification here—hello, Hanson. Hello, Mr. Rankin. Got over those bilious attacks last fall all right, did you? Where's the body?"

Hanson displayed it to him.

Cummings set down his inevitable little black bag, put his hands on his hips, and stared in honest amazement.

"By George!" he said. "It's Miss Olive, all right! Humpf. I'm so dumfounded, I'm utterly speechless. Never in my life was I more dumfounded than I am at this very moment. Why—"

Asey interrupted his monologue several minutes later with the suggestion that he stop being speechless and get to work.

"There's some things we'd sort of like to find out about, Doc. Where d'you want us to move the body, inside?"

Cummings nodded.

"Ordinarily, I'd say wait for the ambulance. But I liked Miss Olive, and I don't like to see her out here like this. Olive Beadle! Of all the people in this world to be shot in the back! Miss Olive! A perfectly nice, pleasant, honest, helpful, unassuming woman, as kindly and as humane and—oh, I don't like this! I don't know what this world's coming to! Without any hesitation, from my own patients, I can name you fifteen people who could be riddled with bullets, and I'd stand up and lead the cheering, but—well, hurry up, hurry up, Hanson! What're you and Asey waiting for? Let's *do* something about this nasty business!"

A few minutes later, Hanson was protesting the doctor's choice of a room.

"This looks like somebody's bedroom, Doc. You think you ought to use it?"

"It's the only bedroom *I* can find," Cummings returned. "Never saw such a place! Regular rabbit warren. Halls, halls, halls! Unless you want to stand and hold her, put her in here, and then go find Mrs.

Doane and warn her I'm using this room—why isn't she around? Where is everyone? I thought you said Jennie was here, Asey. Where's she?"

Asey shook his head.

"Marvelous organizers, you and Hanson!" Cummings said. "Called Carey yet? Hanson, haven't you even called Carey? Well, go call him, man, go call him!"

"I was going to call him," Hanson said, "when I phoned for the boys to come, Doc."

"Haven't you got *any*one here *yet?* What in the world have you people been doing!" Cummings said. "Jennie told me over the phone that you found her at six. She very distinctly said six. Here it is, nearly nine, and you two haven't done one constructive thing that I can see! Where's my bag? Don't let's dally any longer! Rankin, get my bag from the porch, will you?"

"I brought it in," Rankin pointed.

"Well, then, why don't all of you get out and stop getting in my way!" Cummings said. "Close the door behind you!"

"Peppery tonight, isn't he?" Rankin said as he and Asey started up the hall toward the living room.

"He feels bad about this," Asey said. "I don't know as I ever seen him quite so indignant. Huh, I wonder what become of Jennie? An' where's that girl Freddy, that was bein' sent out to tell me things so long ago? I—"

"Asey!" Cummings stuck his head out of the bedroom door. "Asey, come here. I want you!"

Grabbing Asey by the arm, he pulled him into the bedroom and closed the door.

"What's the matter, Doc?"

"You should ask me that! What's the matter with *you?* What's going on here? What's the big idea?"

Asey looked at him in bewilderment. "What you mean, Doc?"

"That woman!" Cummings said. "Look at her! That isn't Miss Olive any more than you are!"

6

Listen, Doc," Asey said gently, "the one thing there don't seem to be any difference of opinion on is that this's Miss Olive Beadle. I know you wish it wasn't, but you identified her yourself. So's Mrs. Doane. So's Rankin."

"I don't care," Cummings retorted, "if she's been identified by the F.B.I., and the President, and the Senate, one by one! I tell you, it's not Miss Olive!"

"But you said, out on the porch, that it was!"

"Yes, yes, and what if I did? That was when I saw her in the light of Hanson's flashlight—was that the only time you saw her, out there, Asey?"

"Nope, I seen her inside, in—"

"In the full glare of lights?"

"Nope, she was in the phone booth, an' there was only candles. But—"

"Well, that explains it, then. I wish," Cummings said, "that you'd do what I say, and look at her, Asey! I didn't suspect anything when just the side lamp was on here, but the minute I put on the overhead lights, it was as plain as day. Look—oh, stop staring at *me*, and look at *her!* That's not hair on her head, that's a gray wig! Look at that make-up! This isn't Miss Olive, Asey, it's someone made up to look like her!"

Asey leaned over the figure on the bed.

"Golly, Doc, it *is* a wig!"

"It is. Very professional job, too, if you ask me. So's the padding—see how she's padded out? That's Miss Olive's coat, all right, and her clothes. She always wears the same sort of plain, tailored things. But it isn't Miss Olive!"

"Who in time," Asey said, "do you think it is, Doc?"

Cummings shrugged.

"I haven't the remotest idea. But I can very shortly show you what she looks like. I can tell you one thing right now. She isn't half Miss Olive's age. Look at the back of her hands. I doubt if she's a third Miss Olive's age. She's just a kid. Humpf! Whyn't you mosey around and see if any young girls are missing, Asey, while I look into this. I'll call you when I'm ready."

Asey paused on his way to the door.

"Couldn't be Freddy Doane, could it, Doc?"

"Never," Cummings said. "It would take more than make-up to blot out Freddy's freckles. Besides, this girl's gray-eyed, and I think she's blonde. Freddy's blue-eyed and dark, and weighs about fifteen pounds more."

"I didn't know you was so intimate with the Doanes," Asey commented.

"I'm not. I just happened to know Freddy because

I treated her for a nasty burn she got about a month ago. I've been doing a lot of business over here in Quisset since old Dr. Martin died. Before you go, Asey, maybe you better tell me what's been going on tonight. Jennie tried to, over the phone, but I couldn't make head nor tail of what she said."

Asey drew a long breath, and for the second time in half an hour gave his concise summary of what had taken place since he and Jennie set out to deliver Syl's clams.

"There you are," he concluded. "We found the body. I took time out to chase somebody, lost him, run into Washy Doane. I come back, the body's there, an' a few minutes later it ain't. An' while I track down a Persian rug an' a dead goat, Jennie finds it. An' now we got it, it ain't who we thought."

"Mrs. Doane," Cummings said, "need never worry about her inn getting bad publicity. Any reporter who turned in a yarn like that would be fired. And if any editor was daft enough to print it, the general public would lose heart after the first paragraph and think it was a printer's error. I never heard such a fantastic yarn—don't turn your head for a moment, Asey, please. Keep on looking at me, and say something. Anything."

"Now is the time," Asey said obediently, "for all good men to come to the aid of the party. What's the matter?"

"I'm trying to figure out," Cummings said, "if what I see in the mirror is a bush moving outside, or a face looking in, or simply a flaw in the glass. By George, I do think there's someone out there, Asey! That *was* a patch of face I saw!"

"Still see it?"

"Uh-huh. Looks like a beady-eyed gnome. He keeps ducking away. I think," Cummings said, "he suspects something!"

"Wonder how I could get outside quick," Asey said. "You got any idea where the nearest door is from here?"

"By the time you find your way through this maze of halls," Cummings said, "that gnome will be an old gray-bearded ogre with arthritis. Why not jump him through the window?"

It seemed the simplest way, and it probably would have been, if the window hadn't stuck tight and resisted every effort on the part of Asey and the doctor to raise it.

"Wa-el," Asey picked up a pair of the doctor's surgical scissors and evened off a broken fingernail, "that's that! I never laid eye on him, did you?"

Cummings snapped off the flashlight and tossed it, with an exclamation of disgust, onto the bureau.

"I had a fine view of two legs," he said. "He's tall for a gnome, and I think I saw some wings on his ankles. And if he kept up the pace he started off at, he's now halfway to Boston. You might have one of Hanson's men posted to catch him if he peeps around again."

"I mean to," Asey said. "I'm also goin' to locate Jennie, an' find that girl Freddy—"

"Wait," Cummings said. "Wait a second before you go, Asey."

"Look, Doc, you been givin' us blazes for dallyin' so, an' now you—"

"Yes, yes, but that was when I had a personal interest in this. Now that I know it isn't Miss Olive," Cummings removed his coat and hung it over a chair back, "my interest is purely professional. I wanted to warn you about Jonathan Rankin, Asey."

"Warn me about him?" Asey asked in some surprise. "What for?"

"Frankly, I'm amazed to notice that you're on such good terms with him," Cummings said. "He's a slippery individual, Asey. I've treated him several times, and I've sent him a dozen bills, and he's never paid the slightest attention to them. That's why I inquired so tenderly after the state of his health just now. I thought if I accented the 'bil' in bilious, he might take the hint. I don't trust that man, and I never have, and I *don't* think you ought to do any more confiding in him!"

The doctor was so vehement about it that Asey raised his eyebrows.

"I wouldn't say I confided in him, Doc. He was the first person I landed on here that I'd ever seen before, an' I asked him questions. He once dropped in at the house a couple of years ago with a letter of introduction from some friend of Bill Porter's. He was lookin' up the Mayo family, an' Jennie give him an earful. He seemed all right to me. I don't think I'd care much for his undiluted company on a month's fishin' trip, say, but he seems pleasant enough. I had quite an entertainin' time with him that afternoon, discussin' various an' sundry Mayos."

"Oh, he can be charming as hell!" Cummings said. "My wife thinks he's wonderful, and positively distinguished looking. She said so. He knows the best people, and he goes everywhere. I know that! When he was over in my office, he couldn't say two words without sticking in something about his friend Princess This, or what Senator Somebody said at dinner the night before. But I tell you, he's a slippery customer, and I wouldn't trust him an inch. I don't *like* men who go around stroking their Vandyke beards anyway. And leering!"

"Who'd you ever see him leer at?" Asey inquired.

"Why, last summer he used to hang around the back stage door at the South Pochet Theater—you know that barn place my wife's so crazy about. Used to drag me there every week." Cummings rolled up his shirt sleeves. "Well, I've seen Rankin there any number of times, standing and leering at all the girls in the dressing rooms. Used to make me sick!"

"Idea you're tryin' to get across is that you don't like Rankin, huh?"

"I don't trust him," Cummings returned. "There's a difference. All right, all right, look quizzical if you want! You don't have to believe me!"

"I was just thinkin'," Asey said, "you sent me a bill last January, an' to the best of my knowledge it's still sittin' on the desk in my livin' room. I forgot it."

"Sometimes you're so damn charitable about

people," Cummings said, "you make me speechless! You take my advice, Asey, and watch out for your friend Rankin. I'll call you when I'm through here."

There was no one in the Inn's living room when Asey returned there. A little hand bell had been placed on the desk, he noticed, and he rang it, but no one came.

"The service here," Asey murmured, "is simply wonderful!"

Walking over to the phone booth, he opened the door, pulled at the cord of the overhead electric light, and looked thoughtfully inside.

Hanson's men would probably manage to find some fingerprints or some bits of microscopic evidence. They usually did. But as far as clues visible to the naked eye were concerned, Mrs. Doane had done a fine, efficient job eradicating them.

Asey shrugged and walked the length of the living room and down the corridor leading from a door to his left.

Almost at once, he bumped violently into Jennie, bustling along and muttering to herself.

"Where you been?" he held out a hand to steady her.

"Land's sakes!" Jennie said in a harassed voice. "You've knocked the breath out of me! Asey, I never! I never in all my life!"

"What's the matter?"

"Well, you let me get into one of those chairs," Jennie said, "an' get pulled together, an' I'll tell you. Here. Come over to this sofa."

Asey helped her get settled, and then asked her again what the matter was.

"Well! I come in from the porch," Jennie said, "an' what do you think, Asey? Mrs. Doane had only got to callin' the doctor then! She was just askin' for his number. What she'd been doin' all the time after she left us, I don't know! So I said I'd talk to him, an' I did. I told him what'd happened, an' to hurry over quick."

Asey nodded. "I wondered about that, an' why he mentioned you an' not her. What then?"

"When I put the phone down, she asked me if I'd had any supper, an' I told her just some sandwiches at the drugstore, an' right away she had me by the arm an' was sweepin' me out to the kitchen. 'Washington,' says she, 'you get busy an' get Mrs. Mayo a good meal. *And*,' says she, 'tell her all about your voyage in the barque *Dexter*.' And out she went! Well!"

"Didn't you follow her?"

"I started to," Jennie said, "but Washy plumped me down onto a chair, an' I tell you, Asey, you might just as well try to get yourself away from an octopus as him!"

"Uh-huh. I noticed out there in the woods," Asey said, "that Washy was kind of a hard man to get away from."

"Hard? I never seen nothin' like him! Asey, I followed 'the barque *Dexter* from Boston around Cape Horn to Sydney, an' then," Jennie said wearily, "all of the way back! I been through two mutinies, I have, an' I lost all the masts three times. Maybe four times.

An' the beef got weevilly! She was awful upset, Asey!"

Asey gave it as his opinion that practically any ship would have been upset under the circumstances.

"I don't mean the barque *Dexter*, Asey! I mean Mrs. Doane! She was worried when I first come in, an' she was worried when she rushed me out to the kitchen an' turned me over to that human windbag! Somethin's wrong. I think it's the daughter."

"Where is she, anyway?" Asey asked.

Jennie shook her head.

"I don't know. I haven't seen any sign of her. I tried so hard, Asey, to get away from that man an' find out what Mrs. Doane was doin'! But every time I got up, he sat me down. I tried to ask him things, but I couldn't get a word in edgeways with the barque *Dexter!* I tell you, when he described them mutinies, I was scared! There he was, dancin' around with a carvin' knife in one hand, an' a leg of lamb in the other, brandishin' 'em—Asey, what you laughin' about? It wasn't a bit funny!"

"Maybe it ain't funny to you now," Asey said, "but in a day or so it'll probably hit your funny bone, too. My, my, I'd like to have seen that! How'd you manage to get away?"

"He went into the pantry to get me some pie, just now, an' I run out! Asey, there's the girl, now!"

Jennie pointed toward the front door.

Freddy Doane came in, took off her dripping raincoat, rolled it up and slung it over the corner desk into the cupboard beyond.

She was just about to vault over the shelf herself, when she became aware of Jennie and Asey. The song she'd been humming stopped abruptly.

"Are you two still here?" She tried to sound severe, but she obviously was in too buoyant a mood to be at all successful. "Look, I *know* you're not Asey Mayo, because I asked the Wellfleet telephone operator if you were home, and she said you weren't. She said Asey Mayo always let her know the minute he came home. Now, honestly, I know you're not tramps or tourists or anything. I know you're from around here somewhere, and you've made a mistake and got this place mixed up with some other inn. But if Mother finds you here after she's sent you away once, she'll simply raise the roof! Mother's in a talky state tonight, anyway. Won't you be lambs and dash off before she sees you?"

"Asey," Jennie said blankly, "you know what *I* think? I think that girl don't know a thing about Miss Olive's bein' killed! She don't know a thing about what's been goin' on here!"

"About what?" the girl walked over to them quickly. "What did you *say?*"

Asey watched Jennie's face as she looked at the girl. Washy had exasperated his cousin, and Mrs. Doane puzzled her, but the daughter was apparently someone more to her liking. A great deal more, Asey mentally amended, as Jennie held out her hand to the girl.

"Come over here, dear, an' sit down. You don't know. I can see you don't. Well, Miss Olive's been killed. That's the size of it. An' this *is* Asey Mayo. I dragged him here to deliver Syl's clams before he even got his foot on his own doorstep this evenin', let alone before he had any chance to let folks know he was back. Do you know *anythin'* about this business of Miss Olive?"

Freddy's blithe buoyancy had completely disappeared. She shook her head slowly as she stared from Asey to Jennie.

"You're not joking," she said at last. "You seem to mean it. But—look, that simply can't be true!"

Jennie assured her that it was.

"When Asey an' I come here with Syl's clams at six, she was in that phone booth yonder. She'd been shot."

"In there? At six? Oh, there's been some frightful mix-up somewhere, then!" Freddy spoke with more than a trace of her mother's emphatic manner. "I was in that booth myself at least twice after Miss Olive left here this afternoon! She left around four-thirty. And now that I think of it, she *did* go in the booth and make a phone call. But I was in that booth later, and besides, I saw Miss Olive drive away!"

"Asey an' I both saw her up to the four corners," Jennie said, "but here she was in that booth when we come at six! You listen, now, an' let me tell you about things!"

"Better wait, Jennie," Asey said, "until—"

"I say it's high time she knew, an' I'm goin' to tell her!" Jennie insisted. "You hush up!"

She went on to relate her version of the story, and,

after two fruitless attempts to interrupt and explain that Dr. Cummings's discovery had considerably altered the situation, Asey gave up and let her continue. While he was still wondering what the effect on Jennie would be when she found out that the body wasn't Miss Olive's at all, Cummings appeared in the hall doorway.

"Hullo, Jennie," he said. "Hullo, Freddy. I say, Asey, I think that gnome's back again—why *don't* Hanson's men get onto their job?"

"I don't even know where Hanson is," Asey said, "or if his fellows are here yet. What did you find out, Doc?"

"You don't know where he is! For the love of God," Cummings said vehemently, "what is the matter with you, Asey? This rushing around with Bill Porter's certainly done something drastic to your efficiency! Find Hanson, and get someone to chase that fellow—you ever had any Peeping Toms here before, Freddy?"

"Peeping Toms?" Freddy repeated. "You mean—uh—someone looking in windows? Why, no!"

"Well, you've apparently got one now. Where's your father, Freddy? In the kitchen? Where's your mother? Hanson's probably with them. Where are they?"

"I don't know," Freddy said. "I just came in. I—er—I've been out. Up to the village. I was just doing an errand." She hesitated a moment and then rather unnecessarily amplified her statement. "Just an errand for Mother."

Cummings, mistaking Asey's interest in the girl's hesitation for indifference to the Peeping Tom problem, expressed himself rather forcibly on the topic of soft living and its relation to brain activity.

"I told you to watch your diet, Asey! You get yourself into a lot of soft, city ways, and what happens? Brain gets as rusty as an old wheelbarrow someone's left out in the rain! I don't know what's the matter with you. Just sluggish—I'll go get Hanson myself! I'll find him! I'll get something *started!*"

He marched out, and again, before Jennie could pick up her story, Asey tried to correct her impression of the identity of the woman who had been shot.

Once again, he had to give up.

"Never saw anything like this!" Cummings said when he marched back a few minutes later. "First it's you, gabbing with two women, and then it's Hanson and three troopers—and this is a murder, mind you! There they are, out in that kitchen, listening to Washy Doane telling them about mutiny on the high seas aboard the schooner Snowdrop, and eating coconut cake! Well, I've got *them* started, I can tell you!"

"Now you got all that worked out of your system," Asey said, "what did you find out, Doc?"

Cummings sat down in one of the chintz-covered chairs and lighted a cigar before replying. He was tremendously pleased with himself. Asey knew all the signs.

"*I've* found out," Cummings said, "a number of interesting and instructive things. Freddy, I'm going to describe someone, and I want you to see if you recognize her. You might know her, too, Jennie. You've seen her, I know. Now, the girl I'm going to describe —what are *you* muttering about, Asey?"

"I was just sort of wonderin'," Asey said, "if you really felt that a quiz program was the ideal way to spend our time right now. I mean, what with nothin' havin' been done accordin' to you an' Hoyle to date, an' things at sixes an' sevens in general?"

"I have a particular reason," Cummings informed him, "for going at this my own way. Now, this girl is about five feet four. She weighs about a hundred and ten. She has very light blonde hair, comes about to her shoulders. Her face is pointed and she has gray eyes. Who is she?"

"Betsey Porter's cousin!" Jennie said triumphantly. "That one from Los Angeles!"

"Who ever said anything about Los Angeles?" Cummings retorted. "I didn't! Freddy, don't you know?" he repeated his description, and then added, "She has a small scar about two inches long above her left wrist."

"It sounds," Freddy said, "like Ann Joyce. She's a girl who stayed here at the Inn last summer. She's in the regular cast of the South Pochet Barn Theater. I didn't recognize her really until you mentioned her little scar. Somehow, I always think of Ann's voice instead of the way she looks. She has a lovely voice."

"Oh, that one!" Jennie said. "If you'd only said somethin' about that voice of hers, I'd have remembered her, too! You an' your five-foot-four! Think people carry yardsticks around with 'em?"

Cummings said tartly that height and weight were usually the first details given in any description.

"The idea being," he added, "that if you know them, you know if the person's a pygmy or a giant! I suppose if I'd said 'Who is a girl with a soft, mellow voice?', you'd have known at once, would you? Humpf. I have my doubts! Freddy, tell me about Ann Joyce. What do you know about her?"

"Well," Freddy said, "she *has* a lovely voice, and she's lovely looking, and I've always liked her. She intended to stay here again this summer, but then she decided she'd better be nearer the Theater, so she's living over at Mrs. Thorne's place in Pochet. The Beeches. But she's here a great deal. Once or twice a day. She's a friend of the Hinghams."

"And isn't she also a friend," Cummings demanded, "of Jonathan Rankin?"

"Oh, yes. She used to be his secretary. In fact, it was Rankin," Freddy said, "who helped her get this job at the Barn Theater when it started last year."

"Hear that, Asey?" Cummings demanded. "Good! Now, Freddy, when you were in my office a few weeks ago, we spoke of Rankin, didn't we? Now, I shan't embarrass you by recalling any of the ribald detail, but without compromising yourself you could assure Asey, couldn't you, that you don't accept Rankin's invitations to the movies, or to dances, or the theater?"

"Well," Freddy's face was crimson, "yes."

"Thank you," Cummings said. "Hear *that*, Asey? Well, bear all this in mind. You see, this Ann Joyce got a touch of laryngitis last summer, and I sprayed her throat hourly so she could go on with her part. I knew who she was the minute I got that wig off." He ignored Jennie's exclamation and Freddy's bewildered murmur. "But I wanted to establish a few facts for you before people knew about her, and before their opinions might be colored, so to speak. Now—"

"What are you talkin' about?" Jennie interrupted.

"Ann Joyce. Now," Cummings said, "I don't know anything about these new laissez-faire methods of detection you seem to have embraced lately, Asey. For all I know, it's the newest wrinkle to track down murderers while sitting on a comfortable sofa. Perhaps police all over the country have got together and decided that they make more progress while munching on a bit of coconut layer cake. I'm no expert. I don't know. But in my feeble opinion, I think *I* should be inclined to toy with the thought of summoning Mister Jonathan Rankin and asking the gentleman a few questions."

"Doctor, I'm awfully mixed up! What's Ann got to do with things?" Freddy asked.

"Why, she's been killed! She's been shot! For the love of God, haven't they even got around to telling you what's happened here?"

Jennie uttered a shrill yelp.

"Another? Somebody else been killed?"

"No, no!" Cummings said. "The same one! The woman you saw wasn't Miss Olive at all, Jennie— didn't Asey tell you? The woman you found was this

Ann Joyce, dressed in Miss Olive's clothes, and made up to look like her. Good job, too. Fooled me till I started to work with a dozen lights on. Freddy, why in blazes would Ann Joyce be dressed up in Miss Olive's clothes? Can you understand the reason for that?"

Freddy said unhappily that she didn't understand the reason for anything.

"Mrs. Mayo's just got through telling me a long story about Miss Olive—and you say now it isn't Miss Olive at all, it's Ann Joyce dressed up like her! I can't imagine why. I suppose it must have something to do with Horace's play. Or some other play. Was she really dressed in Miss Olive's *own* clothes?" Freddy asked. "Really? Miss Olive won't like that part at all. She's funny about her clothes."

"Just what do you mean, funny?" Asey inquired.

"It's hard to explain," Freddy said. "She buys quite expensive things. Nice tweeds—but look, this doesn't matter, does it? The point is that Ann's been killed—and I think it's horrible! Why, she was *here* this morning! That's what matters. Not the clothes."

"Maybe not," Asey said, "but bein' as how Ann Joyce was dressed like her, tell me about Miss Olive's clothes anyway."

"Well, she buys nice things," Freddy said. "But—well, they're always a little dowdy looking, somehow. You can't tell her new things from her old. I ran across a picture of her taken—oh, fifteen years ago—and, except that the skirts were longer, you couldn't have told her outfit from the one she wore today.

Once or twice, Mother and I have sort of tactfully suggested how nice she'd look in some other style, and she's been annoyed. In fact, her clothes are the only topic I've ever known her to get annoyed about. She takes a lot of care of them, presses them herself, and she has lots of 'em. And she knows Ann Joyce, casually. But I'm sure she'd never let Ann borrow her clothes! Oh, it's all mixed up! I don't understand any of it. But it must be something to do with a play. That must be the answer. Horace will know."

"Who's this Horace?" Asey asked. "Rankin spoke of him a couple of times."

"Horace is Elissa Hingham's husband. Mrs. Hingham's one of the backers of the South Pochet Barn Theater. She—"

"I know her!" Cummings interrupted. "Tall, pale, striking-looking woman. Isn't she an opera singer?"

Freddy looked even more confused.

"Well, yes, and no. That is, one of her husbands, Amos Hingham, bought her an opera company once. So I suppose she technically *is* an opera singer. She was for a little while, anyway. She's crazy about the theater, now, and wants to be an actress. Horace is sort of a manager, and assistant director when Bram Reid's busy, and he writes—well, he's a little of everything, Horace is."

"Horace Hingham," Cummings said thoughtfully. "Funny, I don't remember ever seeing his name on the program. I suppose I must have. Hingham. Horace Hingham—"

"Oh, his name isn't Hingham," Freddy said quickly.

"That's *Mrs.* Hingham's name. You see—this is rather complicated, I'm afraid—but people always call her by the name of the husband who bought her the opera company. I don't know why. I presume it's because she was known to more people as Elissa Hingham. She was Mrs. Hingham when she first came here, and we've never called her anything else."

"That still," Asey pointed out, "don't solve the problem of Horace's last name."

Freddy bit her lip.

"Honestly, I can't remember it! Here's Mother," she called to Mrs. Doane, who was just coming along the hall from the kitchen. "Mother! Mother, what's Horace's last name? Isn't it something like Prang?"

Mrs. Doane looked startled.

"Your father asked me that when they came this year, and I really meant to find it out and learn it! We shouldn't call him Horace all the time, and Mr. Hingham would never do—isn't it Anderson, or Patterson, or Peterson? I think it's Patterson. Remind me that I must find out and learn it, Freddy!"

Asey suggested that they might always look in the hotel register.

"You got one, ain't you?"

"Of course!" Freddy went over to the desk and picked up a tooled leather book. "Here. They came two weeks ago. Mrs. Hingham signed. Elissa Hingham—well, what do you know, she forgot to put Horace down! Well, anyway, whatever his last name is, he's Elissa Hingham's husband, and he'll be sure to know why Ann was dressed up. Mother, do you know about all this? D'you know it wasn't Miss Olive at all, but Ann Joyce dressed up in her clothes?"

"What!" Mrs. Doane almost slid into a chair, and for the first time since Asey had met her, she smiled a genuine smile. "It's *not* Miss Olive? Oh, that's the best news I've had—of course," the smile disappeared as she added hurriedly, "I'm sorry about Ann Joyce! That will only add size to the headlines, what with her being on the stage. But anyway, she wasn't staying here! How did she happen to be dressed up in Miss Olive's *clothes?* When did she come here? How—"

"That's what I want to know, in one word!" Jennie said. "How? How did—"

"I never saw Ann around this afternoon, Mother!" Freddy said. "She was here early this morning, and then she went off with Horace to a rehearsal. You were at the desk till three, and I was there after three, but I never saw Ann! How—"

Cummings took Asey's arm.

"Let's get out of this hen-party powwow!" he said. "Maybe I should call it a powhow—get that, Asey? That wasn't bad. Pow-how."

"It was terrible," Asey told him, "an' if you want to know the truth, I can't think of anythin' but a lot of how's, myself!"

"Trouble is, you're trying too hard," Cummings said. "You won't see the trees for the forest. Come up along the hall to this little smoking room." He led the way to it. "Now, sit down and listen to me. You thought I was just taking cracks at Rankin because

I don't like him. But I meant what I said. I don't trust him. And let me tell you this. No stray pot shot from Washy Doane or anybody else killed that girl. That was a neat, cold-blooded, well-thought-out bit of shooting. Someone stood behind her, Asey, took very, very careful aim, and shot her through the heart. She couldn't have suspected what was coming, and she certainly never knew what hit her. And your friend Rankin—"

"What about him?" Asey asked as the doctor relighted his cigar.

"Remember the Pochet Home Guard they organized last fall, about the same time all those women started up their Rifle Corps? Were you here on the Cape Labor Day? I didn't think you were. Well, to stir up enthusiasm, the Home Guard and the Rifle Corps had a shooting match. And your friend Rankin won it with his little pistol. The girl was killed by a good shot. Your friend Rankin is a good shot."

"So, presumably, is Washy Doane," Asey said. "At any rate, he practices."

"But Ann Joyce," Cummings retorted, "was never Washy Doane's secretary! Instead of howing and whating around, you get hold of Rankin! Find out where he was and what he was doing from four till six!"

"From four till six?" Asey said. "You mean, she might have been killed as early as four, Doc? Because Miss Olive used the phone at half-past four or so, an' Freddy used it later. You sure about your timin', Doc?"

"Of course I'm not sure!" Cummings said testily. "If I've said it once, I've said it a thousand times that you can't look at a body and say that person died at two minutes and sixteen seconds past two! Not unless you happened to be standing beside the person, and timed his last breath with a stop watch! I can give you a better estimate of approximately what time she was shot after Carey and I've had a chance to really look into things. My guess is between four to six! You certainly can find out from someone when the Joyce girl came here, and who saw her last, and all that sort of thing. You can make some time estimate yourself, on the basis of her coming here."

Asey, filling his pipe, pointed out that no one appeared to have seen Ann Joyce enter the Inn.

"There's a little problem here, Doc," he went on, "that maybe you ain't considered. That's what's got me feelin' a little floored. Rankin says he give Miss Olive two nickels to phone with. An'—"

"What have Rankin's nickels got to do with the time Ann Joyce was killed?"

"Wa-el," Asey said, "he says he give 'em to her, an' Freddy says she seen Miss Olive leave. But was it Miss Olive, Doc? Was it her, or the girl dressed up like her? Jennie an' I take it for granted it was Miss Olive we seen at the four corners. But was it? We don't know her so well we could swear up an' down it was her. Lots of folks has seen Miss Olive, but nobody's seen the girl Ann Joyce. Now, people know pretty much what Miss Olive wears. They see her coat an' they take her for granted. Nobody's goin' to begin any intensive examination of her, like you did. Now, Doc, s'pose the Joyce girl's been goin' around all day as Miss Olive?"

"What? Asey, you're crazy!"

"Could be," Asey said. "Maybe we seen the girl dressed as Miss Olive, actin' like her. She could have driven back here an' been killed like we figgered at first, around six. Until Miss Olive herself comes back, an' we can find out from her just where she really was, we always got the possibility that sometimes maybe folks who thought they was seein' Miss Olive was really seein' Ann Joyce."

"My God!" Cummings said. "I never thought of that angle—let's find Miss Olive! Where is she?" He went to the door. "I'll bring Freddy here. She ought to know where Miss Olive is."

Freddy shook her head when Asey told her he wanted to find out about a few odds and ends.

"I'll gladly tell you anything I can, but don't expect me to be too alert, will you? I'm just getting myself adjusted to all this. And Mother's just confessed she moved the body from the phone booth, and Father's confessed he was shooting at his target this evening— he knew Mother was out, and that I'd never hear. He even says he took a practice shot past Alfred, too! Alfred's Lady Boop—I mean, Mrs. Clutterfield's chauffeur."

"I know him well," Asey said. "Why'd your father want to scare him?"

"He claims he couldn't resist Alfred's broad beam," Freddy said. "Anyway, Mother's giving him hell, and we're all awfully confused. And none of us can remember seeing Ann after she was here this morning. Mother was at the desk till three, and I was there from three till the lights went out. And we *know* Ann never came through the living room!"

Asey suggested that there was always the possibility of Ann's having entered the Inn by a rear door.

"I suppose so," Freddy said, "but I don't see why she should come in the back way! She never does. Of course, if she sneaked up and swiped Miss Olive's clothes to dress up in, as Mother and I suspect she must have, maybe she *did* come in the back way. I don't know. I'm so confused I can't even guess what might have happened!"

"Where's Miss Olive?" Cummings asked. "Do you know where she is tonight?"

"Now there," Freddy said, "is something Mother just asked me. She just went off, that's all I know."

"Didn't drop any hint as to where she was goin'?" Asey asked.

Freddy shook her head.

"No, it was rather strange! She didn't say a word except that she was dining out. That's unusual, because she has dinner here most of the time. When she does go out, she always says where. She seemed a little excited, too. Mother got worried when I told her that, and she and I were considering phoning the movies— you see, it's one of her regular movie nights. But if she'd gone to the movies, she'd have been back half an hour ago! Mother's really upset."

"Probably she just stopped for a soda," Cummings

said. "Or stopped to see the newsreel on the second show. My wife sometimes sits through both shows."

"But Miss Olive never does!" Freddy said. "She always goes to the first show, has a soda at Johnson's, and is back here by nine-thirty. Usually as the clock is striking. And when I say always, I mean always. If it was anyone else who was half an hour overdue, Mother and I wouldn't give it a thought. But in Miss Olive, it's the equivalent of being missing for three days!"

"S'pose," Asey said, "we phone around to places where she might be. Will you do that, Freddy? An' Doc, I hear a noise out there that suggests Carey an' Hanson's crew. We better see 'em."

"Just one thing first," Cummings said. "Where was Rankin this afternoon, Freddy? Say, from three o'clock on? D'you have any idea?"

Freddy sighed.

"I certainly do! He and Lady Boop and I listened to the radio in the living room."

"You don't mean," Cummings sounded incredulous, "that *all* three of you were there *all* afternoon?"

"Weren't we just!" Freddy said. "I never put in such an afternoon! You see, they were both really waiting to hear that special broadcast of the King and Queen and the President—probably you heard that. Everyone listened. And to kill time," she went on as both Cummings and Asey nodded, "they bickered. Lady Boop wanted to listen to the continued stories she's so crazy about, and Rankin wanted war news and some symphony orchestra. Between the two of 'em, I was almost frothing at the mouth!"

"You mean," Cummings said again, as if he couldn't quite grasp the situation, "that the three of you were there in that room *all* the time? Every minute?"

"If you want proof," Freddy said, "I can tell you the plot of every soap serial from three o'clock on. Rankin gave up at 'Marcella's Rainbow to Love' and went up to the little radio in the alcove at the head of the stairs, and turned on his symphony orchestra as loud as he could on another station—I must say I didn't blame him! Only then, Mrs. Hingham started phoning me at the desk and asking if we please couldn't be a little considerate of her migraine. And when I relayed her message to those two idiots, Lady Boop got sore as a pig and said she refused to be dictated to by Elissa Hingham, and then she bounced up to the hall radio and put on Benny Goodman as loud as she could. And Rankin tap-danced. And they both sang."

"Sounds like quite an afternoon," Asey commented.

"It was. Someday I hope to find out," Freddy said, "why people who get bored on dull days in a hotel do such utterly bizarre things. I'll bet Lady Boop never turns on Benny Goodman in her own home! And I'm sure Rankin never tap-danced before in his life. Anyway, I finally quelled them by getting them an early tea—now there's another peculiar thing I forgot to tell Mother about. Miss Olive came in about a quarter-past four, and she wouldn't stop for a cup of tea! And she *always* does! But today she said no, and went right up to her room, and then she came down in about fifteen minutes, and—that was when she told me she was dining out, by the way—got into her car and drove off."

"Freddy, you disappoint me," Cummings said. "You mean that Rankin was really around all afternoon? Didn't he make any phone calls? Didn't he go near that booth?"

"No. Lady Boop did, and so did I, but—"

"I must confess I'm disappointed!" Cummings said. "Rankin was really here, under your eyes, all the time?"

"Well, he did walk up to the main street with Dad," Freddy said. "About the time Miss Olive left, they went to Tony's for their afternoon beer—they often do if Rankin's here. Then they rushed back for the broadcast at quarter to five. That's why this's so muddled—we were all here! We all listened, Mother, Dad, Lady Boop, Rankin, and I. And Mamie Riggs. She'd been in the dining room, washing the wainscoting—"

"Was she there all afternoon?" Asey interrupted.

"All day, and she'll be there all day tomorrow," Freddy said. "Did you ever wash carved wainscoting? It's a hellish job."

"Uh-huh, Jennie an' Syl an' I do mine every year. Freddy, was the dinin' room doors open or closed?"

"Open. I suggested Mamie close 'em, but she said she guessed she'd listen to the radio. I should have been firm and made her shut them. Mother would have. But it's dull work washing paint, and I never thought till later how Lady Boop and Rankin must have sounded to her. Anyway, we all listened. Then Judge Houghton came for Rankin, and Lady Boop bounced off in a huff to the club when Mother insinuated she might not have clams for dinner. People were there in the living room all the time! And, except for me, Boop was the only one to go near the phone booth. So this must have happened in those few minutes before six, from the time the lights went out, and Dad and I went to get the Delco working, till Asey and Mrs. Mayo came with the clams."

"Did you ever get them lights workin'?" Asey asked. "I wondered."

"No, the regular current came back before we got anywhere. Frankly," Freddy said, "Dad and I are not good mechanics. Neither of us ever understood that Delco. But, you see, the stoves are electric, so Dad was stymied—"

"Humpf!" Cummings said. "I wonder if her watch *was* right!"

"Mine?" Freddy asked. "It usually is."

"Ann Joyce's," Cummings explained. "It was stopped at seven of six. I didn't pay any attention to it, because I'm opposed to the theory that someone died at the exact time their watch stopped. I've seen too many bodies with their watches ticking merrily away, and too many perfectly healthy, living people whose watches stop at the drop of a hat. Humpf! I guess I'll have to take it all back, Asey. I thought I had this figured out."

"You better turn your mind," Asey said thoughtfully, "to other channels. Huh. I had a solution, myself, but that ain't goin' to work. Not if Mamie was washin' paint in the dinin' room."

"What *are* you talkin' about?"

"Ann Joyce. Freddy," Asey said, "phone around all the places you can think of an' see if you can't locate Miss Olive. We ain't got much of a basis to start from till we can talk with her an' get things settled."

He was discussing the wound with Hanson and Cummings when Freddy returned some twenty minutes later.

"Located her?" he inquired.

"No one's seen her!" Freddy said. "She wasn't at the movies, and she hasn't been to Johnson's, she hasn't called on any of the people she ordinarily calls on, and no one has any idea where she might be! And there's nothing going on in town at any of the churches, or the Women's Club, or the War Relief or the Red Cross! Truly, Mother and I are terribly worried! What could have happened to her?"

"Huh!" Asey said. "Happen to know her license number?"

"Her car's a Chevvy sedan, but I don't know what the number is! Maybe Mother might."

Characteristically, Mrs. Doane had the license number on the tip of her tongue.

"Fine," Asey said. "I'll cruise around an' see if I can't find her. May be that she had a flat, or engine trouble, an' is waitin' for the rain to let up before she sets out to phone for help. That's probably the answer. Oh, Doc." He paused at the front door and beckoned to Cummings. "Doc, keep your eye on Jennie. An' see if you can't do some delvin' into this time problem. So long."

He found his own Porter roadster where Sam had

left it on the corner where he had previously parked Syl's truck.

A little wearily, he got in and started off in search of Miss Olive.

Two hours later, having covered all the roads he could think of, and having made a canvass of all the garages within a radius of thirty miles, he turned back to Quisset.

At Joe's gas station at the four corners he stopped on impulse, introduced himself to the attendant who was just closing up the place for the night, and asked if Mrs. Doane had been there for gas around six.

"Sure. She was here from just before the lights went till the current came back. All the time. I told that state trooper so."

"Another thing, you seen Miss Olive tonight?" Asey asked.

"She was here this morning for her weekly check-up," the man said. "I told Freddy Doane so when she called up a little while ago. What? Would she be likely to have engine trouble? I don't see why. She takes good care of that car. It was okay this morning. And if she did have any trouble, she could most likely fix it. She's handy with a car. Knows more about 'em than most women."

Asey frowned as he drove on to the Inn.

This business, he thought, got more and more like a Chinese puzzle. Was it the real Miss Olive who refused tea and drove off from the Inn that afternoon, or was it the girl Ann Joyce, dressed like her? Was it the real Miss Olive or Ann Joyce whom he and Jennie saw?

And, if no one knew that the girl was dressed up like Miss Olive, was it possible that someone had meant to shoot Miss Olive, and got the girl instead?

And, if that was the case, had someone realized their mistake, and since gone after Miss Olive and carried out their original intention of killing her?

It almost began, Asey thought, to look that way.

The Inn driveway seemed filled with cars, so he stopped his roadster a little beyond, got out, and walked through the wet grass toward the Inn.

Just as he stepped on the gravel to cross the driveway between two parked cars, he saw someone duck into the bushes by the porte-cochere.

Asey stood stock-still and watched with interest as the broad figure of Mrs. Clutterfield slowly emerged.

Apparently the lack of any further scrunching of gravel reassured her that she was unobserved, for after listening a moment she tiptoed to the side of the Inn and peeked up into a window.

Then she peeked into another. And still another.

Keeping at a safe distance, Asey quietly followed her on her circuit of the Inn.

Certainly, he thought, not even Dr. Cummings with his love of jumping to conclusions could ever make the error of mistaking Lady Boop for a gnome! No one in their right mind would ever refer to her as a gnome. On the other hand, the face of almost anyone peering in through a screen might possess a certain gnomelike quality, and with that crazy little straw hat perched on the middle of her forehead, Lady Boop looked as much like a gnome as she did like anything else.

Asey walked softly over to her and touched her shoulder as she started her second circuit.

"Ooooh!"

"What," Asey inquired, "do you think you're doin'? What's the idea of all this reconnoiterin'?"

"Ooooh!"

"Why are you—say, can't you do *anythin'* but squeal?"

When it became apparent that Lady Boop couldn't answer his questions in any other manner, Asey took her firmly by the arm and led her indoors to the living room.

Cummings stared at him in amazement as he entered.

"For heaven's sakes, Asey, what's that you've got on your arm? Who's *she?*"

"Meet Mrs. Clutterfield, Doc. It don't hardly seem possible, but there's indications that she might maybe have been our Peepin' Tom."

"Well, she is not!" Cummings said. "One of Hanson's troopers picked him up twenty minutes ago. It was your dear friend Rankin!"

"Ooooh!" Mrs. Clutterfield said. "Policemen! Ooooh! Ooooh! Ooooh!"

"What's the matter with her?" Cummings demanded. "She in pain?"

"I think she's just frightened," Asey said. "What do you mean, a trooper picked up Rankin?"

"She sounds," Cummings said, "like a baby I once saw who'd swallowed a tin whistle. Rankin was peering into windows, Asey. *Claims* he'd seen someone out there and was trying to catch him—"

Freddy came into the living room.

"Did you find Miss Olive? Oh dear, you didn't! This is simply getting worse and worse! Did you tell him about the call, Doctor?"

"No, I was just getting to that," Cummings said. "What do you know, Asey, a man phoned a few minutes ago and said not to expect her back!"

7

Nᴏᴛ to expect her back when? Tonight?" Asey demanded. "Who took the call? What did he say, exactly?"

"I answered," Freddy told him. "I said, 'Whale Inn,' and a man's voice said, 'Is this where Miss Olive Beadle lives?' I said, 'Yes,' and he said, 'Well, don't expect her!' Then he hung up before I had a chance to ask who he was, or how he knew about her, or where she was, or anything else! I called Hanson and told him, right away, and he tried to trace the call. But he couldn't find out anything about it except that it was made in town here. The operator said there'd been a flurry of calls right about then, and she didn't notice who called the Inn. All she knew was that it wasn't a long distance or a toll call."

"What d'you make of that?" Cummings inquired. "That make any sense to you, Asey?"

Asey shrugged. " 'Course," he said slowly, "it's perfectly possible she just happened to do somethin' out of the ordinary tonight, an' wanted Mrs. Doane to know she was all right, but'd be late. On the other hand—"

"On the other hand, she doesn't *do* things out of the ordinary!" Freddy interrupted distractedly. "I wish I could make you understand that! Why, for twenty-six summers, Dad's had exactly the same breakfast ready for her at exactly the same time, and Miss Olive's eaten it at the same table looking out at the same view! She's always back from the movies at nine-thirty. From the Women's Club at nine forty-five! She doesn't *do* things out of the ordinary. And if she had any intentions of doing something out of the ordinary, she'd tell us so! She'd phone herself! She wouldn't have some strange man call here and tell us not to expect her! She—"

Freddy broke off as Hanson entered the living room. He looked distracted, too.

"Where the hell have you been, Asey? I wish you wouldn't go dashing off! Peterson wanted to talk with you before he left. Look, he says there's everything to indicate Colt rifling on the bullet the doc found, and the markings on the bullet show no slippage as it took the rifling, so it's probably from a Colt automatic and not a revolver."

"Huh!" Asey said. "In other words, she probably was killed by a bullet from that twenty-two that was there in the booth with her. Peterson was pretty sure, was he?"

"He said there's always the chance it wasn't, but I think he's sure. He'll phone us back later, and he's going to look up and see if he can't find out who bought the gun—what's the matter with *her?*"

He pointed to Mrs. Clutterfield, who was still squealing at intervals.

"Ooooh!"

"What's the matter with you?" Hanson said brusquely.

"Ooooh! I didn't know a goat was so *important!*"

"What's she talking about?" Hanson appealed to Asey.

"I don't think," Asey said, "it's worth the time to go into it. Tell me, Mrs. Clutterfield, just what *was* you lookin' in windows for, anyway?"

"Ooooh!" Mrs. Clutterfield said. "I saw all these policemen moving around! Alfred was afraid. He *said* there might be trouble. I wanted to see what was going *on!* Really, if it's a matter of a *fine*, I'm sure I can—"

"I'm sure you can, too," Asey said. "Tomorrow mornin', Mrs. Clutterfield, I'll tell you the fine, an' you *will*. Right now, you go up to your room an' stay there!"

Mrs. Clutterfield scurried up the stairs.

"What did you pack her off like that for?" Cummings wanted to know.

"I can't concentrate with her squealin' so," Asey said. "Besides, I'm sure she ain't got a thing to do with this. Her problem is runnin' over a goat."

"What was all that about a fine?" Cummings persisted.

Asey grinned. "That's just a charitable problem, Doc. Where's Rankin?"

"You'll find your friend in the smoking room." Cummings drew on his overcoat and picked up his little black bag. "A blend of tolerant amusement and refined irritation. He was only waiting for a streetcar —I mean, he was only chasing someone *else*. I always enjoy that it-wasn't-me-it-was-two-other-fellows angle. Have fun with him. I'm going to join Carey."

"You're goin' to do more work tonight?" Asey asked in surprise. "Thought you hated workin' up there at night. You always claimed the place didn't have enough light."

"It doesn't," Cummings said. "But there are several things I want to find out. I'll let you know if anything comes up I think would interest you. Good-by."

Asey made his way to the smoking room, where Rankin was reading a Sears Roebuck catalogue.

"Hullo," Rankin looked up. "Why do you look at me that way? Have I aged?"

"Nope," Asey said. "I just never had a good look at you before tonight, what with our either bein' outside or in a car or in a hall. I thought you was older."

"It's the beard," Rankin said. "A wise uncle of mine pointed out years ago that successful genealogists wore beards. People somehow connect beards with ancestors. I'm forty-eight, as a matter of fact. Mayo, I gather it's Ann who's been killed, and not Miss Olive, and I also gather from Cummings's mutterings that he thinks I killed her. I didn't. I was very fond of Ann. But, as I told Cummings, if it'll make the authorities happier, go upstairs and go through my things. Prod into anything that strikes your fancy. You'll find a forty-five Colt in my bureau drawer, and a license to carry it in my pigskin wallet. And—tell me, why does Dr. Cummings dislike me so?"

"Wa-el," Asey said, "I think it's mostly the bill you owe him."

"The bill *I* owe him? But I don't! I left money with Freddy to pay that bill last year, before I went home! If she forgot, why didn't he *send* me a bill? My God!"

"He said that he did, but—"

"He never did! I never got any! How utterly ridiculous, to suspect me of killing Ann because I didn't pay a bill he never sent me! Was that the reason he had me seized by that trooper? I was brought in here and told to wait for you. Nobody explained why."

"Didn't they bring up the matter of somebody lurkin' around peerin' into windows?" Asey asked.

"*I* brought up that matter, myself!" Rankin said. "Look, you remember my cigarette lighter? You threw it at Hanson, and in all that rush after Elissa, I forgot to retrieve it. I'm fond of that lighter, so I went out to see if I could find it. And when I turned the corner of the house, I saw someone dart away from the bushes by one of the side windows. So I sneaked into the bushes and waited to see if the fellow might come back. In my own way, *I* was trying to be helpful. *I* thought that, under the circumstances, someone darting around bushes in a surreptitious fashion was someone to grab and investigate. And while I was lurking there in the bushes, waiting, this trooper grabbed me. I'm sure," Rankin concluded, "that he meant well. So did I."

"I see," Asey said. "Now, tell me about this girl Ann Joyce, will you?"

"She was an awfully bright and talented girl," Rankin said promptly, "and I was very fond of her. She worked for me as my secretary the winter before last. It was admittedly a stopgap job. She wanted to go on the stage. She was good-looking, and she had one of the loveliest voices I ever heard, and I thought she had ability. So I told people about her, and helped her get a job here in the South Pochet Barn Theater last summer. And I don't mind telling you that whatever success the Theater enjoyed was due wholly to Ann. Last winter she got some understudy jobs, and this summer, she came back to the Barn Theater to get more experience."

"Then," Asey said thoughtfully, "you couldn't hardly, in all honesty, refer to her as a star, could you?"

"No. That's why," Rankin said in a troubled voice, "*I* can't begin to understand this business of her being shot! Ann wasn't important, in the sense of her being any colossal, glamourous success in the theater! She wasn't. She was just a talented, ambitious youngster starting to work her way up."

"An' bein' at the foot of the ladder," Asey said, "she wasn't far enough advanced on her career to have what you'd call awful complicatin' problems, was she?"

"She had problems," Rankin returned. "Who doesn't have problems? The problem of getting three meals a day is no less acute in the theater than it is anywhere else!"

"Uh-huh. But there wasn't Hollywood agents fightin' over her," Asey said, "or admirers challengin' each other to duels, or people she'd stepped on yearnin' to pick out her eye teeth. Nobody stood to lose millions because she did this thing instead of that thing. The point I'm makin' is that while her problems mattered to her, they wasn't important an' far reachin' enough to make someone want to kill her."

"I don't see why anyone would want to kill her anyway!" Rankin said. "People liked Ann. She wasn't temperamental. She gets on with everyone. Bram Reid—he's the new director over at the Barn—told me last week he thought Ann would go far, and he added that he'd never found anyone easier to get along with."

"You can't think of anyone you might call an enemy of hers?" Asey asked. "Anyone that might have had a grudge against her?"

Rankin hesitated.

"D'you remember," he said at last, "I told you earlier in the evening that it wasn't fair for you to ask me my opinions of the people at the Inn until I knew who was killed? Well, now I know it was Ann, I'm not going to pretend to pull any punches. The Barn's success last summer was due to Ann. Elissa Hingham's one of the Barn's backers. Elissa's husband, Horace, is—"

"By the way," Asey interrupted, "just for the record, what's Horace's last name?"

"His last name?" Rankin said. "Why, it's—let's see. Sproul, I think. No, it isn't. It's Henderson, or Sanderson, or Martinson, or something. I don't really remember. Anyway, Horace has wit enough to know that Ann is good. Horace is worried that she might get enticed up to that outfit in Weesit, so he's trying hard to see Ann gets all the breaks here, so she'll stay. Ann had a very flattering offer from Weesit, incidentally, but she finally decided she'd learn more here, working with Bram Reid. So—"

"Bram Reid," Asey said. "I seem to connect that name with something. Wasn't he in the movies once?"

"Yes. He was one of the strong silent men around the Pearl White era. Now, d'you get the picture? Horace knows Ann is good, he's doing his best to give her the breaks, and Elissa's jealous as hell. She's always been jealous of his interest in Ann, which is purely professional, and she's always been jealous of Ann's success. She doesn't understand why Ann should get on and get ahead."

"Why not? You said the girl had talent, an'—"

"She has! But Elissa's jealous of anyone who seems to be succeeding without pull, and on their own merits. You see, Mayo, Elissa was a mediocre soprano who kidded a lot of people into thinking she was good. God knows how much money old man Hingham threw away trying to make an opera star of her! She finally gave up her operatic ambitions, but she still thinks she was destined to be something in the theater. I think that's why she married Horace and backed this barn outfit. She's still trying to buy her way into the theater somehow!"

"Huh!" Asey said. "So you think that maybe Mrs. Hingham might—"

"Wait, now," Rankin said. "I'm not through! You asked me if Ann had any enemies or anyone with a grudge against her. Now, Elissa's jealous of Ann's success and Horace's interest in her. I'll go so far as to say that if Ann had an enemy in the world, it's Elissa. But

—and this is a good big but, too. But Elissa was too shrewd to let Ann know how jealous she was. I don't think Ann ever guessed. I'm positive Ann never guessed. Elissa's shrewd enough to know that if Ann got mad and left the Barn the box office would suffer. Elissa never said a word to Ann, ever. She took it all out on Horace. I'll wager that most of her migraine today was due to quarreling with Horace, and most of her quarreling with Horace was over Ann. But she never came out in the open and blew off steam at Ann. So, if she cared that much for the box office, it doesn't seem possible that she'd have killed Ann! What I mean—"

"What you mean," Asey said, "is that Mrs. Hinghan has plenty of motive for killin' the girl, but while killin' the girl might maybe ease her jealous feelin's, it'd hurt her pocketbook maybe more."

"Something like that," Rankin said. "Of course, Elissa is impulsive. There's no reason or logic behind a lot she does. Look at that crazy, involved business of taking that rug away from here! After fussing so much about her migraine, she couldn't suddenly recover sufficiently to rise up and move rugs. Not in front of Mrs. Doane! Not when she's been demanding and getting extra service from Mrs. D. all day long. But she had the impulse to take that rug to the Theater tonight. She could have waited till tomorrow, but she wanted to take it tonight. So she did, using the roof to save her face, so to speak, with Mrs. D. The only person Elissa thinks of is Elissa—and that's just another reason why it doesn't seem that she would harm Ann. She might have wanted to, but she'd have been held back by the thought of the consequences—Mayo, when was Ann killed?"

"Looks," Asey said, "like she was shot in the phone booth just before six."

"I'm sure she wasn't killed before five-thirty," Rankin said. "That was when I left with Judge Houghton. And Lady Boop and I were there in the living room all afternoon." He smiled. "We had a fine time irritating Elissa with the radio and miscellaneous noise. She made the mistake of ordering us, via Freddy, to shut up."

"Freddy told me about that."

"When Lady Boop puts on Benny Goodman," Rankin said, "you can be quite sure she doesn't believe her fellow guest is suffering very badly with migraine. Anyway, we didn't see Ann, and we didn't hear any shot. There's one more thing I'm curious about, Mayo. Where *is* Miss Olive?"

"That's a problem I've been lookin' into," Asey said, "without success. Can you think of any reason why Ann Joyce should be dressed up in her clothes?"

"I can't think of any reason for any of this," Rankin said, "and that least of all. Of course—"

"Of course what?" Asey prompted.

"Well, Miss Olive goes pretty much her own way," Rankin said. "Week after next, when the place gets going, you'll find it full of Lady Boops. Elissa is definitely not a Whale Inn type. She adds glamour to the place, she and Horace, and I think that's why Mrs. D. likes them to stay here. They make the Boops of the world feel worldly. Miss Olive isn't a Whale Inn type, either. She knows all the townspeople, but she doesn't have much to do either with the Boops, or Elissa. She never had much to do with Ann last summer. I mean, they just nodded and said hello to each other. But—this probably isn't worth telling you."

"Go on," Asey said. "Right now I'm eager for crumbs."

"Well, since Miss Olive's been here this year, I've noticed her chatting often with Ann. One day—I don't remember if it was Wednesday or Thursday—Ann picked up Miss Olive's coat from a chair arm and tried it on. Miss Olive looked annoyed and told her to take it off at once, and said something about mockery that I didn't hear. Now, when the doctor told me it was Ann dressed up in Miss Olive's clothes, I just took it for granted she must have done it for something at the Theater. But then I remembered that scene, and I wonder, Mayo. D'you suppose Ann just had the impulse to dress up like her and see if she could fool anyone? Bram Reid's been teaching her a lot about make-up. Maybe, just for the hell of it, she wanted to see if she could get away with being Miss Olive for an afternoon."

"Did you have any suspicions about her when you give her the two nickels for her dime?" Asey asked.

"Not then. Now it occurs to me that she seemed a little excited and breathless. And I never knew her to ask for change before. She's the sort who always has two nickels for your dime. It doesn't seem possible that Ann could fool me, but I find myself wondering if she did! And, Mayo, that brings up something else. Suppose Ann *did* dress up to see if she could get away with being Miss Olive. If she was keeping it a secret, and no one knew what she intended doing, then someone killed her thinking she *was* Miss Olive!"

"Uh-huh."

"Well, my God!" Rankin said, "*that's* fantastic, too, as I told Hanson out there on the porch! D'*you* think someone meant to kill Miss Olive? And *why?*"

Asey shook his head.

"Those questions," he said, "been hauntin' me for what seems like years. Rankin, you wouldn't know about any play where there might be a Miss Olive sort of character, do you?"

"I don't know anything about the Theater's plans," Rankin said. "They don't stick to their schedule. At least, they didn't last year. Sometimes they'll do 'Captain Applejack' for a couple of nights, and then they'll spring some fantastic thing—well, like this fantasy where they needed a pickax and a page boy and a Persian rug! That's Horace's influence. Horace should be able to tell you if Ann was planning to do a character part—but I don't see why she should! She never has. She just does straight ingénue roles! I'm sure she'd have mentioned a character part to me if she'd planned doing one! And it does seem, if she intended to sneak in here and swipe Miss Olive's clothes, she'd have tipped me off, or told Freddy, or someone! Where are you going?"

"I'm goin'," Asey said, "to see if I can't get started, like, an' put my finger on somethin'. I don't much care what. To quote Doc Cummings, 'I'm speechless with too much speculation.'"

"Want me to stay here in seclusion?" Rankin asked.

"Wa-el," Asey said with a grin, "I don't think you're the peeper we want unless you was peepin' around here a little after six."

"I wasn't. I was with Judge Houghton," Rankin told him. "He asked me to dinner, forgetting it was his housekeeper's night off. So he and I broiled a steak, and we were just settling down for an evening of the Houghton family tree when he got a call from some distressed client up the Cape. I don't know what time I came back—but you were here then, weren't you? Have you tried to locate Miss Olive?"

"I've scoured around everywhere," Asey said, "but Lord knows where she is! I'm torn right now between the desire to track her down, an' to get hold of the Hinghams an' pump them. Only trouble is, until I find out where the real Miss Olive went, an' what she did, it's kind of aimless tryin' to pump anybody. You ain't sure which you seen an' give nickels to, an' I ain't sure which Jennie an' I seen at the four corners. There ain't really any place where you can focus your mind an' start from."

Rankin said that all he'd tried to do, personally, was to focus his mind on motives.

"And look at the state of confusion I'm in! But certainly Hanson's men can find fingerprints and things like that!"

Asey smiled.

"A phone booth," he said, "is sort of a lair for assorted fingerprints, when you stop an' think of it. Or, at least, it would be if Mrs. Doane hadn't been kind enough to clean it out so nice after she moved the body. Just her movin' it from the booth to the porch ain't been any aid, exactly, either. An' if there'd happened to of been prints on that gun, Mrs. Doane probably wiped 'em off. Wa-el, I'll be seein' you."

He didn't know, he admitted to himself as he stepped into the hall, exactly where he intended going or what he intended to do, but he was tired of talking, and of people's if's and how's. Any situation, even one as confused and complicated as this seemed at the moment, simplified itself after you thought about it a little. Usually it was the if's and what's of other people that made it confused in the first place.

The door at the end of the hall was ajar, and Asey paused in the act of pushing it open to listen to the voice of Jennie soaring high in argument with Hanson, in the living room beyond. Then Mrs. Doane and Freddy chimed in, and then the bass voice of one of Hanson's troopers.

Asey stood for a moment and listened, mentally noting that if he answered half the questions they professed to have waiting for him on the tip of their tongues he would be talking for the rest of the night.

With a weary sigh, he turned back up the hall. He didn't feel like being pounced on, and he didn't want any more problems broached than the ones which were already besetting him.

He tiptoed past Rankin in the smoking room, quietly opened a window at the end of the hall, removed the window screen, and slid over the sill outdoors.

The rain had turned to a drizzle while he was driving around hunting Miss Olive, and now the drizzle had turned to a thick, wet, clammy fog that cut the light from the street lamps down to a small, bulging glow.

Asey walked over to a bench near a birdbath, and sat down. It had been hard enough trying to find Miss Olive's black Chevvy sedan in a light rain, and now, with this fog, it seemed a little senseless to go driving from one road to another when you couldn't see any more of cars than the blur of their headlights. He could always round up the Hinghams and ask them questions. Horace of the elusive last name ought to be able to tell whether Ann Joyce was costuming herself for some prospective play, or whether she was dressing up for fun.

And even if it were for some play, and Horace knew about it, Asey thought, that didn't advance things very much. Then you'd only have to delve around and find out how many other people might have known, too, and if the person who shot Ann Joyce in Miss Olive's clothes had known she was masquerading and was counting on that fact to confuse everyone, they would hardly admit the fact. And if only Horace knew, then you were right back where you started, and someone was shooting Ann Joyce instead of Miss Olive, and thinking it was the latter.

Asey put his feet up on the bench and pulled out his pipe.

The thing was nothing but possibilities. If Ann Joyce had been pretending to be Miss Olive all day, she ought to have had Miss Olive's car, and the car should be around, now. Perhaps, Asey thought, it might have been parked out behind the Inn somewhere when he and Jennie came. He hadn't seen any trace of it when he chased the prowler who knocked over the clams, but that didn't mean that the car couldn't have been there. And still might be. If the fog cleared, or if Miss Olive didn't return by daylight, Hanson's men would have to scour around.

But if Ann Joyce had Miss Olive's car, then where was Miss Olive now, and where had she been all day? And where was she keeping herself?

And why?

Asey sat up straight on the bench.

Was it possible that Miss Olive knew all about this?

Everyone had mentioned her peculiar attitude about her clothes. Freddy spoke of it. Rankin said Miss Olive made Ann remove the coat she had tried on. Everyone seemed to agree that Miss Olive never would have lent Ann her clothes to dress up in.

But suppose she had?

Suppose, Asey thought, that Miss Olive knew she was in some sort of danger, and had deliberately allowed, maybe even encouraged, Ann Joyce to dress like her?

Asey shook his head and dismissed the thought at once.

That might work out if Miss Olive were someone like the impulsive Mrs. Hingham, but not for anyone as settled in her ways as Miss Olive seemed to be. If he had gleaned from people one idea that evening, Asey thought, it was that Miss Olive Beadle was not a person about whom danger and excitement lurked.

Offhand, he never remembered a case where there was so little apparent reason to do away with the two people most involved.

There the two of them were, a struggling young actress with a lovely voice and a middle-aged school-teacher with steel-rimmed glasses. No vast fortunes were involved, no angry lovers, no irate husbands. Just two women from whose death nobody appeared to derive any benefit, and for whom no one apparently had a single harsh or unkind word. Even Doc Cummings, whose irony could occasionally be spread out with a butter knife, had carried the torch for Miss Olive. Even Rankin, with his knack for dissecting people in a few well-chosen phrases, could say nothing unpleasant about his ex-secretary Ann Joyce.

Asey puffed thoughtfully at his pipe.

No one had yanked him into a corner and poured into his ear any reports of violent quarrels or sinister threats. Aside from Mrs. Hingham's jealousy, which didn't seem to weigh as heavily as her pocketbook, no motive for anyone's shooting Ann Joyce had cropped up. No one could even bring themselves to think up any motive whatsoever for anyone's shooting Miss Olive.

And if there was a dearth of motives, Asey thought, there was a positive desert of clews. No shreds of tweed, no cigarette butts smeared with lipstick, no quaint cameo pins, no gobs of chewing gum, or anything else. There weren't even any obviously false clews that you could dangle in anyone's face and demand explanations for.

That, at least, was the way it seemed.

But, of course, there was a motive, Asey told himself. There always was. There had to be.

There were clews, too, if only he had the brains to recognize them as such.

The whole trouble was that he had let himself be distracted. He had wasted his time, chasing would-be actresses with rugs, investigating fat ladies and dead goats, brooding about Mrs. Doane's moving the body and trying to make away with the gun, wondering about odds and ends like the apparent lamblike innocence of Washy Doane and Freddy Doane's long absence earlier in the evening. And in between times, he'd let people talk his ear off.

Perhaps Doc Cummings was right, Asey thought. Perhaps all this rushing around with Bill Porter had done something to his mind.

"What I want," he murmured aloud, "is a few roots!"

He had thought, once that evening, that he had actually landed on a root, until Freddy mentioned that cleaning woman and nipped the root in mid-air.

It was such a simple, logical, sensible root that it appealed to Asey, and neither Cummings nor Hanson nor anyone else had given it a thought. At least, they hadn't mentioned it.

They had all simply taken it for granted that Ann Joyce must have been killed inside that telephone booth.

It never seemed to have occurred to any of them that if it had been so easy for Mrs. Doane to have moved that body from the booth to the porch, it must have been just as easy for someone else to have placed the body there in the first place!

The back door of the booth, that led into the narrow hall, could just as well have been used for an entrance as it had been used by Mrs. Doane for an exit. While Freddy and Rankin and Lady Boop and everyone else moved around in the living room, the body could have been inserted in the booth from the other side, without any of them being a whit the wiser.

It had seemed such a likely idea, Asey thought a little sadly, and it had been such a clear, distinct picture that he'd visualized!

In his mind's eye, he could still see someone stealthily slipping in through the French doors of the dining room, bearing the body across the dining room to the kitchen hall, pausing and listening, then walking rapidly along to the narrow hall, a dozen feet beyond to the left. Then, after more waiting and listening outside the booth door, the final dangerous moment of placing the body on the little chair inside the booth, of putting the gun and glasses on the floor. And then the cautious, stealthy business of slipping away, back across the hall and through the dining room, and out of the Inn.

But the presence of the cleaning woman in the dining room knocked all that conjectured pantomime into a couple of cocked hats.

It did even more. It also put an abrupt stop to another thought Asey had been toying with, that Ann

Joyce might just possibly have been shot upstairs in the Inn and brought down in one of the two elevators Rankin had mentioned. What with so many people wandering around the living room, the elevator in the alcove couldn't under any circumstances have been used. But the elevator to the dining room had seemed a magnificent possibility until this cleaning woman reared her head. And the fact of her keeping the dining-room doors open even made it difficult to see how anyone might have sneaked in the back way without being spotted by her in the hall.

Not, Asey thought, that he liked the idea of anyone's having sneaked in by the back door anyway. It was too great a distance from the kitchen ell to that phone booth, and a person bringing in a body that way would run too many chances of being observed. The possibility of Washy's being in the vicinity would have to be considered, just as someone had to consider the possibility of Freddy or Mrs. Doane being at the desk in the living room. If Washy had seen Alfred clearly enough from the woods to take a pot shot at him, Washy ought to have noticed anyone else lurking around.

Asey knocked out his pipe.

The possibility that Alfred himself might have carried a body into the Inn was, on the one hand, too absurd to consider seriously, and, on the other hand, not quite absurd enough to ignore entirely. Alfred was fat. Alfred possessed, as Washy put it, a broad beam. From a distance, any addition to Alfred's broad beam would not be as obvious as it might be in the case of a narrower person. In the dusk of evening, Alfred with a body might not appear visibly encumbered to Washy, in the woods.

Asey couldn't bring himself to consider Lady Boop and Alfred as a pair of murderers, but it might not do any harm to seek out Washy and have a talk with him about Alfred, just in case. Even though Lady Boop was as rich as Croesus, there had been something fishy in her giving Alfred a cool thousand dollars in cash to keep in his wallet for little eventualities like dead goats.

And, although Asey hadn't considered that particular angle of the situation before, he couldn't stake his oath that the goat was the only thing Alfred had buried. And, after all, Miss Olive was still missing.

"If that goat was a red herrin'," Asey murmured to himself, "I'm goin' to look one plumb dumb fool!"

He strode over toward the kitchen ell.

The lights went out before he got there, and as he peered around the corner, Washy, in a belted Mackinaw and with his little blue knitted cap on his head, sidled out the kitchen door and started down the path.

He didn't exactly run, but he walked so rapidly on tiptoe that the effect was the same, and he held his head down and his shoulders crouched a little, as if he were trying to make himself small.

With a puzzled look on his face, Asey watched for a moment, and then quietly set off down the path after him.

He heard a crackling sound as Washy left the path and skirted the brush pile, and then the soft crunching of his sneakers as he hurried along down another gravel path.

Keeping well behind him, Asey followed him around a small pond, through a pine woods, and down a little sloping hill to the bay shore.

Washy paused for a moment at the edge of the beach grass and then continued more slowly toward the gaunt outlines of a bathhouse that loomed out of the fog.

Waves lapped on the shore beyond, and a bell buoy rang hollowly from Quisset Harbor, and then Asey heard the rattle of keys and the click of a padlock.

Washy swung open the bathhouse door, emerged a moment later with a shovel, and then began to dig industriously in the sand.

After a few moments he stopped, jabbed his shovel upright into the sand, and took something from the pocket of his Mackinaw.

Asey strolled forward.

His hands were in the pockets of his coat, and he almost sauntered up to Washy, but he was ready to meet anything from a frontal attack with the shovel to what used to be Washy's *pièce de résistance*, a sort of elementary flying tackle.

"By gorry, it's you, Asey!" Washy said in a voice of pleased relief. "I must say I'm glad! I been tryin' to get hold of you all evenin' long to see what you thought was best for me to do about these cussed things. Here. You take 'em."

He held out a flat fifty cigarette tin.

Asey took it with caution. Washy was also a past master of the extended hand and the hearty grip. And when you came to and picked yourself up, you found your arm was broken.

"What's this, Washy?"

"It's them cussed papers. Honest, Asey, I been like to go crazy, with them cussed cops stickin' their cussed noses into everything, for fear they'd find 'em an' start askin' my wife—say, you met my wife now, ain't you?"

"Uh-huh."

"Then you know if they find these papers an' ask her about 'em, I'm a goner! I kept thinkin' I'd be all right as soon as Miss Olive come back. But with her away, no one wouldn't ever believe me. Anyhow, now you got 'em," he hooked his arm chummily in Asey's, "an' everything's okay. My, my, it's good to get them cussed things off my mind, I can tell you. Come on back up to the house, Asey, an' let's us talk about the ole days—"

"Wait up," Asey disengaged himself warily. He still didn't trust Washy even in this mood of benign good humor. "What's all this about papers?"

"Oh, they're in the box. Come on out of this damp an' fog an'—"

"Hold on, Washy! Come back here! What are these papers, an' what's the idea of buryin' 'em?"

"I told you!" Washy said impatiently. "I don't want them cussed cops to take 'em to my wife an' ask her any questions about 'em, because then I'd be a goner! So I thought I'd just bury 'em out of the way till Miss Olive come back, because then people'd believe me— say, Asey, you don't think nothin' happened to her, do you?"

"I hope not. Washy, stop dancin' around, an' tell me what these papers are!"

"They're just the notes." Washy took Asey's arm again. "She wouldn't never take 'em, you see. She said she trusted me. But I said, 'Miss Olive, with a sum of money like that, you got to have a note.' I told her that ten years ago. So I makes out a note. N'en as I paid her back, I made out other notes. She gives me a receipt every time I pay her back. The receipts is in that box, too."

"Do I understand," Asey was honestly bewildered, "that you owe her money?"

"Only two thousand now," Washy said with pride. "I paid back the other five."

"Washy," Asey said, "come over here an' sit down on these bathhouse steps an' let me get this straightened out. Miss Olive once lent you seven thousand dollars?"

"Yes, sir," Washy said. "An' you know what? My wife, she don't know it!"

He leaned his head back and laughed until his little blue cap fell off and tears rolled down his cheeks.

"What for?" Asey asked.

Washy misunderstood his question. "Say, you'd laugh, if you knew my wife better! Why, say, my wife knows everything, she does, Asey! She knows more'n Old Tantabogus, like Custer Mayo used to say. She knows everything goin'. Except about this! You see, ten years ago the bank foreclosed. Kind of hard, times was then. An' the cussedest part was, Asey, I had the money to pay 'em with, only it was all tied up in this schooner. Ever know Sim Smith? He was kind of a crazy feller, Sim was, but he was a good trader, an' he'd been tradin' around the South Seas for years, see, an' I was partners with him in this schooner. That's where my money was tied up. I knew I'd get the money back all right, someday, but the bank, it had to get paid cash money then, see?"

Asey nodded.

"Well," Washy continued, "I was feelin' pretty blue about it all when Miss Olive come to me one day, out in the kitchen, an' said she knew how things was, an' she'd like to lend me the cash money to pay the bank. Only she didn't want Mrs. Doane to know. So—"

"Why not?"

"Miss Olive said Mrs. Doane'd make a lot of fuss over her, an' things wouldn't be the same, an' nothin' but hard feelin's ever come when one woman lent another woman money—I think she was right, don't you, Asey? Women are funny about loanin' money, always seemed to me. Well, to make a long story short, Miss Olive an' I fixed it so's it seemed like the money come from Sim Smith. Even made up a letter," Washy laughed at the thought, "an' pretended to lose the envelope. An' we paid up the bank. N'en, you see, whenever I get a hunk of money from Sim, I pay it over to Miss Olive. An' when them cussed cops started pokin' around tonight, I thought to myself, I wasn't goin' to have this spoiled now if I could help it. It'd look awful funny if they asked my wife to explain about the notes an' she didn't know, see, an' nobody'd believe *me* if Miss Olive wasn't there."

"Washy, where in time'd Miss Olive get this cash money to pay you with? They told me she was a schoolteacher."

"Oh, she's one of them careful ones, I guess," Washy said. "Think of it, my wife not knowin' about this! When I get the last cent paid up, I'm goin' to tell her an' show her the notes, an' that's goin' to be a great day, Asey, I can tell you! My wife's always talkin' about how she finances things an' how smart she is about money. It's goin' to be a shock to her when she finds out how this Inn got financed by *me!* I get an awful lot of comfort out of this business, sometimes, just thinkin' about it. Asey, you don't think anything's happened to Miss Olive tonight, do you?"

"I don't know." Asey opened the tin box, struck a match, and held up one of the papers. It was a note, all right. Washy was apparently telling the truth. "Where d'you keep these papers usually?"

"Hid in the kitchen."

"An' your wife don't know? You're sure she don't?" Asey closed the tin box.

"If my wife knew," Washy said, "she wouldn't keep it a secret—I guess you ain't seen much of her."

"I've seen enough," Asey said, and mentally added that he'd seen enough to know how Mrs. Doane might react to the news that her precious Inn wasn't as free and clear as she thought it was. And suppose that Washy had got tired of paying. Suppose—

"I hope you noticed," Washy said proudly, "that I pay her six per cent interest, too. I pay that regular, out of my own pay, an' what I pick up shootin' crap with fellers like Rankin around the Inn."

"Where's that gun of yours?" Asey said. "Got it in your pocket now?"

"Oh, I give that to one of them cops," Washy said. "I told him I had a gun, an' a license, an' give 'em to him, right away. I used to be kind of a wild feller, you know, till I got married. I didn't want anybody suspectin' me of anything to do with killin' Miss Olive— that was when they thought it was her. I was afraid if you got to rememberin' anything about me when I was young, you might think I'd been cuttin' loose. But I tell you, Asey, I ain't cut loose since I had my wife around. I guess you can understand that. But you know what I was thinkin' tonight?"

"What?"

"I was thinkin', if anyone's harmed Miss Olive," Washy said, "I don't know but what I might cut loose enough to make up for all them quiet years. I'd like to locate her, Asey, an' be sure she was all right. Can't you figger out some way we can find her?"

"I done my best," Asey assured him. "Tell me one more thing, Washy. This feller Alfred. Lady Boop's chauffeur. You seen him go into the Inn this evenin'—"

"I told them cops I took a pot shot at him," Washy said with a snicker. "I couldn't help myself. I always wanted to, an' there he stood outlined against that ell, big as a barge! I know I hadn't ought to of, but I couldn't help myself. I just had to, Asey."

"Wasn't carryin' anythin', was he?" Asey asked. "Like a large bundle, maybe?"

Washy laughed.

"Say, you couldn't tell, with him! Once I seen him walk in that kind of waddle of his from the garage to the car, an' it wasn't till ten minutes later that I realized he'd been luggin' a tire all the time! He ain't such a bad shot. Used to be a cop, you know."

"Alfred? He was a cop?"

"Yup," Washy said. "Till he got kicked off of the force for bribery an' corruption—'course, *he* never told me *that* part. He just said he didn't see no future in bein' a cop, so he quit. But one of the other chauffeurs that comes from Boston told me Alfred got kicked off of the force for takin' bribes. Seems like he couldn't never let a chance get by him to make a few dollars. For a cop, he ain't such a bad shot," Washy added thoughtfully. "He shoots with me, sometimes. Seems like folks do a lot more shootin' nowadays than they used to, Asey. Fellers around town used to laugh at me for pottin' away, but then last winter after they started up this Home Guard thing, they started comin' over here an' askin' me to show 'em how to shoot. Why, even Horace, he's come out an' pulled a trigger once or twice! 'Course, he always closes his eyes tight, first— say, Asey, anyone think to look in her room?"

"Whose?"

"Miss Olive's. I don't know's I ever knew it to happen," Washy said, "but I been thinkin' maybe she might of come in an' gone to bed with a headache or somethin'. Seems like somebody ought to of seen her come in, if she did, or her car'd be here, but she's a quiet sort of person. Don't make any noise. She might have come in without any of us hearin' her. 'Course, I know whoever called up said not to expect her, but just the same, she might be back anyway. You can't never tell."

"What do you make of that call?" Asey asked.

"Oh, I think Freddy got it wrong. You know," Washy lowered his voice, "she's got this feller, Freddy has, an' my wife don't like him, an' Freddy's kind of worked up about things. She don't pay attention. Absent-minded, like. Other day I asked her to get a pound of sausage an' a dozen yeast cakes, an' she waltzed back with twelve pounds of sausage an' a piece of cheese cake! Her mind just ain't *on* things. Tonight in there, when she was talkin' with that head cop, I noticed she made any number of mistakes. I didn't say nothin', because I knew if I pointed 'em out her mother'd jump on her—my wife's a great jumper, you noticed that?"

"Uh-huh. Mistakes like what, Washy?"

"Like about this afternoon. She kept tellin' that cop that there was somebody in the livin' room all the time, every single minute, an' *I* know for a fact there wasn't! She an' Rankin an' Lady Boop was out in my kitchen at least twice, all three of 'em, together, yellin' for food. Couldn't have been anybody in the livin' room *then*, now, could there?"

"Huh!" Asey saw the remains of his theory about the phone booth's rear door disappearing forever.

"An' she kept sayin' we was all in the livin' room durin' that special broadcast, too!"

"Wasn't you?" Asey said.

"Why, we all come together to hear it, but we didn't stay put, like Freddy made that cop think! The laundry man come just as the King started to speak, an' I had to get up an' give him the laundry, an' my wife went off while the Queen was speakin', to get Lady

Boop a handkerchief—think of her, cryin' her eyes out for the British," Washy said, "but she wouldn't give 'em ten cents if her life depended on it! An' Rankin went out durin' that music in the middle of it to get his raincoat he'd left down here—begun to look awful stormy about then. An' then Mamie Riggs got up an' left after the President'd spoke a minute or two. Mamie's a kind of a die-hard Republican, you know. So what I think about that call Freddy took tonight, Asey, is just that she made another mistake again. She looked sort of dreamy, like, earlier, I noticed. Between you an' me, I think he's around here somewheres."

"Who? The feller that shot Ann Joyce?"

"I don't know nothin' about him. I mean Freddy's feller. 'Course, no one's asked *me*," Washy said, "but what I think is, if she wants him, an' he's all right, why then, let her have him! Seems a nice feller. Wrote me a nice letter explainin' how he felt about everythin', an' all. *I* ain't got nothin' against him, but my wife's got other ideas for Freddy, an' she gets after the girl, an' Freddy gets all worked up. So probably what happened about that call is that someone just asked Freddy for Miss Olive, an' said she could expect him to call back, an' Freddy got it wrong."

Asey got up from the bathhouse steps.

"Huh!" he said. "Anyway, that may explain why people been peerin' around, an' where Freddy was, an' why she was so gay when she come in! I think you gone a long way toward clearin' up some things, Washy, but you sure landed me a flock of other problems!"

Washy said in a hurt voice he was sure he didn't see how he'd done any such thing.

"I only told you what you asked!" he added.

"Uh-huh. An' added a money problem that's got considerable ramifications," Asey said, "an' give everyone a gun an' Alfred a criminal career, as you might say, an' balled up this timin' business to a fare-thee-well. But, anyway, I think you got somethin' in bringin' up her room. 'Course, Hanson's boys must of looked it over by now, but I think I'll take a look at Miss Olive's room myself. I wonder, could I get to it without bein' seen, Washy? I kind of took a private oath, a little while ago, that I wasn't goin' to be pounced on an' asked a lot of questions till I felt like it. People been gettin' in my hair. Where is her room?"

"I'll show you. What you ought to do is to make like you're deaf," Washy said. "Like when the boarders—gorry, it's good my wife ain't here! She don't let me call 'em boarders. She makes me call 'em guests. Anyways, when they clutter up my kitchen wantin' recipes, I just hold my hand up to my ear an' say 'Hay? Hay? Hay?' An' they give up. My clam chowder's kind of celebrated, you know, an' people always want to know how I make that. 'Course, like Custer Mayo used to say, first thing in makin' a Cape Cod clam chowder is to get Cape Cod clams. Now, I always—"

Washy chatted on about Cape Cod clam chowder and his own particular version of it as he and Asey walked back to the Inn.

"Gorry," he said, as they neared the brush pile, "see them car lights! Looks like there was even more of 'em millin' around! But what I say, Asey, is you can't begin to tell no New Yorker about clam chowder because they don't even know what a clam is. They call quohaugs clams, an' when you try to tell 'em that clams ain't the same as quohaugs, they don't know what you're talkin' about. Like I said to one of 'em last summer, I said, 'Lady, if you don't know the difference between a clam an' a quohaug, then there's no wonder you New Yorkers don't feel no sense of shame when you stuff your clam chowder up with a lot of canned tomatoes!' They just don't know no better, I guess."

"Washy," Asey said, "who do you think shot that girl?"

"Gorry, Asey, I don't know! Don't seem to me it could of been anybody hereabouts! She got along fine with folks when she stayed here last summer—my wife always likes to have an actress or two around, or somebody mixed up with the theater, you know. Kind of sets up the rest, an' gives 'em something to gawp at an' talk about."

"Don't you know somebody that didn't like her?" Asey persisted. "Can't you think of any reason why somebody might have wanted to kill her?"

"To tell you the truth," Washy said, "I don't know much about the boarders—I mean, the guests. Most of the time I'm right out in my kitchen. This Joyce girl seemed nice an' pleasant, an' I'll say for her she always cleaned up her plate! Always had a pleasant word when you seen her. 'Nice dinner,' she'd say. Or 'Nice lunch.' Or something like that. 'Course, I *did* wonder about the Hinghams. But then that seemed kind of silly, when

Horace can't even fire off a twenty-two at a target without closin' his eyes an' flinchin'. Last summer I might have wondered about Rankin, but that's all over now."

"What's all over?" Asey asked.

"Why, he was kind of smitten with her last summer," Washy said, "but she turned him down in August. He told me all about it one afternoon over a glass of beer up to Tony's. I don't think he felt bad about it. Between you an' me, I think he was relieved. He's the sort that'll take one of Tony's waitresses to a dance one night, an' my wife an' Miss Olive to a church fair the next, an' play rummy with me the next—see that third window from the end, right by that cornice? That's Miss Olive's window. She's had that same room for twenty-six years, an' if you wanted to, Asey, I don't see why you couldn't shinny up an' get in there without anyone knowin'. Rankin's got the corner room, an' Lady Boop's got two rooms on the other side."

"I'll go up the shed lattice," Asey said, "an' walk over—huh. I wish I didn't have on these city shoes. Them rooves look slippery."

"You can always sneak up the back stairs," Washy suggested. "I can go in an' keep people busy. Room Five, it is."

Asey looked at him curiously. "Room Five's Mrs. Hingham's, ain't it?"

"Nope. The Hinghams is on the other side of the house. Miss Olive's Five."

"But Room Five's what Mrs. Hingham come out of this evenin'!" Asey said. "She'd been in there havin' her migraine—real or imaginary, I don't know which! Anyway, that's the room she come out of when Jennie an' I yowled around in the hall outside!"

"I guess you maybe just made a mistake," Washy said. "Mrs. Hingham's door always has a big sign stuck on it. Says, 'Don't Disturb.' Nobody ever pays any attention to it, but if any maid ever takes it off, Mrs. Hingham marches out an' sticks it back on again! I tell you, Room Five's Miss Olive's, an' she's had it for twenty-six years, an'—look up to her window, quick, Asey! I'd swear I just seen a little light flicker, like someone strikin' a match in there!"

8

"GIMME your sneakers, Washy!" Asey kicked off his leather-soled brogues. "Gimme—oh, I can't wait! Gimme that knife of yours, if you got it! Hustle up!"

Grabbing the ugly little knife Washy drew from his pocket, Asey raced over the wet grass in his stocking feet and was up the shed lattice with a catlike agility that left Washy gaping.

His lower jaw was almost dangling on his chest as he watched Asey's progress across the shed roof, down to the lower level of the next ell roof, up again and over the railing of a sun deck, then up and along a precarious strip of gutter.

"Gorry!" Washy murmured in admiration. "Custer Mayo always claimed that feller was part rubber ball! Well, by gorry!"

He held his breath as Asey pulled himself, apparently by the skin of his fingernails, to a position beside Miss Olive's window.

Washy had been right about something flickering, Asey thought, as he dug his toes into the gutter.

There had been someone in Miss Olive's room. And there still was someone in there, moving about!

He thrust his hand into his coat pocket for Washy's knife, and wished that Mrs. Doane had been less extravagant with her guests' screening. Copper wire screens were all very nice, but a simple length of netting across the window would have made his job here something less than a cinch.

As he raised his hand to slash across the screening, the knife slipped from his grasp and fell.

Mercifully, it didn't fall far. Only to the gutter. He could feel it with his foot. But it made enough of a clatter to put anyone inside the room on their guard.

Asey edged himself down, grabbed at the knife, got it, and was once again ready to slash the screening when the lights flashed on in the room.

Muttering under his breath, Asey peered through the slats of the Venetian blind.

It was his Cousin Jennie standing there in the doorway, looking dubiously and a little guiltily around.

Asey tapped on the screen.

The location of the sound puzzled her for a moment, but at last she walked over to the window, raised a slat of the blind, and peered somewhat ineffectually out.

"Lift the blind an' open the window!" Asey said impatiently. "Hurry up!"

Jennie struggled with the blind, finally solved the problem by ducking around in front of it, opened the window, and asked him sharply what he thought he was doing anyway.

"Scaring me near to death! What you doin' out there, playin' Superman?"

"Unhook the screen, will you? Hurry up! Jennie, you been in this room before? Just a minute ago? Did you light a match in here?"

"Gracious, no! What'd I be lightin' matches in here for? How'd you get out there? Where," she added as Asey swung one leg over the window sill, "are your best shoes?"

"I don't know. Jennie, who'd you see as you come in here? Who was in this room?"

"Nobody."

"Nobody except *who?* Listen, this is important! Who'd you see out in the hall? Outside the room? Did you see anybody comin' up the stairs?"

"Not a soul, Asey! Everybody's down in the livin' room—a couple of men come an' they're takin' pictures of the phone booth for Hanson, an' Doc Cummings phoned just now an' said he was on his way back here to see you—what's all this about, anyway? Where you think you're rushin' to?"

"I want to find who was in here! Come on!" Asey strode past her into the hall. "Take the rooms on that side an' yell if you see anybody. I'll take this side."

Five minutes later they met at the other end of the hall.

"*I* didn't see anybody anywhere," Jennie said. "Did you? I looked under beds an' in closets, too. My, I'm all out of breath!"

"Wasn't Lady Boop in her room?"

"Mrs. Clutterfield? Oh, she's been downstairs a long

time," Jennie said. "She ain't quite so scared as she was, but she still kind of jumps ever time Hanson walks past her—Asey, what is all this about?"

"I don't know," Asey said. "That's what I'm tryin' to find out—hullo, Washy," he added, as the latter appeared at the head of the rear stairs, "*you* see anybody?"

"Gorry, no!" Washy said. "Was there someone? I figgered there must be, when you didn't call out to me or make no noise, so I beat it inside quick to the hall outside the dinin' room. Nobody come down these back stairs, an' nobody used the elevators, either. You can always tell when anybody uses them, because it cuts the lights for a second when they start an' stop."

"Huh!" Asey said. "An' you're sure you didn't pass no one on the main stairs, Jennie?"

Jennie told him acidly she guessed she knew when she passed someone and when she didn't.

"How's about an attic?" Asey asked Washy.

"See that hatch?" Washy pointed up to the ceiling. "That's the only way you can get to the attic, through that hatch. We made so many changes here, we had to cut out the attic steps altogether. It's hooked, see? Nobody's gone through that. An' this other wing," he pointed to a bolted door, "that ain't been opened up for the season yet. Nobody went through that door an' bolted it after 'em, that's one sure thing!"

"Somebody," Asey said, "was in that room! I know they was! I heard someone movin'! Huh! Ain't got any secret panels around, have you, Washy?"

"We did used to have a slave hole once," Washy

said, "over in the old wing. But we use that for a linen
closet now, an' we don't ever speak of it as a slave hole
no more. Scared the boarders—gorry, there I go again!
Scared the guests stiff, I don't know why. Nope, Asey,
we ain't got any passageways or secret panels—believe
me, I'd know if there was! I ripped this place apart an'
put it together again with my own bare hands too many
times not to know every nail an' lathe by heart! Nobody ever got away off of this floor by any secret
panels. No sireebob!"

Asey leaned against the newel post at the head of the
rear stairs, smoothed out the brim of his now thoroughly battered gray felt hat, and looked down
thoughtfully at his wet feet.

"I wonder," he said at last, "if this is what the newspapers call bein' confronted by a seemin'ly blank wall,
or if we just reached a sort of impasse. Huh! I wonder
what he was doin', an' what he was after, an' how he
got away, an' I wonder if our prowler an' peeper *was*
Freddy's boy friend! Washy, hang around outside an'
keep your eyes peeled, will you? I know somebody was
here, an' there's always the off chance that if we scared
him away before he finished whatever he was up to,
maybe he'll try comin' back. You stand watch."

"Aye, aye," Washy said. And then he paused on the
stairs, and added, "Wasn't no sign of Miss Olive havin'
been in her room, was there?"

"Not that I could see, but I didn't get more'n a
glimpse of the room," Asey told him. "I'm goin' back
there now. Take care outside, now, an' grab anybody

you see actin' stealthy—only don't go for any of Hanson's fellers."

"I'm comin' with you, Asey," Jennie announced.

"Now I think of it," Asey said, "what was you doin' in Miss Olive's room, anyways? What brought you upstairs here?"

Jennie hesitated.

"Well," she said, "for one thing, I got to thinkin' about her. I got to thinkin', now if I could just take a look at her room I could tell an awful lot more about her. I thought maybe if you looked at her things, you'd find everythin' in order, but some one thing different, like. You see what I'm drivin' at?"

"Uh-huh," Asey said. "Sort of. You mean, for all she sounds so set in her ways, there might be some little quirk nobody noticed that'd account for her bein' away tonight." He opened the door of Room Five. "I hadn't thought of that, but it seems likely. Jennie, did you happen to notice the number on this door?"

Jennie nodded vigorously.

"I certainly did! That's the other thing I got to thinkin' about. Mrs. Doane was talkin' to Hanson 'cause he said he'd have to search all the rooms, an' she said somethin' about Room Five; she said Miss Olive'd had Room Five for twenty-six years. Now, this *was* the room Mrs. Hingham come out of, wasn't it? It wasn't Room Fifteen at all, but Room Five! Mrs. Doane said I just made a mistake, but I felt *sure* it was Five. That's why I excused myself an' come up here now, to have a look around an' see what the number was. I still don't trust Mrs. Doane much, an' that fat Mrs. Clutterfield's takin' in every single thing, for all she seems so scared! Kind of a pretty room, ain't it, Asey?"

Asey agreed as he looked around. It was a pleasant room, with white painted woodwork and flowered wallpaper, hooked rugs, several comfortable-looking armchairs, and a small, chintz-covered chaise longue. There was a tufted quilt on the spool bed, a spinet desk in the far corner, several cases of books along one wall, and a pair of white-framed flower prints on either side of the window through which he'd come.

"I love Venetian blinds," Jennie said wistfully. "I always wanted Venetian blinds. I don't know why, but it just always seemed to me if I could only have some white Venetian blinds with red tapes in my kitchen, an' a new inlaid linoleum floor, dark red with a white pattern cut out in the middle, I wouldn't ask for nothin' more. Not for a long time, anyways. Asey, what d'you suppose Mrs. Hingham was doin' in here?"

"What do you think?" Asey returned.

"Well, *I* think—'course, you'll laugh at me! But I wonder if it wasn't Mrs. Hingham, that woman that rushed through the livin' room an' you said was only a piece of my imagination? Don't you suppose it *was* her, dressed up in Miss Olive's clothes?"

"Jennie, how much harder do you want to make this?" Asey demanded.

"Think it'd be all right if I took a look around in the closet? Because," Jennie said with a gleam in her eye, "if I was to find a coat that was damp, an' things hung up different from the rest—"

"If I thought there was three Miss Olives wanderin' around," Asey said, "I should curl up in that waste-basket an' ask you to toss me out into the incinerator! But golly, Jennie, you know, she could have, at that! Officially, she was in bed with a headache, but we don't know for sure! Nobody sat by her bed an' held her hand all the time. Let's see. She was here when Rankin an' Lady Boop was playin' the radio this afternoon, because she complained to Freddy, down at the desk. No one mentioned her listenin' to that broadcast, though, that everyone else listened to! No reason why she couldn't have slipped out, I s'pose. Everybody just sort of took it for granted she was in her bed, writhin' with the agony of her migraine. Huh! Jennie, you suppose you an' me got treated to an' took in by a sample of her actin'?"

"Oh dear, all the clothes in this closet's dry!" Jennie said in disappointment. "Dry as a bone! An' what a lot of coats she's got all alike! Brownish tweed, bluish tweed, grayish tweed, greenish tweed, an' just sort of mottledy tweed! Her dresses're all the same style, too, with them white collars an' cuffs. Ain't that a shame, Asey, nothin's even the least bit damp! There's a lot of empty hangers, but you can't guess anythin' from them—Asey, what you lookin' at? Oh, pictures!" Jennie crossed over to where he was standing by the spinet desk. "S'pose that's her mother, in the old-fashioned gold frame? Who's in that folder?"

She picked up a leather picture folder and examined it interestedly.

"Asey, what a nice thing! I don't know's I ever seen

any like this. You open it up, see, an' instead of there just bein' places for two pictures, there's these other leaves, like, an' you can twist it around so's any picture you fancy can be on top. She had this snap of those two men in white coats—oh, look!"

Asey leaned over her shoulder and looked at the photograph she was pointing to. It was a faded brown photograph of a bewhiskered, stern-appearing man who stood in front of a tall, viciously spiked iron fence. His left hand was placed stiffly on a high chair in which a sad baby sat bolt upright. Beyond the baby stood a petulant-looking girl of about sixteen. Behind the trio was a flight of perilously steep marble steps, flanked by two enormous jardinieres stuffed with plumed grasses.

"I seen that before!" Jennie announced triumphantly.

"So've I," Asey returned. "Them painted marble steps, an' that spiked fence, an' them jars of grass was what you might call standard equipment in every photographer's studio in the country some sixty years ago."

"I'm not talkin' about the scenery! I mean the people! I seen 'em before. Now, let's see, where'd I ever see that picture before? Asey, while I'm thinkin', you get down an' look under the bed. That's where I'd stuff things if I took 'em off in a hurry. 'Member, we heard the bed squeak, too, just before Mrs. Hingham come out. Let's see. Now *why* do I keep thinkin' of Mr. Philpotts!"

"I wouldn't know," Asey said as he knelt down. "Who in time is Mr. Philpotts, anyway?"

"That nice minister we used to have about five or six years ago. Asey, what you got? Did you find somethin'?"

Asey brought out from under the bed a tweed coat, a blue wool dress with white collar and cuffs, a blue felt hat, and a pair of gloves.

"They was all rolled up in a ball behind that cardboard box," he said. "The coat ain't much more'n damp, now, but the rug where it was lyin' is soakin' wet."

Jennie sat down in one of the armchairs and beamed with satisfaction.

"There!" she said. "There! Now you take it all back about me an' my seein' things! I *did* see someone go past me in the livin' room, an' it was Mrs. Hingham dressed in these clothes of Miss Olive's. An' she *did* come up the stairs an' come in here! An' then she took off these things of Miss Olive's an' put on her own striped house coat. Now, was I right?"

"Looks like you was," Asey said. "Looks like you still are, for that matter. She must've slipped out while the rest was listenin' to the radio, an' not come back till you seen her come in. Huh! 'Member you said you was goin' to sit right there in the hall till you found out what'd been goin' on? She must have heard you an' decided you meant it. So she decided she'd bluff us away, an' breezed out past us like she was the Queen of Sheba ridin' on a white charger. She was good, Jennie. I hand it to her. I never suspected nothin'."

"Neither'd I," Jennie said. "I just felt awful kind of small. Then when she heard Mrs. Doane talkin' to us a few minutes later, she come down an' said all that about bein' so bothered by us, she needed a doctor. Guess she figgered Mrs. Doane'd get rid of us pretty quick, if she thought we was botherin' her guests! An' did you notice no doctor ever come? I asked Mrs. Doane about that, an' she said that after she an' Freddy fussed around Mrs. Hingham for a while—that was after she ordered us an' the clams away—why, Mrs. Hingham changed her mind about havin' a doctor, an' said she'd take two more pills."

"I wonder, does Mrs. Doane think Mrs. Hingham's still in her room?"

"I guess she does," Jennie said. "I heard her tell Freddy a little while ago she guessed them pills done the trick in quietin' Elissa. But didn't you tell me, while you was eatin' them drugstore sandwiches, that Mrs. Hingham'd gone out?"

"Uh-huh. She departed some time ago, with a rug. An' Room Fifteen was empty still when I looked into it just now. Say, *why* was everybody seized with an impulse to dress up like Miss Olive this afternoon?"

Jennie shrugged.

"Search me. I wish I could remember about that picture!" She got up from her chair and walked back over to the desk. "What a lot of people in white coats Miss Olive knows. There's two more of 'em in this folder. S'pose they're all doctors? Here's a snap of the Inn—oh, look, Asey! Here's one of Mrs. Doane, an' Freddy, an' Washy with his white cap, an' this must be Miss Olive herself—come see this snapshot, Asey!"

"Uh-huh," Asey continued to scan the titles in the bookcase.

"Come here an' look!" Jennie insisted.

"I must say the woman don't go in much for light readin'," Asey said. "I don't even know how to pronounce the names of most of these books, let alone what they mean. Hefty readin', I'd say—what's the matter, Jennie?"

"Look at this picture! That's Ann Joyce on the steps, see, next to Miss Olive? Asey, they look alike!" Jennie said excitedly. "Asey, d'you s'pose—"

"Now listen, don't go insinuatin' things!"

"But they do look alike! Asey, s'pose it's her daughter!"

"From what I heard about Miss Olive," Asey said, "I think you're comin' close to malignin' her, Jennie. Don't let yourself get so carried away. They both got the same kind of pointed chins, but Ann Joyce don't look half so much like Miss Olive as she looks like Freddy, if you'll just stop an' think."

"Hm," Jennie said. "Yes, that's true. It's the way they got their hair. Hm. The Joyce girl's only twenty-one, Mrs. Doane said, an' Miss Olive's been here for twenty-six years. Hm. I suppose it ain't very likely— Asey, maybe that's why even Mrs. Doane didn't realize it wasn't Miss Olive when she first seen her there in the booth. The girl looked a little like Miss Olive to begin with, what with that pointed chin an' kind of broad forehead. Asey, this other picture of them three in front of that iron fence is drivin' me crazy, tryin' to remember where I seen it before! All I can think of is Mr. Philpotts! What's that note on the bureau?"

"What note?" Asey had turned back again to the bookcase and was thoughtfully scanning more titles.

"Beside the brush!" Jennie went over and picked it up. "Asey! Asey Mayo!"

"What's the matter now?"

"Asey, they ought to have come up here before! *Listen* to this note. *Listen* to it! It says, 'Dear Miss Olive. Well, I've gone and done it, and I hope you won't be too annoyed with the results! Now I'm setting off to see how many people I can take in and fool —won't it be too wonderful if it works!' It's signed 'Ann.' An' there's a lot of exclamation marks! Asey, look at this! For mercy's sakes, what do you make of it? *Did* Miss Olive know Ann was goin' to dress up, an' this was just to let her know she'd set out? Or *didn't* Miss Olive know, an' Ann left this to break the news to her? An' who was the girl aimin' to take in, an' fool? An' what was supposed to work? You s'pose there was some kind of plan? Asey, if Miss Olive knew, an' there was a plan—no, it don't seem possible from what we know of her that she'd ever let the girl dress up like her if she thought any harm'd come of it! I wish if she had to leave a note, she'd left one that said more!"

Asey agreed dryly that it would have been more convenient of her.

"What was both the girl an' Mrs. Hingham dressed up like her for?" Jennie demanded. "S'pose Miss Olive knew about Mrs. Hingham? An' whether she knew or not, where's Miss Olive now? Why—"

Five minutes later, Jennie paused.

"Uh-huh," Asey said.

"You ain't listenin'! Asey, can't you stop starin' off into space an' tell me the answers to some of them things?"

"Your guess's just as good as mine."

"Another thing I want to know about!" Jennie went on. "You listenin' to me? Well, nobody's tried to harm you, have they? But most usually when you get mixed up in this kind of thing, why someone tries to shoot you, or tampers with your car so you'll get hurt in it, or somethin' like that. Nobody's done that tonight, have they?"

"Nope."

"Well," Jennie said, "mightn't that mean that the person that shot the girl's gone away, or anyway that he ain't around here bein' active?"

"Could be so," Asey said, "but I'd say it meant the person knows he's perfectly safe, an' I ain't even warm. No need for him to bother with me while he's got me flounderin' around, so balled up I don't even know when the girl was killed!"

"Why, I didn't think there was any trouble about that part!" Jennie said. "I heard the doc tell Hanson something about the phone booth, an' a few minutes to six, an' how the girl's watch was stopped—"

"Uh-huh, I know all that. But first, before the doc heard much of the story, he said she was shot sometime between four an' six. You know, Jennie, the doc pretends he won't never tell the time a person dies till he can prove it an' swear it on a stack of Bibles, but I notice he's got a way of guessin' pretty accurate, right off the bat! I ain't a bit sure of this few minutes before six part, or even if she was shot there."

"Why, for mercy's sakes," Jennie said, "why'd you want to think she was shot any place else? *That's* where she was!"

"Uh-huh. But the chair in that phone booth downstairs faces the side of the booth," Asey said. "The phone itself's on the side wall, mind, not the back wall that opens into the hall. There ain't a lot of leeway there to shoot anyone in the back. I don't say it couldn't have been done, but it'd have been mighty hard. If she'd been sittin' down—gimme a spool out of that workbasket on the table. Look, this spool's her, see? Now, gimme that crochet hook. This is the other person. Now, if she's sittin' down, there ain't hardly space enough behind her for anybody to squeeze in there, let alone hold a gun in her back an' shoot her! See what I mean?"

"I could!" Jennie said. "Gimme the crochet hook. Look, *this* way!"

"Yup. But then," Asey pointed out, "your bullet'd have gone in at an angle, see, an' the doc never mentioned anythin' like that."

"Well, where do you think she was killed, then? How'd anyone get her in the booth?"

"If it wasn't hard for Mrs. Doane to move her out, it wouldn't have been hard for someone to put her in there. Don't ask me any more questions, Jennie! I don't know the answers. An' this guessin' of mine here may be way off. Probably is. Must be, if I ain't even warm enough so's nobody bothers to favor me with a casual pot shot—"

He broke off as something crackled sharply against the Venetian blind.

Jennie uttered a shrill squeal of terror and jumped from her chair, but Asey looked at the little pieces of gravel on the rug and grinned as he strode over to the window.

"Ahoy, Asey!" Washy called up hoarsely. "Ahoy! I can't find nobody!"

"Keep on watchin', anyway," Asey told him.

When he turned around, Jennie was viewing with acute dismay the contents of the workbasket, strewn all over the floor.

"How'd that happen?" Asey inquired.

"Oh dear, ain't that an awful mess! I had the basket in my hand when I jumped, an' it popped right up into the air—my, that gravel startled me! Help me pick things up, will you? I looked under so many beds in such a rush, I'm stiff an' creakin' from bendin' over. I'm tired, anyways. You know it's most one o'clock?"

"Feel like callin' it a day an' goin' home?" Asey knelt down and started to gather up the spools.

"I thought," Jennie sounded discouraged, "that I'd be a big help to you, Asey. It always seemed to me when you had cases like this before that I'd have guessed things an' figgered things, right off. Maybe not as fast as you, but anyway as fast as Hanson. But I guess it's easy enough after someone's shown you. He—oh, don't stuff things back that way, Asey! It was just about the neatest workbasket I ever seen, an' we mustn't leave it all messy!"

"There!" Asey gave her the basket and tossed the last spool into her lap. "See anythin' I missed?"

"Seems like there'd ought to be a pincushion," Jennie said. "There's always a—Asey, that's another thing!"

"What? Where?" Asey looked around on the rug.

"Not on the floor, ninny! I mean, the pincushion's somethin' else I don't understand. Look, when we first come here tonight, didn't I pick up a pincushion off the floor in the livin' room? It was a pincushion that looked like a tomato, *wasn't* it?"

Asey thought for a moment.

"I don't know's I remember—whoa! Yes, I do, too! Just about the time it dawned on me that this was Mrs. Mercer's Boardin' House, you bent over an' picked somethin' up. An' I asked you what it was, an' you said you thought first it was a tomato, but it was just a pincushion, an' you put it into a sewin' basket on the long table down there. I remember it now. What about it?"

"Why, tonight while we was waitin' there in the livin' room, while you was off huntin' Miss Olive, Mrs. Doane picked up the sewin' basket an' started darnin' a sock. I said, just to kind of make conversation, that I'd picked up her pincushion off the floor, an' she said she was very fond of that pincushion because it was her mother's, an' so different from most—shaped like an orange! So I said—now, Asey, stop lookin' at them pictures an' listen to me! I said, what *I* picked up was a tomato, an' she said to take the basket an' look for myself, there wasn't any tomato there, only the orange, an' I must just have made a mistake with the candle-light an' all. Well, like I said, I was gettin' tired of havin' people tell me I just made a mistake, an' I got sort of mad, an' Freddy stepped in quick an' said that Miss Olive had a tomato that belonged to *her* mother, a real old-fashioned tomato pincushion—"

"What's that?" Asey said. "Say that again."

Jennie repeated it. "I wasn't so upset an' worried that I couldn't tell a red tomato from an orange orange! I said so, too, but Mrs. Doane just smiled that sort of superior smile of hers, an' said I could see, couldn't I, that there wasn't any tomato there then!"

"Wasn't there?"

"No!" Jennie said. "I looked through that basket twice!"

"Did you hunt around anywheres beside the sewin' basket?"

"I was just mad enough," Jennie said, "that I pawed around the floor for it, an' peered among the magazines on the table, an' I even poked in the flower bowl there. I tell you, it's exasperatin', when you know you picked somethin' up an' put it in a certain place, not to find it there, or anywheres near it! An' Mrs. Doane sittin' there with that kind of smirky look on her face, like I was just a stupid fool that didn't know what I was doin'! Freddy an' Rankin an' Washy all helped me hunt—they was polite enough, an' they pawed things around on that table every which way. But it was plain to see they thought I'd made a mistake, too. After a while, I got to wonderin' if maybe I wasn't wrong, because they all thought so—but just the samey, I was positive sure I'd picked up a tomato pincushion an' put it in that basket. Now, what do you think—Asey, what's the matter with you? You looked glum as a fish two minutes ago, an' now you're grinnin' from ear to ear!"

"Cousin, d'you realize what you done?"

"What *I* done?" Jennie sniffed. "Well, I must *say*, if I'd realized all the fuss an' bother an' to-do there'd be over a simple little thing like my pickin' up a pincushion, let me tell you I'd have let it lay right there on the floor! Mercy's sakes! A body'd think—"

"You got me wrong," Asey interrupted. "I don't think it's bad. I think it's good. I think it's more'n good. I think it's just about the best thing that's happened here tonight!"

9

What you done, Jennie," Asey continued, "is to put your finger *on* somethin', see?"

"I never!" Jennie said with spirit. "I didn't put my finger on it, Asey Mayo! I tell you, I picked up that pincushion. With my hand!"

Asey's grin widened.

"An' presented it to me on a platter," he said. "Just so. Look, there was somethin' belongin' to Miss Olive, Jennie. On the floor. You pick it up an' put it somewheres, but—it ain't there now!"

"I can't help that! I—"

"Wait. It must be Miss Olive's pincushion, all right. You say Freddy said she had a tomato pincushion. But there's none in her own basket here, is there? An' you said yourself it was the neatest basket you ever seen! That tomato pincushion ought to of been right *here*. Only you found it downstairs on the floor. So that means that somebody—"

"Asey, you feel all right?" Jennie inquired anxiously. "Don't you think you better go lie down somewheres? You're talkin' kind of wild!"

"Look," Asey said, "all night I been tryin' to see

what in time really went on here! Somewheres, in back of Ann Joyce masqueradin' as Miss Olive, an' apparently Mrs. Hingham doin' the same, an' Mrs. Doane movin' that body, an' in back of all this mess an' mix-up an' confusion an' contradiction, there's the truth. Someone either killed the girl thinkin' she *was* Miss Olive, or else they shot her as herself. There don't seem to be no motive for anyone's killin' either of 'em. Leavin' aside the problems of where an' when the girl was killed, an' who anyone thought she was, here in this pincushion business, you got somethin'. You got somethin' that indicates that someone was here an' took the pincushion, an' somehow dropped it downstairs, an' then cared enough about it to come back an' remove it—"

"I bet," Jennie said, "it was that fellow that knocked over the clams, Asey! That's what he was snoopin' around for! Don't you s'pose that's the fellow the doc seen, too? He was tryin' to get in an' get the pincushion!"

"May be," Asey said. "Seems logical. But the big point is, at last we got somethin' belongin' to Miss Olive that somebody seems to of wanted! We don't need to waste time speculatin' if she left the pincushion down there on the livin' room floor herself. Folks as neat as her don't go strewin' their belongin's around. An' if this belonged to Miss Olive's mother, like Freddy told you, then probably she's just as choice of it as Mrs. Doane is of her mother's orange model."

"But look here, Asey," Jennie's forehead was screwed up into a frown, "what'd anyone want a little ole pincushion for, for mercy's sakes? I see what you mean, all right, but I think it's kind of a silly idea, Asey! If it was jewels or money or somethin' valuable, I can see why someone might want to steal it—but stealin' away a little ole tomato pincushion seems to me about as silly a thing as I ever heard!"

"That's just it!" Asey said. "It's so silly an' unimportant that I didn't even remember your pickin' the thing up at first! But s'pose Miss Olive's got somethin' someone wants. There's a motive for killin' her. I'll grant you that a little ole tomato pincushion ain't in the same class with a diamond an' platinum necklace, but it's perfectly possible that the pincushion might be more valuable—"

"I'd like to know how!" Jennie said.

"It ain't necessarily the thing or the value of the thing that matters, Jennie," Asey said. "It's what the thing means to someone, or the value it's got to someone else."

"You s'pose the girl might have taken the pincushion?" Jennie wanted to know. "You don't s'pose Miss Olive might of killed the girl herself? S'pose she was mad at the girl dressin' up like her? Wouldn't it be awful, after how sorry an' worried we been about Miss Olive, if she was—oh, no. I guess," Jennie said wearily, "that I'll just get along home an' make myself a nice cup of tea an' go to bed! You, too. Maybe the real answer'll come to you over night."

"I think I got enough now," Asey said reflectively, "to tackle them an' bluff somethin' useful out of 'em. But this pincushion—"

"Oh, that pincushion! I just wish I hadn't said a single thing about it! Asey, here you got this note; an' there's those pictures on the desk that I still think makes it sort of look like Miss Olive an' the girl was somehow related; an' you got them damp clothes. You got all that. An' what can you think of? Just a little ole pincushion! I tell you that a nice cup of tea—*what's* the matter *now?*" she added, as Asey walked over to the window and peered out through the Venetian blind.

"I thought I heard my car start up!" Asey said.

"You never did—*see*, you're jumpy! You ought to rest an'—"

"Well for the love of Pete!"

"Asey, come back here! Where you goin'?"

"Goin' to rescue my car!"

"You mustn't go out that window! Come back here! Asey, are you stark ravin' mad! Come back!"

Jennie hustled over to the window, struggled again with the Venetian blind, and finally ducked around in front of it in time to see Asey land on the lawn below, scramble to his feet, and dash toward the driveway.

She could just make out the sleek lines of Asey's chromium-plated roadster sliding off through the fog.

Jumping into the coupé parked at the head of the driveway, Asey started it, backed out, and set out in pursuit of his roadster.

He was not, he thought grimly, going to let Lady Boop smash up a practically brand new Porter, just because she liked to drive!

He had expected to be able to overhaul the roadster

without any difficulty, but he could just barely make out the taillights ahead in the fog.

It dawned on him, after a moment or two, that Lady Boop was really driving! She wasn't seesawing or weaving or swaying as she had in the big sedan. She was driving like a human being, on her own side of the road, and her rate of speed was steadily increasing.

"If she should ever find out what that car *can* do!" Asey murmured unhappily. "Oh!"

The thought made him shudder, and caused his foot to jam down on the accelerator.

Like the other instruments on the dashboard, the speedometer didn't work, but Asey estimated that the car was going just a little slower than it had been. Like Syl's truck, the coupé's engine made a lot of noise and throbbed violently, but apparently nothing could compel it to pick up speed.

And meanwhile the Porter's taillights had decreased to mere pin points, barely visible in the thick fog.

Lady Boop, Asey decided, was finding out what the car could do, all right!

He practically stood on the accelerator, but the coupé continued to slow down, little by little.

At the North Quisset fork, the coupé's engine gave a little cough and stopped entirely, just as the red light flashed off and Lady Boop started across the intersection.

Asey got out, raced for the roadster, grabbed at the top bracket and hung on, and at the same time kicked forward at the door button with his foot.

A moment later he swung himself inside the car and landed heavily on the leather seat beside Mrs. Clutterfield.

"Ooooh!" she said.

"What do you think you're doin'!" Asey demanded breathlessly as he reached forward and snapped off the ignition. "What do you—"

"Did you see me?" Mrs. Clutterfield turned a beaming face toward him. "I drove!"

"You certainly did! You—"

"I hit eighty," Mrs. Clutterfield said with simple pride.

"I don't doubt it!" Asey said. "What—"

"I never saw anything like it before in my life!" Mrs. Clutterfield told him. "No feet!"

"What?"

"No feet! You don't have to do anything at all with your feet! That's what the trouble was," Mrs. Clutterfield said. "I was always so worried about my feet, I couldn't think to watch the road! Did you see how wonderfully I steered? Did you see me—what kind of car is this?"

"It's a Porter Sixteen, an' it belongs to me," Asey said. "I might add that it's a special custom-built job, that it don't grow on trees, an' if you'd hurt it, the cost would have been somethin' more than considerable, Mrs. Clutterfield. What in time made you take—"

"What will you sell it for?"

"What'll I *sell* it for? I won't," Asey said. "With Bill Porter goin' into the tank an' airplane engine business, the chances of my gettin' another car like this for some time is mighty slim. Now, why'd you take this? Where'd you get the nerve to—"

"Mr. Mayo—you see, *I* know who you are!" Mrs. Clutterfield waggled an arch finger at him. "I found out all about you! Mr. Mayo, I'll pay any price you ask for this car. I've got to have this car! I've got to!"

"You can't," Asey said flatly. "You—wait a sec. How much do you spend a year runnin' over things? An' payin' out in bribes an' in buyin' antiques to square your conscience?"

"Oh, a great deal!" Mrs. Clutterfield said. "Mr. Fredley at the bank says I spend a great deal too much on the car, and Alfred. But if I had a car like this, I could drive myself! I wouldn't need Alfred! I'm sure I wouldn't ever run over anything again!"

"Tell you what," Asey said. "I'll let you drive this till I can get you another Porter from the factory— after all, you don't want a flashy roadster like this! You want a nice, unpretentious, ladylike sedan, or a coupé—"

"I love roadsters!" Mrs. Clutterfield said. "I always wanted a roadster!"

"Wa-el," Asey said, "I'll order you one like this, then. But you can't have this particular model. It's got sort of special innards. I can have Bill get you the streamlinedest model he's got, an' have it dolled up any way that strikes your fancy. Plated with silver, if you want. But in return—don't you think you might fork out somethin' to some worthy cause, maybe, an' kind of show your gratitude in a nice, practical way?"

"Why, if I didn't have Alfred," Mrs. Clutterfield

said, "I could afford to do lots of things! Alfred costs so much!"

"How much?"

She told him, and Asey whistled at the sum she named.

"I don't think," he said, "that you'd even feel an ambulance a month! Golly, Mrs. Clutterfield, he's been bleedin' you! An' to think I let him ease me out of that century note! Huh! Well, now we got this settled, you get over here an' I'll drive back to the Inn!"

Mrs. Clutterfield absolutely refused to move.

"You said I could have this until you got me another, and I'm going to have it, and I won't move! I won't stir from this wheel!"

Asey sighed.

"Well, I s'pose if you got here, you can get back," he said. "Look, what impelled you to take this, anyway?"

"I saw someone outside," Mrs. Clutterfield said, "when I opened the living-room window for a breath of air—it was so stuffy in there with all those policemen! I slipped out without saying a word to anyone, because I thought from his cap that it was—"

"Washy Doane," Asey said.

"Oh, no, not Mr. Doane! I thought it was Alfred. But it wasn't. It was a soldier!"

"A soldier?" Asey said. "You mean, one of Hanson's troopers?"

"No, a soldier. A regular soldier. It rather surprised me, too," Mrs. Clutterfield said. "He didn't see me at first, and I followed him across the lawn to your car.

He stood looking at it several minutes, and then he caught sight of me, and walked quite quickly away up the road. And it was such a beautiful-looking car, and so unusual, that I went over and looked at it. And then I got in—so *easy* to get into, isn't it? No steps to trip over. And I pressed this little button, and away it went. Just like a saucy little whiff of down!"

"That's the first time in my memory," Asey said, "that anyone ever called a Porter Sixteen a whiff of down! Huh. A soldier—now I wonder if it's humanly possible that Jennie an' I got caught up with! I s'pose someone might've recognized her an' give her name, but—oh, well, there's no use tryin' to figger that out. Mrs. Clutterfield, where do you think we'd be likely to find the Hinghams? Neither of 'em had come back to the Inn when you went out, had they?"

"Oh, they never get home from the Theater till all hours! Three in the morning is early for them, and with the bustle of getting ready for the opening, week after next, they've been even later than usual these last few nights. Don't you think that barn makes a *dear* little theater? So cozy! Perhaps, if you want to find them now," Mrs. Clutterfield said eagerly, "I could drive you over to the Theater?"

Asey hesitated.

"Wa-el," he said, "a bargain's a bargain, I s'pose. Drive me over there. Only, till you get the feel of this craft, don't let's hit eighty, huh? It's kind of foggy, you know."

"I only hit eighty for a second, really! Just before I saw that red light and stopped. Lovely brakes, aren't they? Just touch them, and the car stops so nicely! Really, I feel so confident in this, I think—now don't you laugh, Mr. Mayo! But I really think I could *back!* I really do!"

"Maybe right now it would be simpler," Asey said hurriedly, "if you just went ahead an' turned around in front of the monument. Not that I want to discourage you from backin', you understand. You only got to push in that yellow button. But—uh—it's such a nice wide space there by the monument!"

"I think I'll back," Mrs. Clutterfield said with finality. "I *feel* like backing. *This* button?"

Asey held his breath.

But he admitted honestly, after they were safely turned around, that he couldn't have done a neater job himself.

En route to the South Pochet Barn Theater, Mrs. Clutterfield's driving was nothing less than masterly, and Asey told her so when he got out.

"I won't be long," he added. "Mind waitin'?"

"Ooooh!" Mrs. Clutterfield said, "I'm just so happy, I don't care how long you are, Mr. Mayo! I always *knew* I could drive, if I just kept on trying! Have you any road maps?"

"I think there's some in one of them compartments. Here. I'll get 'em for you. Here's a light. Here's the radio. Okay?"

"I think it's just wonderful! Now I'm going to sit back and dream!" Mrs. Clutterfield announced. "I'm going to plan my trip to Mexico—Alfred never would go there, but now I'm going to drive, all by myself!"

Asey bent over and removed the ignition key.

"Just a precautionary measure, Mrs. Barney Oldfield —I mean, Mrs. Clutterfield! I don't want to have to hike clear to Xochimilco for transportation when I come out!"

He paused for a moment in the Theater's little lobby and looked thoughtfully at two pictures of Ann Joyce tacked on a portion of the pine boarding.

Then he went on inside.

A pale, tired-looking young man in shorts and a striped blazer was coming wearily up the center aisle. He didn't even notice Asey until the latter put out his hand and stopped him.

"Say, son, is Mrs. Hingham here?"

"Backstage." He ran a hand through his rather long blonde hair. "If it's more telegrams, don't wait for an answer. She's in a hideous mood."

"How d'you get backstage?"

The fellow waved his hand vaguely toward the bare stage.

"There's a door. You can't miss it. You can't miss her, either."

He stumbled on past Asey and out of the Theater, and Asey, with a shrug, walked down the inclined floor to the door the young man had apparently meant.

Mrs. Hingham swung open the door as Asey reached for the knob, and for a moment the two of them stood looking at each other.

She was in a hideous mood all right, Asey thought. There were spots of dark color on her high cheekbones, and her eyes were flashing with anger.

She recognized him, too, and that seemed to add to her general state of bad temper.

Before she could explode a word of the speech she was obviously preparing to fire at him, Asey pointed his finger at her and waggled it in Hanson's best menacing manner.

"I want you!" he said sharply. "I'm Asey Mayo. Sent here by Lieutenant Hanson of the state police. He wants to see you about the murder of Ann Joyce this afternoon. Come along!"

If he had announced his firm determination to tar her, feather her, and hang her from the nearest tree, Asey thought, Mrs. Hingham couldn't have wilted any quicker than she did.

After taking a stumbling little step backwards, she put both hands against the wall as if to prop herself up, and stood there, wide-eyed and trembling.

In the glare of the unshaded overhead light she looked much older, Asey noticed, than he'd guessed at first. She wasn't any thirty-five. She was nearer fifty, and probably a lot more.

"You mean I'm—I'm under arrest?" she almost choked over the words.

"You will be, soon as you get to the barracks," Asey decided to lay it on thick. "Unless you can explain a lot of things Lieutenant Hanson wants to know about."

"I can explain anything! Anything! Anything at all! Anything!"

"Sit down!" Asey pointed to a crate on the floor.

Then, adopting Hanson's favorite prosecuting-attorney pose, he started in.

Mrs. Hingham was so anxious to explain anything he wanted to know that her answers to his questions tumbled from her lips, and sometimes she talked so rapidly that her words were unintelligible, and Asey had to make her stop and repeat them.

Her story was simple enough, and it provided the solution to much that he wanted to know, although none of it appeared to concern Ann Joyce.

It seemed that Bram Reid, the director, had read and liked and wanted to produce, later in the season, a play whose leading character was a middle-aged schoolteacher. Mrs. Hingham at once picked the part for herself, but neither Horace nor Bram Reid would even entertain the suggestion that she do it.

"They laughed at me! They said a *real* actress had to play that part! They wanted Isabelle Mallery and wired her right away—they didn't *care* how much she'd cost! We've already run beyond our budget! We can't afford to pay Mallery a thousand a week, and she won't come for a penny less! Bram talked with her by phone yesterday, and she wants all her expenses besides! We can't afford that! I told them so. I begged them to let me do the part, and we argued about it all yesterday and all last night till my poor head was whirling! Simply whirling!"

"I see," Asey said. "That settles your migraine today, don't it?"

Mrs. Hingham looked as if she'd like to hurl a brick at him.

"An' that's why," Asey continued, "you decided you'd dress up like Miss Olive this afternoon, huh, an' show 'em how good you could be? I see. So you went in an' swiped Miss Olive's clothes—what time was that?"

"Oh, about half-past five! I don't know. That hateful Rankin and that fool Clutterfield had finally turned off the radio—they'd kept the hideous thing on full blast all afternoon, just to irritate me! I never heard such a frightful din in my life!" Mrs. Hingham cringed at the thought of it. "Anyway, I slipped in and put on some of Miss Olive's clothes—deadly things! And slipped out the back door. But I never saw Ann Joyce! I haven't seen her since early morning when she went off to rehearsal! I don't know anything about Ann, or what might have happened to her! I didn't—"

"You see anyone lurkin' around when you left?" Asey interrupted.

"Only that fat chauffeur. Mrs. Clutterfield's."

"Huh!" Asey said. "So it was you an' not Mrs. Doane he seen at the back door. Was the electric lights out then?"

Mrs. Hingham said that the street lights went out just as she reached the road in front of the Inn. Dramatically, and with gestures, she described the terrific rain, and how she'd run every step of the way to the house where Bram Reid was staying.

"I wanted to catch him before he left—I knew he was going out because one of the times I phoned him today I asked him to dine with me, and he said he had a date. I caught him just as he was getting into his car. And he said—" her voice broke, "he said, 'Elissa, you certainly look like a wolf in sheep's clothing!' He knew me! He knew me right away!"

Mrs. Hingham burst into tears.

Asey bit his lip to keep from grinning, and waited until she recovered herself.

"He told me," Mrs. Hingham said, "to go home and take the clothes off! He said, 'Take them off, Mrs. Fiske, and be your age!' "

"An' you did, I see," Asey said. "An' what with havin' been dealt that heavy blow by Bram Reid, you was too worked up to notice Jennie there in the livin' room, huh?"

Mrs. Hingham nodded.

"As I went up the stairs someone screamed, and frightened me—I had such an eerie feeling when I entered the Inn then, anyway! And I was simply a terrified pulp when that woman clumped upstairs after me! All I wanted then was to get out of those hideous tweeds before Miss Olive came back—those plain, intelligent women are so serious about their deadly clothes! I thought if I kept quiet, this other woman would go away. But at last, I decided to—er—"

"Bluff your way past us," Asey said. "Uh-huh. An' nobody could find fault with that piece of actin'. Now, what about this rug business?"

Mrs. Hingham presented him with an elaborate and rather poignant explanation. She had refused to lend the rug to Bram Reid for the opening play. Bram had begged her for it, but she had been adamant. Back in her own room, after she had taken several pills to ease the hideous pain of her whirling head, she began to realize how selfish she was. She decided to let Bram have the rug.

"At once! Right *then!*" Mrs. Hingham said. "And the moment I decided that, my poor head cleared! Isn't that remarkable? I slipped down and phoned Ronnie to come and get me and the rug, and bring us right over here. And he did."

"In short," Asey said, "you used the rug for one last try to wheedle Bram Reid into lettin' you have that part, huh? That was your big gesture. I see. Now, about Ann Joyce—"

Mrs. Hingham burst into a flood of praise for Ann Joyce. Ann was a sterling young actress, a fine girl, admirable in every respect, and definitely destined for great successes. If ill had befallen Ann, however, Mrs. Hingham wanted to reiterate her statement that she, personally, knew nothing about it and had nothing to do with it. She loved Ann. Ann was like a sister. She had helped Ann get her start in the South Pochet Barn Theater. If Ann had been murdered, the loss to the Theater would be beyond belief.

Asey let her talk herself out.

"But," he said at last, "did Ann know of this play Bram Reid wanted to do?"

"Why, no! No, I never mentioned it to her. Of course, I suppose Horace might—I wonder," Mrs. Hingham's voice lost the note of enthusiastic warmth which she had used while speaking of Ann's virtues. "I wonder if that's what he meant! Oh, no! No, it couldn't be! She's only a little ingénue! He'd never have considered the chit for *that* part! Never! I wonder, though—he *was* arguing with Bram! I wonder!"

Mrs. Hingham began to breathe heavily.

"Where's Bram Reid now?" Asey asked.

"I don't know! Back where he lives in Quisset, I suppose!" Mrs. Hingham was now practically seething. "He wasn't here at all tonight. He phoned he had important business to attend to!"

"Where's Horace?"

"I don't know!"

From the harshness of her tone, Asey gathered that she didn't much care, either.

"I don't know anything about Horace!" Mrs. Hingham went on. "I want to—look, I've answered all your questions, haven't I? And I've told you the truth! I swear I have! Is there anything more you want to ask me? Do I *have* to go to the police barracks?"

"That's up to Lieutenant Hanson," Asey told her. "You go back to the Inn an' talk with him an' see what he decides—you got any way to get back there? Got a car? Maybe you better come with me."

"In a police car?" Mrs. Hingham wet her lips. "Uh—do you have room for my things? I've got quite a lot that must go back to the Inn tonight. Most of it's in Ronnie's car already. And I want to take back that Windsor chair. Mr. Doane's going to repair it—wouldn't it be all right if I just went with Ronnie?"

"Wa-el," Asey said. "Wa-el—"

It didn't matter a bit to him how she went back to the Inn, he thought, but he didn't want to let her off too easily, after his initial threatening outburst and prosecuting-attorney manner.

"We were going right away, anyway!" Mrs. Hingham said. "And Ronnie drives fast!"

"Uh-huh. I think I had some brief experience with Ronnie's drivin'," Asey said. "Wasn't he the feller that brought you an' the rug here? Well, go along with him, then. See Hanson right away, an' tell him all you told me. Tell him I'll be right back, only I got a little errand to attend to first."

Mrs. Hingham looked as if she had just been granted a stay of execution, Asey thought, as he walked back through the lobby. Rankin had been right when he said that the only person Elissa Hingham thought of was herself. At the first suggestion that she might get into trouble, she dropped her Queen of Sheba attitude like a hot cake.

He strolled on out to the roadster, where Mrs. Clutterfield was all but buried in road maps.

"Figgered out your route?" he inquired as he got in.

"I've thought and thought," Mrs. Clutterfield told him seriously, "and I think I've made my choice. I think I'll go via Dedham."

Asey looked at her. "You mean, via Dedham, Mass.?"

"Dedham's so pretty, I always think," Mrs. Clutterfield missed the irony of Asey's question. "Have you found out anything useful from Mrs. Hingham? Did she tell you why Ann Joyce was dressed up like Miss Olive?"

"Nope, but I think I know why, now. There's a play Ann wanted a part in, I think. It was a middle-aged part, an' Ann'd never taken one like it, an' I think this dressin' up was to show folks how much she could make herself look the part."

"D'you suppose Miss Olive *knew* about it?"

"I don't know. I hope Horace or Bram Reid can settle that. Mrs. Clutterfield, isn't that place the girl stayed, the Beeches, near here somewheres?"

"Just down by the shore." Mrs. Clutterfield waved a hand toward the fog. "Down there."

"I think we'll drop by," Asey said. "Hanson said he'd send someone there as soon as his fellers come, but nobody's said nothin' about it. Want to drive me over there, please?"

Pushing the road maps out of her way, Mrs. Clutterfield backed the roadster around without even a preliminary quiver, and a few minutes later drew up neatly in front of the Beeches, whose sign said simply, "Guests —Meals—Open."

A distraught-looking woman in a gray bathrobe answered Asey's knocks.

"Sorry to disturb you," Asey said, "but has a state trooper—"

"They've all just gone. All of them—aren't you Asey Mayo? Well, I'm Martha Thorne. Isn't there some way to keep people from taking pictures of this place? What are they taking so many pictures for?"

Asey shook his head.

"To tell you the truth," he said, "I never pretended to understand this picture business. Sometimes they take 'em, an' sometimes they don't. Seems to depend on how they feel."

"Well, they've waked everybody up and kept this place in an uproar, taking pictures!" Mrs. Thorne said. "*Why* should they take pictures of that poor girl's room? It's the barest place! She's never there except to sleep. There's nothing there but a few clothes! I wish you'd come and see the room, and tell me why in the world they made such a fuss about it!"

"I'd like to," Asey said. "I was goin' to ask you if you'd show me where she lived."

He followed her along a succession of halls, and finally she opened a door.

"Here. Look. Those are all the things she has. You could put that poor girl's belongings into a suitcase. Everything—except, of course, for that packing case! Heavens, I suppose if they'd known that was hers, they'd have had everything out of it and taken pictures of that, too!"

"What packin' case?" Asey inquired.

"It's out here in the hall. See? It came from the estate of some relation of hers who'd died, and she's hardly touched the things, she's been so busy. I don't know what in the world she'd ever have done with the things, anyway! It was just old stuff! She took out those bronze book ends, and that awful plaster cat— see, in there on her bureau? They took dozens of pictures of that cat! I can't think why, can you?"

Asey picked up the cat and looked at it.

"Nope. I guess Hanson's got another of them photographers that likes to enter prize contests. He had one once that drove him nuts, gettin' angle shots of evidence—hey!"

He put down the cat and pointed to a picture on the bureau.

It was a duplicate picture of the bewhiskered man, the baby, and the girl that Jennie had noticed in Miss Olive's folder!

"Oh, that," Mrs. Thorne said. "That came from the packing box."

"Who are they?"

"She didn t know," Mrs. Thorne said. "It was just *in* things, with that cat and the book ends. I told her the man looked to me like a minister. Doesn't he look like a minister to you?"

"Philpotts!" Asey said. "*That's* why Jennie thought of Philpotts! He does look sort of ministerial!'"

"He was an awfully nice man, wasn't he?" Mrs. Thorne said. "He had so many pictures of ministers in that exhibition, too."

"What exhibition?" Asey demanded.

"Why," Mrs. Thorne said, "he collected pictures of all the ministers who'd ever been in any of the churches he joined together, and had an exhibition of them. He wrote little histories of each one, and what happened while they served—didn't you know about that? I thought that's what you meant when you mentioned Mr. Philpotts."

Asey looked thoughtfully at the picture.

"I wonder, now. Is this one of them ministers, or did Jennie just think he looked like one, an' that reminded her of this Philpotts? This is sort of peculiar, this is."

"There's writing on the back," Mrs. Thorne turned the picture over. "See, it's very faint. It says, 'Henry with Lucy and Juanita.' It *is* peculiar, now you speak of it. I thought he looked like a minister, but I never connected him with that exhibition. He must have been a most unusual man, that Ferdinand."

"That *who?*" Asey stared at her.

"Ferdinand."

"Who in time was he?"

"He was the photographer in—well, it would be Quisset now, but in those days it was Pochet. Just think, it never occurred to me when Ann showed me this, but it *is* one of Ferdinand's pictures! Those jardinieres of grass, and that spiked iron railing are in every family picture for miles around. Ferdinand must have taken pictures of half the Cape. And what amazes me," Mrs. Thorne added, "isn't just the way his pictures kept—they never faded out white, like some—but the way people kept his pictures. I suppose that's why, though. They kept, and so people kept them."

"Looky here," Asey said, "Ann Joyce wasn't a Cape Codder, was she? Was her folks Cape Codders?"

"Her folks are dead," Mrs. Thorne said. "She's an orphan. She had several younger brothers, she told me, but they all died in the 'flu epidemic when she was little. I don't think she has any family at all, except this cousin on her mother's side who died. And I'm sure she told me she was born in New York state. She lives in New York now. Of course, Cape Codders spread out, but people always know if they *do* come from the Cape—are you going to take that picture with you?"

"Uh-huh. I wonder," Asey said, "where are those pictures now that Mr. Philpotts had in his exhibition?"

"Why, he just borrowed them from people!" Mrs. Thorne said. "I suppose he gave them back afterwards —is this important, this picture? Is it a clew?"

"I don't know," Asey told her honestly, "if it's a clew, or just a sort of puzzle. If this feller with the whiskers really was a minister, then most likely this picture don't mean much. You know, whenever ministers left a church, they used to give everybody a picture of themselves—we got a raft of ministers at home in albums. On the other hand, it's sort of an odd coincidence to have this picture turnin' up here now, considerin'! Huh. Did the girl mention any new play she wanted to be in?"

"No, she didn't say much about her work. But she's seemed kind of excited these last couple of days," Mrs. Thorne said. "I told those troopers so. And I told them that she hadn't any fights or quarrels with anyone, nor any enemy in the world. She was a nice girl! As nice a girl—"

"Uh-huh. Mrs. Hingham," Asey said hurriedly before Mrs. Thorne had a chance to launch into any recital of Ann's sterling virtues, "she told me as much just a little while ago. I'm goin' along now, but if you remember anythin' about this picture, like who Old Whiskers is, I wish you'd contrive to let me know."

"Angie Harris's mother could probably tell you. She's ninety-five," Mrs. Thorne said, "and remembers everything. Particularly about ministers. She told Mr. Philpotts lots of things."

"Thanks," Asey said. "I think I'll look into her tomorrow."

He returned to the roadster, where Mrs. Clutterfield greeted him with an arch salute.

"Where to, sir?" she asked brightly.

Asey frowned. "I'm torn," he said. "I got this yen to tear a ninety-five-year-old woman out of her bed at —what time is it, quarter to two? An' at the same time I want to see this Bram Reid, an' I want to see Horace. Huh. I guess I better see him first. Back to the Inn, please. Tell me, you happen to know Horace's last name?"

"His *last* name?" Like everyone else, Mrs. Clutterfield seemed dumfounded at the suggestion that Horace might possess a last name. "Why, Hingham, of course! Oh, no, it couldn't be Hingham, could it? Let me see. I'm sure I must have heard it! Horace Ump. It's a little, short name. Ull. Pell. Dill. Ball. Or was it more like Whittaker? Isn't that strange, I can't remember!"

"Neither can anyone else," Asey said. "What's Horace like, that people remember only half of him?"

"Why, you saw him," Mrs. Clutterfield said. "He must have passed by you when you went into the Theater to see Mrs. Hingham. He had on shorts and a blazer—"

"What? Shorts an' a blazer? *That* fellow! If I was drivin'," Asey said, "we'd be strugglin' in a ditch this instant! You mean, that blonde youth? Him! He couldn't have been more than twenty!"

"He was twenty-six last month. He's a nice boy, but always so tired looking, and always wanting a quarter from someone to buy cigarettes with. He often borrows money from Alfred—really, I've often thought that if Mrs. Hingham were as fond of Horace as she seems, she should really make him a small allowance. Just so he would have a little pocket money. Mr. Mayo."

"Uh-huh." Asey said. "Good drivers watch the road."

"Mr. Mayo," Mrs. Clutterfield spoke to the windshield wiper, "of course, all *I* know about crime is what I read in the headlines, and I can't *ever* solve those little daily mystery cartoons they have next to Orphan Annie, but, d'you know, a little bird has just told me where Miss Olive went!"

"Where?"

"You know," Mrs. Clutterfield said coyly, "I think Miss Olive has a crush on Bram Reid! I do. I mean it! She doesn't often talk to people, but last week she and I were both sitting out on the lawn just after Bram had left with Horace, and I said wasn't he still marvelous looking! And d'you know what? She unbent! Actually—"

"The road," Asey said. "Don't get so worked up that you forget the road, now!"

"I'm sorry! But she confessed she'd seen every one of Bram Reid's pictures, and some of them four or five times! I gathered she was dying to meet him and talk with him, but she was too shy just to walk up and speak to him. She's awfully shy, really. And when Freddy said tonight—she was talking to that police lieutenant and giving him a description of what Miss Olive was wearing this afternoon—when she said Miss Olive wore a gray hat with a feather, I almost spoke up then.

I was busy with my tea, and I hadn't noticed her hat. But that's her new one. She bought it in Hyannis yesterday. It just happened," Mrs. Clutterfield added diffidently, "that *I* happened to go into the same shop later, and it just happened in the course of my conversation with the salesgirl that she mentioned an old customer from the Whale Inn who'd just left, and I said *I* stayed at the Whale Inn, and I wondered—"

"In short, you found out she bought a new gray hat with a feather, huh? Where," Asey said, "do you think Miss Olive went tonight?"

"To the White Horse Grill. You see, while we were talking about Bram Reid, she and I, I suggested that if she ever wanted to see him, she had only to go to the White Horse Grill. Horace told me Bram Reid always has dinner there. Now, Mr. Mayo, I can't even do those little mystery cartoons, but I've been wondering if maybe it couldn't be something as simple as that? She just went to see Bram Reid!"

"You suggestin' she eloped with him after dinner?" Asey inquired dryly.

"No, indeed! Only, because she was wearing that new hat, I decided she must be going somewhere special. You don't," Mrs. Clutterfield pointed out, "wear a new hat if it looks as stormy out as it began to when she left! At least, I don't think *I* would. I'm sure Miss Olive never would. She's so particular about her clothes. *I* can't guess what she might have done since dinner, Mr. Mayo. I *told* you I wasn't a bit good at this sort of thing. But *I* think she went to Sketicket, to the White Horse Grill, to look at Bram Reid."

"I don't know," Asey said slowly, "why your guess as to what Miss Olive done ain't as good as mine, or anybody else's. Whereabouts in Sketicket is this White Horse place? I don't seem to remember anythin' of that name."

"It used to be the Casa Valencia," Mrs. Clutterfield said, "until about a month ago. Then it got all done over and became the White Horse Grill—"

"Whoa!" Asey said. "That's on the road to Provincetown! I wonder, now! I wonder if—golly, I'm torn! I ought to get back to the Inn, but if Jennie an' I seen the real Miss Olive, that's the way she was headin' from the four corners. I wonder if the place's open all night, like the Valencia used to be?"

"I think so. Shall we go there? I'm *dying*," Mrs. Clutterfield said, "to try the new highway! We just simply ought to *float!*"

She floated at such a pace that Asey cautioned her gently.

"The cops don't often stop this car, but—uh—it's still foggy. Ease her off a bit."

"To think," Mrs. Clutterfield said, "that Alfred always considered forty-five going *fast!* Mr. Mayo, they're still open at the White Horse. See the lights?"

"Pull in," Asey said. "I'll go in an' ask. Never any harm in askin'."

He didn't think she noticed that he removed the ignition key as he stepped out of the car, but she commented on the fact in a hurt voice as he closed the door.

"You don't trust me, Mr. Mayo!"

"No, ma'am," Asey said. "Not on a six-lane highway! At the rate you're learnin', I wouldn't put it past you to shuffle off to Buffalo without a word of warnin'. I probably won't be two shakes in here—"

But a half hour passed before he emerged, and his face, as he got into the roadster, was a study.

"Whatever's the matter, Mr. Mayo?" Mrs. Clutterfield said. "You look just the way I feel when I try to solve the daily mystery cartoon. Was she there?"

"Uh-huh, she was. Mrs. Clutterfield, I wish you'd explain somethin' to me. Why is it that each additional thing I find out, that ought by rights to make things that much easier, only balls things up all the more? You land on a fact, an' you say to yourself that it'll settle this or that, but it only just opens up a lot of alleyways!"

"Exactly!" Mrs. Clutterfield nodded her head enthusiastically. "That's exactly the way *I* feel about the daily mystery cartoon! She went to see Bram Reid, didn't she?"

"Uh-huh. Washy tells me things," Asey said. "Jennie tells me things. So does Rankin. An' Freddy. An' Mrs. Doane. Everyone tells me things. An' if they provide me with one answer, then they stick on a dozen questions—now, listen to this one! An' it cost me a young fortune in tips to pull it out of the hired help. Miss Olive come here a few minutes after six, in her little sedan. Horace was waitin' for her. They talked together a minute an' then sat down. Horace got up an' made a phone call. While he was phonin', Bram Reid come. The three of 'em had dinner together, an'—"

"How simply splendid for Miss Olive to meet him at last, after simply worshiping him from afar all these years! I'm so glad!" Mrs. Clutterfield said. "I'll wager she was positively thrilled to tears. But Mr. Mayo— why *Horace?*"

"That's what I told you!" Asey said. "Get one thing explained, an' somethin' else crops up. Horace was awful nervous, accordin' to the waiter—"

"*That's* not unusual!" Mrs. Clutterfield interrupted. "He's nervous most of the time. Mrs. Hingham often makes scenes, you know. She always wants to know where Horace is and what he's doing, every minute, and I suppose the poor boy was afraid she'd come and drag him away."

"Horace kept watchin' the door," Asey said, "an' after gulpin' down about half his dinner, he went out to his car an' drove away. Miss Olive an' Bram Reid finished their meals, an' then she went off in her car, toward Provincetown, an' Bram Reid made a phone call, an' then he went off in his car toward Quisset!"

"I think I see what you mean," Mrs. Clutterfield said. "You at least know Miss Olive dined here—I'm *so* glad I remembered that gray hat with the feather! But you're still in the dark about where she's been since, and where she is now. My, my, it's rather provoking, isn't it?"

"That sort of sums it up," Asey said. "I s'pose the main trouble here is that this problem's kind of divided up. This ain't just a question of somebody bein' killed, now find out why, now find out how. Problem here is, find out who was s'posed to be shot, an' then figger from there. Huh! When I found out about that pin-cushion, I thought I'd landed for sure on the why of this business, but now I got doubts!"

"Which of them d'you think was meant to be killed?" Mrs. Clutterfield demanded. "Certainly not Miss Olive! *I* can't imagine *anyone's* wanting to hurt her!"

"Nobody can imagine anyone's wanting to harm Ann Joyce, either," Asey returned.

Mrs. Clutterfield clucked her tongue and said she personally felt this whole affair was harder, much harder, than any mystery cartoon she'd ever seen.

"I still don't see why Horace was here," she added. "It appears as if they had a date, doesn't it? What do you make of that, Mr. Mayo?"

"This is all speculatin'," Asey said, "but I think that Ann Joyce wanted the middle-aged part in the play Mrs. Hingham told me about. Now, Mrs. Hingham said that Horace an' Bram Reid had been arguin', presumably about the castin' of that part. If Bram Reid wanted Ann to have it, there wouldn't hardly be no argument. So you can figger that he didn't think she could do it, an' Horace thought she could. See?"

"Not quite," Mrs. Clutterfield said. "But do go on, Mr. Mayo! This is fascinating, listening to you! I feel like Dr. Watson!"

Asey swallowed.

"Wa-el, Doc," he said, "s'pose Horace an' Ann cooked up a little plan between 'em. If you found out that Miss Olive was one of Bram Reid's fans, I guess anybody could find out. What I mean is," he added hurriedly, "she didn't make no deep secret of it. So s'pose Horace asks Miss Olive to dinner to meet Bram Reid. I wonder, now, if that wouldn't be how it happened that Ann got Miss Olive's clothes? They ask her to dinner to meet Bram on one hand, an' then in the next breath, they beg her to lend Ann an outfit of her clothes—"

"Freddy Doane thought that Ann just slipped in and took them!" Mrs. Clutterfield said.

"Uh-huh. But she left a note. If she'd just swiped 'em, she'd probably just have sneaked 'em out like Mrs. Hingham did."

"Mrs. *Hingham?* What—"

"Don't let's go into that now," Asey said. "It's just one more complicatin' factor, even if it did give me a chance to find out about this play angle. S'pose that Horace an' Ann threw out meetin' an' dinin' with Bram Reid as bait to get Miss Olive to lend Ann an outfit. Oho, I'm dumb! I'm gettin' old an' feeble, Mrs. Clutterfield! I just begin to catch on! Miss Olive was goin' to help, see? Get it?"

"No, but do go on! It's frightfully exciting! How could Miss Olive help? Not that she wouldn't probably have been terribly thrilled to!"

"Sure, that's it! Bram Reid an' the Theater an' all is out of her line. She'd jump at the chance of helpin'! Look, Horace an' Miss Olive an' Bram Reid are to sit down an' have their dinner. Long about dessert, say, Miss Olive is to skip out to powder her nose—"

"She doesn't use any make-up, ever!"

"Wa-el, she's to skip out. An' Ann Joyce, dressed

like her, is to come back. Now d'you see how that would work out? If Bram Reid didn't catch on right away—an' with all them rose-shaded lights in there, I think he'd have been fooled for a few minutes—then Ann had him, see? That explains why Horace phoned —I bet he was the one who called an' asked for mess beetle! That's why he was so nervous an' worried! Ann never showed up, an' he went off to try an' locate her!"

"Where," Mrs. Clutterfield inquired, "is Miss Olive now?"

Asey shrugged.

"At least we made some progress," he said. "We know she headed toward Provincetown around seven-thirty. Mrs. Clutterfield, we'll go back to the Inn now. I still got this yen to chat with Angie Harris's aged mother, an' I want to see Bram Reid. But I bet you he don't know a thing about this plan! I bet nobody let on, when Ann didn't come. An' I bet you Horace knows lots—golly, to think I had that child by the arm an' let him go! Golly, why didn't someone tell me he was a babe in arms, instead of broodin' about his last name! Back to the Inn, Mrs. Clutterfield, an' you needn't spare the horses, this trip!"

Mrs. Clutterfield's face was flushed with triumph when she headed the Porter into the Whale Inn's graveled driveway.

"If Alfred," she said softly, "could have seen that! My, my!"

"Alfred," Asey returned as she drew the Porter up smoothly by the porte-cochere, "would've died of apoplexy just the other side of North Quisset. Huh! Just for fun, take Rankin for a drive tomorrow. He don't relish speed. You're good, Lady Boop! I hand it to you. Come the revolution, I'll get you a job at the Porter provin' track."

"It sounds too, too fascinating—ooooh, there's Horace's car, see?" Mrs. Clutterfield pointed. "He's gone and left it out by the turntable again, and Mrs. Doane will be so provoked with him for not putting it into the garage. But Horace claims he's so tired when he gets back that simply the thought of the garage doors utterly exhausts him, and—"

She broke off as Dr. Cummings stomped down the front steps to the roadster.

"Asey Mayo, I wish to God before you go tearing off on junkets you'd have the common decency to tell people where you could be found! Didn't anyone give you my message? Didn't anyone tell you I was coming back here with some highly important information for you?"

"Golly!" Asey said as he got out of the car, "now you speak of it, Jennie did murmur somethin' about your havin' phoned, but I was so busy then, broodin' about pincushions an' lookin' at the name in them books, it slipped my mind entirely!"

"Indeed!" Cummings retorted. "And did Jennie happen to murmur that I was up at three this morning, and do you realize it's now practically three o'clock tomorrow morning? When people all but break their necks to try and supply you with vital information, it seems you might—"

"You mean, Doc, you found Miss Olive?" Asey demanded.

"Who said anything about finding Miss Olive!" Cummings held open the front door for Mrs. Clutterfield and informed Asey in a whisper that the woman ought to diet. "My God, man, haven't *you* found her? What have you been doing? What's the matter with you? Seems to me you set out to locate that woman six months ago! I don't know where Miss Olive is! Finding schoolteachers isn't *my* department—look, what I've got to tell you is about that gun, Asey. The tool marks on the rifling of a bullet from that twenty-two we found with the girl don't match those on the bullet that killed her. Hear that?"

"Honest? What—"

"Furthermore," Cummings said, "I know it'll interest you to hear that it's Mrs. Hingham's gun."

"*Hers?*"

"She bought it," Cummings said. "When I came back here, I brought the gun with me, and Hanson confronted her with it when she came in a while ago. After a stormy interview, she admitted the gun was hers, and even dug out the fancy case it came in—see it on the table? She claims the outfit, case and gun, was in her bottom bureau drawer and someone must have stolen it."

"Huh! What in time," Asey said, "would she be buyin' guns for? Did she explain that?"

"Claims she bought it for her husband to practice shooting with," Cummings said, "so if he was drafted he'd know which end of a gun you pointed, or words to that general effect. Washy Doane says that Horace has used the gun perhaps twice. Says he closes his eyes—"

"Uh-huh. Washy told me about Horace's shootin', an' after havin' had a glimpse of the fellow, I understand that part," Asey said. "Horace ain't too rugged —they all gone to bed?"

"Mrs. Hingham's retired with acute migraine—genuine, I think. Hanson was feeling so thwarted by the time she came, he let loose in his best manner. You know, finger pointing and yelling 'Aha' and generally acting like a trial lawyer in a B picture. Your charming friend Rankin has also retired, yawning, after a few gentle cracks at me—"

"Before I forget it, an' before you malign my charmin' friend Rankin any more, Doc, I must tell you that he never got any of the bills you sent him."

"I don't believe it!"

"He told me he left money to pay you with Freddy, an' took it for granted she did, an' how was he to know if you never billed him for his debts," Asey said.

"That's utter, rank, blatant nonsense!" Cummings retorted. "I mailed those bills to the bank he said he was working for. The Empire National. He was tracking down some heirs for an estate they were handling. He told me all about it. I'm *sure* it was the Empire National!"

"I'm sure, too," Mrs. Clutterfield said. "Because he knows Mr. Fredley."

"There, see?" Cummings said. "I tell you, that man's

simply a fourflusher, that's all! And look, one of the troopers chased someone he thought was a prowler, but it turned out to be a soldier. And—"

"Again? Is Freddy up?" Asey interrupted. "I'm beginnin' to have this suspicion that maybe perhaps this comes in her department!"

"She's in the kitchen with Washy and Jennie. We were plying ourselves with coffee," Cummings said, "to keep awake. Why should Freddy—"

"You go get her," Asey said, "an' while you're doin' that, I'll go rouse Horace. He's the feller I'm most eager to see, right now."

"Wait!" Cummings said. "Horace isn't here, Asey. He hasn't come back yet. That sent Sister Hingham into a frenzy, when she found that out."

"But his car's here!" Mrs. Clutterfield said. "Down by the turntable. Those lovely headlights of Mr. Mayo's car showed it up the minute I turned into the driveway! Of course he's home!"

"Maybe his car's here," Cummings said, "but *he* certainly isn't. We went through all that with Sister Hingham half an hour or so ago. She didn't say anything about his car. She simply said he *had* to be here. But he's not. And he certainly hasn't come in since. I've been right here, and I know!"

"Is Hanson here?" Asey asked suddenly. "No? Well, he left some men, didn't he? We'll get 'em together, Doc, an' you an' Washy an' I, we'll have a hunt for Horace! If his car's here, he must be. An' I want him!"

It was after five that morning, when the fog at last

lifted, that Washy Doane found Horace, down on the sand by the bathhouse.

Like Ann Joyce, he had been shot in the back, through the heart.

There was a gun lying beside him, and Dr. Cummings gulped as he picked it up.

"Asey, look at that tag!" he said in a weak voice. "I put on that tag, myself! Asey, this is the same twenty-two that Ann Joyce wasn't shot with before!"

10

HALF an hour later Dr. Cummings sat down on the bathhouse steps beside Asey and tossed the bedraggled remains of a chewed-up cigar at a horseshoe crab.

"Never in all my days," he clamped a fresh cigar between his teeth, "have I ever seen anything like this. Never! I'm speechless, Asey. Speechless, I tell you. I have only one consolation. It seems reasonable to believe that no one shot Horace thinking he was either Ann Joyce or Miss Olive. Effeminate as he was, they couldn't have made that error! They knew who they were shooting, this trip, and we know, too—Asey, who was that soldier who popped out of the fog and helped the troopers hunt? Was he the same soldier they found hanging around before? Who *is* he? What in blazes has *he* got to do with things?"

"Wa-el," Asey puffed at his pipe, "I got him cleared up, Doc. Seems he's Freddy's beau."

"That buck private?"

"Uh-huh. Seems he was gettin' along fine in the world bein' a copy writer in an advertisin' agency, an' then he done some recruitin' ads, an' he got so fired with patriotism he up an' enlisted. Seems whereas Mrs. Doane could tolerate the idea of a copy writer as a son-in-law, she couldn't stomach the notion of a buck private, an' so a considerable number of problems arose. If Washy'd only gone into more detail about him last night, I'd of got him settled sooner."

"What's he doing, lurking around here? Is he on leave?"

"Nope. Seems the next problem of his outfit is the defense of Quisset Harbor from attempted invasion, an' his colonel got the idea that the other side might be doin' some preliminary spyin', so he hit on the idea of preinvasion counterespionage, as you might say. This feller's it. He dropped off that convoy Jennie an' I met at the four corners. I gather," Asey said, "that he didn't consider the job a hardship, an' I ain't sure the job wasn't his idea in the first place. He was hangin' around tryin' to see Freddy without rousin' Mrs. Doane— I guess what he seen in his peerin' through windows amazed him a lot. He didn't know what kind of a place he'd landed into! Anyway, he ain't never got connected with Freddy yet. All her bouncin' around this evenin' was from her gettin' a letter he sent, he thinks, sayin' he was goin' to try to see her soon. Invasion ain't due till tomorrow some time, so I guess they'll manage to get together, all right."

Cummings kicked at a piece of seaweed.

"Asey, why in blazes was this fellow Smith shot?"

"Smith?"

"That's what the draft registration card in his wallet said. Horace Smith—what's so funny about that? Sometimes," Cummings said, "you stump me, Asey! Anyway, of all the innocuous-looking individuals— did he lisp?"

"Not exactly. Why?"

"Oh, he looks as if he might have lisped, that's all. *De mortuis*, and all that sort of thing, Asey, but he frankly isn't my idea of a stalwart specimen of young American manhood. I'll take Freddy's buck private, any day. Humpf. I suppose Mrs. Hingham felt it was a feather in her cap to capture one so young. Why was he shot, Asey?"

"He knew too much," Asey said. "An' I'm inclined to think, Doc, that someone's made a mistake in killin' him. I think if someone had let him alone, an' let him talk to me, the chances are good that he'd have answered some questions but just set up a lot more, like everyone else has done to date. But now that someone's gone so far as to kill him, I kind of guess I'm on the track at last. I guess it was the girl that was meant to be killed, all right. I guess someone besides Horace knew about her intention to dress up like Miss Olive, an' so they grabbed the opportunity to kill her while she was dressed up, to spread confusion. Which, I must say, they sure done!"

"Humpf. And you said you thought Miss Olive knew—d'you realize, Asey, that woman's never turned up yet?"

"Uh-huh. I do. How long was Smith—you can't guess how funny that Smith part is, Doc! How long's he been dead?"

"An hour or two. I don't think," Cummings said unhappily, "that I can face going to work on him. I know just what I'll find, that *he* wasn't shot by that twenty-two, either. I know it! Asey, who swiped that gun from the living room?"

"You ought to be able to guess more about that than me," Asey said. "You was there. So was Hanson."

"Well, it's Hanson's fault!" Cummings said defensively. "I brought the gun there, but he ought to have known enough to take it back when he left. Someone must have sneaked it out of that fancy case—well, someone had every chance. They could have taken it any one of half a dozen times when the living room was empty, before you came back with Mrs. Butterfield."

"Clutterfield."

"Butterfield, Clutterfield, what does it matter!" Cummings said wearily. "You know who I mean—and I'll never understand how you happened to let her drive the pride of your life, either! I suppose, Asey, that with all the to-do of finding Horace, someone could have slipped into the living room while we were all out hunting him, couldn't they? And swiped the gun then, and then sneaked down here and laid it beside him, having shot him with something else to begin with. I suppose—my God, I'm tired of supposing! Let's get back to the Inn. You got any plans now?"

"I wonder," Asey said, as they walked through the beach grass, "what time an oldest inhabitant gets up? Early as six, you think?"

Cummings stopped and stared at him and shook his head.

"Are you stark mad, Asey? Jennie told me how you raved and raved about a tomato pincushion, and then hurled yourself out of an upstairs window! I give you my word, I can't make out what's come over you! You *feel* all right?" he asked anxiously. "No headaches, or dizzy feelings? Or—"

"I feel fine," Asey said, "except I'm hungry an' I'm tired. But havin' hung on this thing this far, I'm goin' to see it through to the bitter end."

"Of course," Cummings said, "those clothes you have on make you *look* different—Asey, where in blazes are your shoes, man! Why are you going around barefoot? You haven't—look here, you haven't joined a *cult*, have you?"

Asey grinned.

"Nope. I had shoes, but I shed 'em for some second-story work, an' I had socks, but they got so torn while I was patterin' around huntin' Horace, I shed them, too. Let's see, now. I could rouse Bram Reid an' talk to him, *even* though I don't think he knows a thing about this masqueradin'. I ought to talk—"

"Have you forgotten Miss Olive entirely?" Cummings interrupted acidly. "She's missing, you know!"

"Uh-huh, but one of Hanson's troopers said that a description of her an' her car'd been put out over the teletype, an' it seems to me that ought to bring her to light sooner or later. Just as soon, anyways, as my racin' around tryin' to locate her would. I ought to talk with Mrs. Hingham, I s'pose. She was gettin' good an' sore at Horace, in her mind, before she left that barn theater place. I wouldn't put this past her, in one way. She bluffed me once. On the other hand, she's awful choice of her own skin—Doc, if Angie Harris's aged mother can only remember about Ferdinand's picture of Old Whiskers an' the baby, I'm goin' to be a lot happier about this, I think!"

"Mad!" Cummings said unhappily. "Stark, staring mad! Mad as a hatter—what's the matter with *her?*"

He pointed to Jennie, who was running down the path to meet them.

"I seen you," she said breathlessly. "I been waitin' for you—Asey, there's a soldier up there to the Inn! D'you suppose he's after me for bustin' up that line at the four corners? Do you?"

"No," Asey said. "I'm sure he ain't. He's Freddy Doane's boy friend."

"Oh, my!" Jennie fanned herself with her hand. "My, I been all a twitter! Asey, I guess you better just drive me home! If what I been through since six last night is detectin', then I don't want no more of it, ever! Will you drive me home?"

"Sure. By the time I got you home an' had a bite to eat," Asey said, "I guess even the oldest inhabitant ought to be up an' stirrin'—what is it?"

Jennie drew him to one side, out of earshot of the doctor.

"Asey, will you do something for me before we go? I feel terrible about it. Kind of ashamed. But I went back up in Miss Olive's room, again, after I was there with you. Just to look around again, that's all. But I played with them Venetian blinds— I know I hadn't ought to of. But I did. An'—an'—"

"An' what? Don't look so downcast, Jennie! What happened?"

"I broke 'em," Jennie said in a small voice. "Asey, you suppose you could mend the ole things?"

"I guess I maybe most likely could," Asey told her. "Sure."

"Can you? So's Mrs. Doane won't know? She's looked down her nose at me so much already, I don't know's I could stand her smirkin' at me any more! She won't never come right out an' *say* I didn't have no business up in that room—which I know I didn't! But she'll *look* it! Could you manage to slip up an' fix 'em now, before we go home?"

"I'll take a whack at 'em," Asey said. "Was it one of the tapes that busted, or the roller gadget that angles 'em, or what?"

"I don't know what it was, but I got the pieces right here." Jennie opened her pocketbook. "They almost been burnin' a hole in me! They sort of popped an' scattered around all over the floor, an' you should of seen me scurryin' to pick 'em up an' put 'em in my pocketbook before somebody come! I been so worried —I hate bustin' other people's things! Here. Here's the spring part. Here's a metal thing. Here's that round part like a fountain pen, an' this other big piece, an' here's the two little pieces. There! You think you can fix it up?"

Asey stared down at the six pieces she had deposited in his hand.

"What's the matter?" Jennie demanded. "Oh, dear! Can't you fix it so's she won't ever know what I done?"

"Jennie, where did these come from? From a Venetion *blind?*"

"Yes!" Jennie said miserably. "I was fiddlin' with it, an'—I *told* you I always wanted 'em! An' I reached up an' pushed aside that little kind of hood part over the top to see how it worked, an' these popped out! It didn't seem to hurt the blind so *much*," she added. "It seemed to work pretty good without 'em, but they belong in the works *somewheres*, Asey, an' I did count on your bein' able to fit 'em back in!"

"Cousin," Asey said briskly, "who's the Venetian blind man over home?"

"Harry Barclay has lovely ones, but you couldn't match these, I'm 'fraid! You mean, *we'll* have to get a new one?"

"I mean," Asey said, "*you* can have new ones. All you want. Have two at each window, if you want. Have your pink-an'-blue striped floor, too, or whatever it was you wanted. Have it inlaid with purple, if you like—"

"Asey, come back here!" Jennie said. "Come back here— Doc, yell at him to come back here!"

"No use," Cummings said. "Man's mad. Can't do a thing with him. Going barefoot, you notice that?"

"Must be something wrong!" Jennie said. "I'm *worried* about him! Tellin' me to get a pink-an'-blue striped floor, an' inlay it with purple!"

"A pink-and-blue striped floor, and inlay it with purple? My God, Jennie, he's worse than I thought! Where'd he go? Into the Inn? Let's hurry and get hold of him before he does anything really silly!"

By the time they reached the Inn, Asey was striding toward his roadster, talking earnestly to Washy Doane, and before they could do more than yell at him the Porter streaked out of the driveway.

Cummings shook his head and frowned.

"Usually when he drives that way, he's got something!" he said. "Washy, what did he say to you? Did he make sense?"

"Told me he wanted his shoes," Washy said. "I picked 'em up when he kicked 'em off last night. I give him the shoes, an' off he went— Doc, ain't anyone found out yet where Miss Olive went?"

"Nobody," Cummings said, "has found out nothing —I mean, anything! My God, how do I get mixed up in this kind of thing? Jennie, how in blazes did you manage to get mixed up in this?"

"I was just tryin' to deliver Syl's clams on time," Jennie said. "That's all! Well, anyway, I don't think Asey's goin' far or plans to be gone long. He promised to take me home, an' I know he wouldn't never leave me stranded here. I s'pose," she added philosophically, "the only thing to do is to set down an' wait some more!"

"I wish," Cummings said slowly, "I wish I knew if he'd really got this, or if he's as daft as he seems. I guess, Jennie, that I'll sit down and wait with you!"

At noon they were still waiting for Asey, and Washy Doane was still audibly wondering where Miss Olive could be.

It was after one o'clock when the Porter slipped into

the driveway and came to a stop by the porte-cochere.

Freddy Doane, followed by her soldier boy friend, rushed out to Asey as he was starting up the front steps.

"Asey, thank heavens you're back, we've simply been going berserk!" Freddy said. "Have you found Miss Olive yet? Where've you been? And look, Mother's in such a state about Horace and everything, she's never said even one cross word to Phil, and once she patted his shoulder! Isn't that magnificent? Come on in—everybody's in the kitchen eating lunch! It never happened before, but Dr. Cummings wandered in there for something to eat, and now everyone's out there making sandwiches and getting into Dad's hair— and what *did* you do to Lady Boop? She's a new woman! Why don't you say where you've been and what you've been doing, Asey? Tell us everything!"

"If you'd just give me a chance to open my mouth," Asey said, "I might. Is everything okay here?"

"Comparatively speaking, yes," Freddy said. "I mean, no one else has been killed! Asey, where have you *been?*"

"Hither an' yon," Asey said. "I seen Bram Reid, an'—"

"Oh, we know that! He told us so!" Freddy said. "Where else?"

"I dropped in on the oldest inhabitant, Mrs. Harris. Very sprightly ole lady, she is, an'—"

"Yes, yes, we know that! Jennie found that out. And we know you made a million phone calls, too. But where've you been since?"

"I borrowed Bill's plane," Asey said, "an' flew up to Boston an' back. Refreshin' little trip—look, everythin's really okay here, is it?"

"Yes, yes! Will you—"

Asey turned around and went back to the car.

"Okay, Miss Olive," he said. "I guess you can come—"

"Miss Olive!" Freddy said. "Is she in there? I didn't see her! Oh, Miss Olive! Oh, I'm so glad— I'm so happy— I'm so *relieved!* Miss Olive, this is Phil! Miss Olive, where've you been? Where did he find you?"

"I found her a long while ago," Asey said. "About two shakes after I left here—didn't Bram Reid tell you? Huh. Come to think of it, I guess I told him not to, didn't I? Come along, Miss Olive. We might as well get this over with. Come along out to the kitchen an' let's get you settled!"

Her appearance in the kitchen doorway raised an immediate din, which Asey promptly put a stop to.

"Just a sec," he said, "before you get goin'. Let's have that pincushion, Rankin!"

Rankin's hand came out of his pocket with a gun in it, but before his finger had a chance to squeeze the trigger Washy Doane's rolling pin had knocked him over backwards to the floor.

"Gun was empty," Washy informed Asey. "I unloaded it, like you told me before you left. He never guessed, neither. But I couldn't resist boppin' somebody after all these years—huh, I guess that hit him kind of hard, didn't it, Doc?"

"You know damn well you did!" Cummings said.

"And look at the job I've got, stitching him up! Oh, I wish people would stop and think, before they give in to impulses like yours, Washy, that *I'm* the man that has to sew up the pieces! There's a pincushion in his pocket, all right. Here, Asey, catch."

He tossed the red tomato pincushion to Asey, who, in turn, presented it to Miss Olive.

"Here," he said. "I think if you slice it—yup, I think I'm right. What seems to be a stem is a key. See if it ain't."

With his carving knife, Washy divided the pincushion in two, and, with pride, displayed the thin key imbedded in the wadding.

"What's that for, Miss Olive?" Freddy demanded. "What's that the key to?"

Miss Olive shook her head.

"I don't know, dear. I've had the pincushion for years, and never knew of the key's existence! I knew there was a hard stem in the middle, but I never suspected it might be a key! How amazing! It certainly proves that my cousin was quite wrong about the pincushion!"

"What d'you mean?" Asey asked quickly.

"The pincushion was mailed to her about twenty years ago," Miss Olive said. "Just mailed, done up in brown paper, without any sender's address or any explanation at all. My cousin, Mrs. John Beadle, puzzled about it, and finally decided it was one that had belonged to my mother—she'd been Mrs. John Beadle, too, you see—and was supposedly stolen from her by a maid, and that the maid had mailed it back in a fit of conscience. It was an explanation that never began to satisfy me, but I took the pincushion when my cousin offered it to me, feeling that if it had been my mother's, I should keep it. Mr. Mayo, how did you know about the key?"

"Look, Miss Olive," Cummings got up from the floor where he had been kneeling beside Rankin, "how did Asey find you? Where've you been?"

"He stopped me in the village early this morning, as I was driving back here, and took me to his friends the Porters. I've been there until he picked me up a few minutes ago, and really," Miss Olive said rather wistfully, "I don't know much of anything that's gone on. Mr. Mayo, how did you know about the key?"

"I guessed it," Asey said. "The pincushion wasn't of much value itself, so I figgered there must be somethin' of value in it. Couldn't be big, or you'd have found out about it, an' I had a hunch it might be a key. Now, I'm goin' to Rankin's room an' see if he don't have, somewhere among his things, the explanations I still want. So—"

"You see here, Asey Mayo!" Jennie said. "I ain't goin' to wait a speck longer to understand about all this! I want to know—"

"So do I," Freddy said. "Did Rankin really—"

"*I* want to know, too," Cummings said, "but I point out to you that I've got to sew this fellow up. Asey, for goodness' sake, wait till *I* can hear this!"

The clock which had gone on a rampage and struck twenty-two the night before was chiming two when the group, with the exception of Rankin, gathered together in the Inn's living room.

"Of course," Cummings said airily, "I knew all the time it would be Rankin. I said so. I told you so countless times. I—Asey, how the hell did you ever find out it was him, anyway?"

"When Jennie give me the conversion unit, I knew for sure," Asey said, "though I'd had my doubts about him, off an' on, before that. You see, Doc, what Jennie thought was part of a Venetian blind was a Colt forty-five twenty-two conversion unit."

"And what in the name of all that's holy," Cummings demanded, "is *that?*"

"To Jennie," Asey said with a grin, "it's an integral part of a Venetian blind. She popped them loose parts she picked up off the floor into her handbag so quick, she never troubled to read the name on the slide assembly. Rankin's gun was a forty-five, an' he kept it in his bureau drawer, an' told me so, an' urged me to look at it. You got it there, Hanson? See, it's a Government Model of 1911, Doc. With this unit Jennie found, you can convert it in two shakes into a twenty-two. I don't think there's any doubt it'll turn out that this's the twenty-two that killed both Horace an' Ann Joyce."

"I already found out, while I was waiting for you this forenoon," Cummings said, "that Horace was killed by a bullet from the same gun that killed the girl. Incidentally, I must tell you that Rankin's first words, when he came to, concerned you, Asey. It seems he expected you'd be away from the Cape. In fact, he was rather counting on your absence. Tell me, how did you guess about Rankin? When did you begin to suspect him?" ·

"Wa-el," Asey said, "when the only apparent link I could find between Miss Olive an' the girl was in each of 'em havin' the same picture of the same man with whiskers, an' in each of 'em faintly resemblin' each other—"

"Why, they both did have pointed chins!" Freddy said. "Mother, you spoke of it, once!"

"Jennie noticed that," Asey said. "Anyway, you wonder if they're related, an' you think of family. Rankin was a genealogist, an' families was his business. You give me a good shove in the right direction, Doc, when you mentioned the bank Rankin worked for, an' his diggin' up heirs for estates."

"Asey, is this *that* sort of thing?" Cummings demanded. "Who's the heir?"

"Way it stands now, Miss Olive—golly, Miss Olive, I never thought to tell you!" Asey said. "It's your mother's sister's estate, an' it's kind of a thumpin' big one, too."

"But I'm afraid," Miss Olive said gently, "that there's some mistake! My mother never had a sister. Of course, my mother died when I was born, but no one ever mentioned her having a sister. I never heard of one!"

"But she did," Asey said. "Know that picture of the stern-lookin' man with whiskers, standin' in front of the spiked fence? An' there's a baby—"

"He was my grandfather, and the baby was my mother."

"An' the older girl was your mother's sister," Asey said.

"How simply amazing! I remember asking who she was, once, and being told it was a neighbor's child!"

"It was your mother's sister," Asey said, "an' your aunt. An' her great-grandchild was Ann Joyce."

"Now how the hell," Cummings said in awe, "did you find that out?"

"Angie Harris's mother has a memory," Asey said, "that's several centuries long, an' like nothin' I ever met up with on this earth. Right off the bat, she recognized the man with the whiskers in the picture I took from Ann Joyce's room. He was the Reverend Henry Upjohn, who once preached in town here, an' he had two daughters, Lucy an' Juanita, Lucy bein' the baby. An' the Reverend Henry's wife died when Lucy was born, Miss Olive, just as your mother, Lucy, died when you was born."

"I knew that," Miss Olive said.

"Well," Asey continued, "it seems that one day the Reverend Henry took Lucy visitin', an' when he come home, he found Juanita'd eloped with an itinerant music teacher named Marcy Joyce. Juanita'd always been crazy about music, an' talked wild about wantin' to be an actress. That didn't set well with the Reverend Henry, one bit, so after she run away he disowned her, in effect. Mrs. Harris says he never mentioned Juanita's name again. That's most likely why your mother wasn't ever told about her errin' older sister. A short time after she run away, the Reverend Henry moved to Baltimore. He didn't leave no pictures for his congregation, like most ministers did when they left, but this enterprisin' photographer named Ferdinand, he printed up a lot of the Reverend Henry an' his two daughters, an' sold 'em. An' because Juanita's runnin' away'd caused quite a flurry in town, a lot of people bought 'em. Mrs. Harris dug one out of her attic. She didn't know what'd become of Lucy an' the Reverend Henry, but I s'pose," Asey concluded, "Lucy grew up an' married a Mr. Beadle."

"He was a ship chandler," Miss Olive said, "and he died when I was three. I was brought up by his family. So my mother was actually born here in town? I wonder if perhaps that can be why the place has always attracted me."

"You'll find," Asey said, "that your grandmother is buried in the old cemetery. Mr. Philpotts's wife is buried near her, Jennie—you were pretty hot on that, you were!"

"How does Ann come into this?" Mrs. Doane asked. "How did you find out about that?"

"Juanita married the music teacher, Marcy Joyce. They had a son, Marcy—I got this out of Rankin's papers. Joyce died of pneumonia, an' Juanita left the child when he was a couple of years old an' was never heard from again. Joyce's family brought the boy up, an' he married, an' had a son, who was Ann's father. She had other brothers, Mrs. Thorne told me, but they died. In short, Ann's the great-granddaughter of Juanita Upjohn."

"I'm speechless!" Cummings said. "What about this estate Miss Olive's the heir to, Asey?"

"Wa-el, about a year an' a half ago—I went to Boston for this part, an' bullied some Porter Motors directors into gettin' the dope from friends of theirs connected with the Empire National—'bout a year an' a half ago, a woman named Allstadt died in New York. Juanita Allstadt—"

"Juanita?" Freddy interrupted excitedly. "*Our* Juanita, the one who ran away with Marcy Joyce?"

"Whoa up. She was the wife of Willem Allstadt, who was very rich, an' a famous yachtsman, an' after he died around nineteen-twelve, she went into seclusion an' got kind of queer. She didn't see people, an' didn't often leave her apartment, an' meals were left outside her door. She had one ole servant, an' after the servant died, the apartment hotel folks had an awful time even gettin' inside her place to get it cleaned proper. She paid for everythin' with bills. An' when she died, it turned out she was rollin' in money, an' there wasn't no Allstadts left, an' there wasn't no will, an' the Empire National was pretty unhappy about it all. On her marriage certificate, this Mrs. Allstadt was Juanita Juan. An' when that got known, hundreds of folks named Juan appeared on the scene, an' the bank got unhappier than ever. Finally they hired Rankin to see if he could track down the heirs. An'—"

"I get it. He found out everything," Cummings said. "Only, how did he plan to profit by it?"

"Not so fast. Remember, Doc, you've started from Quisset. Rankin had to work it out the hard way. He had to go through Mrs. Allstadt's things—papers an' all. An' finally he asked the bank for a secretary, an' they sent him a girl named Ann Joyce. Now, Rankin'd found out that Juanita Allstadt had been Juanita Juan, a famous actress of the nineties, an' finally he located some ole lady in an actors' home who told him she was sure Juan was an assumed name. How he caught on to Ann bein' related we can only guess till we've pumped him. But maybe he noticed a resemblance, like the pointed chin. Maybe she knew she had a great-grand-mother named Juanita, an' said so. Anyway, Rankin looked into the matter—without tellin' her—an' found out who her great-grandmother was. There's pages an' pages of how he found out, upstairs in his papers. Last summer, Rankin asked Ann to marry him. Get it?"

"Gorry be!" Washy said. "There's one part I knew, anyway!"

"Uh-huh. An' in trackin' down Juanita Upjohn who got to be Juanita Marcy, he got back to the Upjohns, an' Miss Olive."

"How perfectly amazing!" Miss Olive said in her quiet voice. "D'you know, he asked me to marry him, last September. And several times this winter. And only last week, after I came!"

Asey grinned. "I guess he knew about you, all right! I s'pose, if Ann had accepted him, your relationship an' your part in this wouldn't ever have been brought up, an' if you'd accepted him, Ann's wouldn't. He was pretty safe there. Uh—I gather you didn't accept him?"

"I thought," Miss Olive said, "that he was being rather absurd. I told him so."

"Which I don't think endeared you to him much," Asey told her. "Now, consider. Rankin's done his best to get Ann, an' you. Ann don't know what's behind this. You don't. But a little while ago, a cousin of Ann's dies, an' a packin' case of odds an' ends of her things is sent to Ann. In it is a picture of the Reverend Henry an' his two daughters. Now, from what I picked up, I don't think Ann was one bit dumb. While she worked for Rankin on this Allstadt estate, she saw pictures of Juanita. She knew what Juanita looked like. An' here in this packin' case is a picture of her, an' the name's written on the back. What d'you suppose happened then? Your guess is as good as mine."

"She took it to Rankin," Cummings said. "She said, 'Here, look, maybe I'm related,' or words to that effect."

"I think so," Asey said. "I think, too, that she'd maybe begun to suspect that Rankin *had* found out somethin' about her bein' connected with Juanita Allstadt's estate. I think she asked Rankin to look into it for her, an' then when he dallied, I think maybe she went so far as to threaten to get a lawyer an' look into it herself, if Rankin didn't get busy. I think somethin' like that was what goaded Rankin into action. An' this play about the middle-aged schoolteacher give him an opportunity so golden he couldn't let it get by."

"What d'you mean?" Miss Olive asked.

"Bram Reid told me this mornin' that a day or two after the play was brought up Ann told him that Rankin had given her a sublime idea. She said it was a great secret, but he'd see."

"You mean that her dressing up like me was Rankin's idea, originally?" Miss Olive said.

Asey nodded.

"Uh-huh, I think so. I'm sure of it. He suggested she dress up like you, an' I think planned it out with her, an' somehow got her not to mention his part in it. You see, if you can get someone to keep a plan secret, an' then you shoot 'em, the results is inclined to be bafflin'. But Ann gave a hint to Bram Reid, an' I think she told Horace more than Rankin thought she would. That's why Horace got shot."

"But see here," Freddy said, "how did he shoot Ann? How could he have done it? We were here in this room all afternoon, Mrs. Clutterfield, and Rankin and I! And he wasn't out of sight!"

" 'Marcella's Rainbow to Love,' " Asey said, "is a half-hour program, Freddy. I got stumped by that first, until I looked it up in the mornin' paper today. Rankin was upstairs durin' it, wasn't he? Durin' that time, Ann got dressed up as Miss Olive an' wrote her a note. Then she showed herself to Rankin. An' while Marcella was goin' on down here, Rankin had a symphony concert goin' on the radio upstairs, an' you never heard the shot. Then he whisked Ann into his room—Hanson, look around that bathroom floor, up there, don't forget—after hidin' the conversion unit of his forty-five in the Venetian blind in Miss Olive's room."

"Why in *my* room?"

"I'll get to that. Then Rankin came down, an' clowned around with Mrs. Clutterfield, an' then come the special broadcast everyone listened to, that Rankin knew about an' counted on—"

"Mr. Mayo," Miss Olive said, "d'you mean that when

he walked downstairs with me, and gave me nickels for my dime to phone with, he had just shot Ann?"

"Uh-huh. Did you get the party he told you to phone?"

"No. I didn't understand that. He said I'd had a call, but there wasn't any such number—when I came out of the booth, he'd gone."

"Just so. But he'd planted in people's minds the thought that you was alive an' well when you come downstairs with him, an' that he left before you come out of the booth. The number he give you was a fake. Anyway, everybody gathered around for the special broadcast. An' the laundryman come. An' just afterwards, Rankin went out to get his raincoat at the bathhouse, Washy told me. An'—"

"And he came back with it," Freddy said, "and then he went off with the Judge! Now, how did he get Ann's body downstairs? Tell me that?"

"Laundry chute," Asey said. "I asked Washy if there was secret panels or passageways, last night, an' he said no. But I looked before I went rushin' off this mornin', an' there's a laundry chute next to Rankin's room, an' it comes out in that narrow hall behind the phone booth. What Rankin done was to roll up his raincoat an' stick it near the house—say, behind a bush, or somethin'. Durin' the music part of that broadcast, he just went a few steps away, an' then popped back in. He was safe as he could be. Everyone was listenin'. He rushed upstairs, put the body down the chute, come down the back stairs, took it out an' put it into the booth, draped the glasses on the floor with the gun he stole from Mrs. Hingham, an' then picked up his rain-coat from outside, an' come back in. On the face of it, he'd rushed to the bathhouse an' back."

"Huh!" Jennie said. "What a horrid man! I never did care much for men with pointed beards! Asey, was that how the person got away from upstairs last night, when we hunted around so? Did he use that chute?"

"That was Rankin," Asey said. "I think he was get-tin' his conversion unit out of Miss Olive's blind, where he'd put it. He needed it for Horace. Then I s'pose he stuck it back in a hurry after shootin' him, so it was there when Jennie found it. When was you there, Jennie?"

"Just before you come back with Mrs. Clutterfield. Rankin was in the kitchen drinking coffee."

"Then you got it soon after he put it back," Asey said. "He left it there, because I think, Miss Olive, that he was sore with you, an' I think he hoped you might get involved. To pay you back for turnin' him down. What hurt that scheme was the weather. He did some fine plannin', but he couldn't account for them lights. That was primarily Jennie's work. You see, ordinarily someone'd have been at the desk here in the livin' room all the time. It'd have been awful hard to try an' find when that body was put in the booth, when it was finally found. But the lights goin' out, an' Freddy hop-pin' out with Washy to try an' fix the Delco, that left a gap when the room here was empty, an' led us to think of around six as bein' the time she was killed."

"There was her watch!" Freddy said.

"But it doesn't go," Cummings said. "You can't make

it go. Mainspring's broken, I found out. How about the pincushion, Asey?"

Asey smiled.

"I think you'll find he took that the time he killed Ann. He didn't want to stick it in his coat pocket, where it'd make a bulge. So after he got his raincoat, after comin' downstairs, he stuck it in the pocket of that. I looked, just now, an' the raincoat pocket's got a big hole. He forgot that, an' so the pincushion dropped out on the floor here. An'—"

"An' I *did* pick it up," Jennie looked triumphantly at Mrs. Doane. "Just like I said! Only Rankin took it out of your basket again!"

"He was most likely so anxious to get off with Judge Houghton, who sure made a nice reliable alibi," Asey said, "that he didn't discover about losin' the pincushion right off. My, I was dumb! There he made so much fuss, huntin' a lighter, as he pretended, but it never occurred to me for a long time that after he got the lighter he never used it! In fact, I think he palmed that lighter to alibi his huntin' around outside. After Jennie found that unit, things all fit together," Asey added thoughtfully. "I begun to remember his huntin' the lighter. An' how he described people to me—accurate enough, but colorin' things to fit in best for him. I remembered how Washy spoke of his goin' out for the raincoat just after the laundryman come—an' in my phonin' around, I found that the laundryman always come within a couple of minutes of the same time. Rankin was waitin' for him, see, so there wouldn't be no slip-up about the chute."

"How about Horace?" Cummings asked.

"Rankin must have got panicky about him. He got his forty-five an' unit, an' waited for him to come back. An' got him to stroll down to the bathhouse, an' shot him. I think it was a lot later that he sneaked out the twenty-two from its case an' stuck it beside Horace. He had plenty of opportunity, with all of us, includin' him, huntin'."

"Miss Olive," Mrs. Doane said, "where in the world *were* you last night?"

"Well," Miss Olive seemed a little embarassed, "I— er—"

"Mrs. Clutterfield helped me guess that one," Asey said. "To boil it down, part of the plan thought up to impress Bram Reid with Ann's ability to handle this older role involved havin' Miss Olive an' Horace an' Bram Reid dine together. Then Miss Olive was to slip out, an' Ann, dressed in her clothes, was to slip back, the point bein' to prove to Bram Reid that Ann was a good actress. When Ann didn't turn up, Miss Olive an' Bram Reid got to talkin' about another play, an' the upshot of that was that the two of 'em went to Provincetown an' talked most of the night with the author. That's where Miss Olive was comin' back from when I spotted her this mornin'."

"It was really an amazing thing for me to do," Miss Olive's cheeks were pink. "And I never did anything like it before. And truly, Mrs. Doane, I'm sorry I upset you. Bram Reid said he'd call you and explain that I'd be late, but he apparently phrased it badly. You see, this play had to do with my line of work."

"Schoolteachin'?" Jennie asked.

"Er—well—"

"She ain't a schoolteacher," Asey said.

"What!" Everyone in the room spoke in unison.

"Of course she is, Asey!" Jennie said severely. "Everyone knows it!"

"I knew she wasn't when I seen the books in her room," Asey said. "An' when I finally placed her name, like it was written in them books, I found myself wonderin' if maybe she *hadn't* killed Ann. There's a lot of difference between Miss Olive, a nice schoolteacher, an' O. E. Beadle, who invented Solution R280, that they was so busy talkin' about in Washington last week! I think Rankin hoped that the O. E. Beadle angle would make people suspicious of her."

"Miss Olive!" Freddy said. "Aren't you a teacher, really? What are you?"

"A chemist," Miss Olive said, and bit her lip. "I never meant to deceive you, really, but you just all took it for granted that I was a schoolteacher, and—well, people are more at home with schoolteachers, somehow. And Solution R280 isn't really a fair sample of my work, Mr. Mayo! That was really just an accident!"

"Uh-huh. Biggest new explosive anyone's invented in years, an' you make it sound like somethin' you tossed off in your spare time! But I see your point, Miss Olive. People, particularly here in town, would be a lot more comfortable with you if they didn't know your part in R280, an' the rest. Well, I don't see why anyone should tell on you now, after all these years! Now—"

"Wait, Mr. Mayo," Miss Olive said. "The key. What about the key in the pincushion?"

"You'll find that all up in Rankin's papers, an' I guess it's the part I didn't quite get from the bank. After Willem Allstadt died, Juanita had times when she was sort of odd. In some of the papers in her apartment there was a letter nobody could make much out of. Began 'Dear Sister' an' it said she was sendin' a pincushion to 'dear sister,' an' it was very important. The pincushion had belonged to mother—she'd mean your grandmother, Miss Olive—an' it was the key to a lot. The letter was unfinished. Maybe she forgot to finish it, maybe she decided not to, maybe it was in one of the periods when she was queer. Anyway, the pincushion got sent, an' the letter didn't. Seems, if she knew your mother's name, that she must have made some effort to find her sister. The bank'll solve the key for you, anyways, an' know where it belongs—it's a vault key, an' I guess it'll probably prove who Juanita was, an' solve your claims."

"D'you think," Miss Olive said, "that after Rankin got that pincushion, perhaps he might have—"

"Killed you? I don't know. I'm sort of afraid he planned to," Asey said. "That's why I carted you off to Bill Porter's while I was away. I know one thing Rankin planned, though, after failin' to cut himself into the Allstadt money by gettin' either you or Ann to marry him. He wasn't ever goin' to reveal anythin' about either of you. He was goin' to leave you out in the cold an' get the money for himself. He was goin' to fake claims an' make himself the heir."

"How could he?" Cummings demanded.

"He'd got the pincushion," Asey said. "With the key, he could get all the things in the vault box. An' upstairs, you'll find some lovely papers, the beginnin' of the faked proof he was goin' to produce about himself bein' the heir. It's all up there, in black an' white."

"You don't mean," Hanson said, "he left evidence like that lying around loose for anyone to see!"

Asey smiled.

"Why not? Without your knowin' all this, them papers of his wouldn't mean a thing to you, Hanson, or anybody else. The beauty of all this was how safe it all was. An' now, Jennie, I guess we'll go home an' order Venetian blinds an' plaid floors!"

It was nearly five o'clock when the Porter, which Asey had wrenched with difficulty from Mrs. Clutterfield, rolled into the driveway of his home in Wellfleet.

"There's Cousin Hat at the door!" Jennie said. "Oh dear, Mrs. Doane's give me back the Inn clam business she took away last evenin', an' I know Syl'll be glad, but I feel like a criminal, leavin' him with Cousin Hat so long! I oughtn't to—everythin' all right, Hat?"

"Well," Hat said, "Bill Porter just phoned. He's comin' for Asey at six. Got to go right back to Washin'-ton, he says. An' Syl wonders if maybe Asey could do him a favor first?"

"What?" Asey asked.

"Well, they phoned from the Penniwinnick Inn, an' want some clams—"

"No!" Asey said.

"But some of Mrs. Bemis's old boarders is havin' a

reunion, an' they want chowder—guess you could deliver the clams, couldn't you, Asey?"

Asey and Jennie looked at each other, and Jennie shook her head.

"I wouldn't tempt fate!" she said. "Not after what I been through on *this* clam-deliverin' expedition!"

"But it ain't tourists! It's old, *old* boarders—"

"No, Hat," Asey said. "No. I might take a chance for tourists, but if Jennie an' I learned one thing in the last twenty-three hours, it's that clams an' perennial boarders don't mix!"